Prisoner of Steel and Shadow

Meg Anne

ISBN: 978-1-951738-38-9 (Paperback Edition)

Cover Art by Story Wrappers

Edited by Mo Sytsma of Comma Sutra Editorial

Proofread by Dominique Laura

For everyone who sent me a message begging for Ronan's story.

And then kept begging.

The only thing I dread more than being wrapped in your forsaken arms…

Is the thought that I may never be again.

— AURORA JAMES

PRISONER OF STEEL AND SHADOW

AUTHOR'S NOTE

Prisoner of Steel & Shadow contains mature and graphic content that is not suitable for all audiences. Such content includes murder, references to suicide and suicidal thoughts, infertility, explicit violence and gore. **Reader discretion is advised.**

A detailed list of content and trigger warnings is available on my website.

CHAPTER 1

RONAN

Reyna is dead.

Five years without so much as a murmur of her whereabouts and today, finally, the harshest truth. The Night Stalker queen, Elysia's most ruthless assassin, the woman he'd searched high and low for, was never coming back. They found her body.

As soon as the news reached him, the small ember of hope, that sole kernel of warmth remaining within him, guttered out. He wasn't even an echo of who he'd once been. That would imply part of that man remained, but any tenderness he once had withered away, leaving something hard and brittle in its absence. Traits such as empathy, kindness, and humor were such foreign concepts he couldn't recall the last time he'd employed them.

When weeks without sign of her turned to months and then years, he'd spiraled deeper into sorrow that quickly turned to obsession. Some might even call it madness. It was then he began seeking out the blackest parts of his soul, clinging to them in his effort to find some sort of outlet for the bottomless grief he could not purge.

She was supposed to be it, his happily ever after. The woman he'd grow old with. The one who'd spend long days—and longer nights— in his bed. The one to bear his children and teach them how to channel the wild spirits they'd inherited from their parents into a life that wouldn't see them tamed completely. They were supposed to live out their days together, the mundane transformed into something remarkable because she'd be at his side until the Mother called them both home.

He'd had plans. So many fucking plans. All of them centered around *her*.

And she was dead.

Stolen from him before he could tell her what she meant to him. He never even got the chance to let her know she was the one who ultimately repaired the battered remains of his heart—nay, his very soul—only for it to be shattered beyond recognition in the wake of losing her.

So what was left for him here?

What purpose remained now that the one reason he had to crawl out of bed each morning had just been ripped away from him?

Gritting his teeth, Ronan acknowledged another harsh truth, though this one came with a wave of icy acceptance.

Nothing.

There was *nothing* left.

He'd been broken once before and barely recovered then. There was no coming back this time. Not for him. Not without her.

He couldn't live like this anymore, half a man, devoid of purpose— of hope.

He refused.

Adjusting the hood of his cloak to ensure it concealed his entirely too recognizable face, Ronan shoved open the door to a tavern no respectable person would dare enter and stalked across the ale-and-vomit-splattered floor to the notice board against the far wall. A hush settled over the room as the patrons within watched him tear a piece of parchment off, the quiet interrupted by shocked gasps when they realized which bounty he held in his hands.

Lukas Nightshade, the Bargainer. Infamous blackguard, notorious thief, and criminal kingpin. Gifted in four of the five magic branches, he was the third most powerful person in the realm, falling just after the Kiri and her Mate *if* the rumors were to be believed. He'd only evaded capture for so long because no one had ever seen his face and lived to share the tale.

Thus, the unclaimed bounty. The contract was so yellowed and faded with age that it had become a running joke that time would do the job before a proper merc.

Only an utter fool—or man with a death wish—would dare to attempt it.

Ronan didn't know who'd posted it, which would matter if he'd had any intention of claiming the reward. But he wasn't doing this for the money. This was about release. Even if that wasn't the case, a man in his position could never claim the bounty. He was a member of the Kiri's Circle. One of the five famed Chosen sworn in service of their queen. The vows he'd made to her, the ones proclaiming him a man of honor who'd act only according to her will, forbade it. They were the same vows he upheld in the light of day but dropped as soon as the sun went down. There was no honor in what he did under cover of darkness, though perhaps there was a grim sense of justice.

A vigilante's justice.

The Butcher's justice.

It was a moniker Ronan donned as easily as this cape. One he welcomed. Because when he set aside his title of Shield, the sacred protector, he became something else. Something darker, born of violence and rage rather than loyalty and obedience.

It was a name spoken of in whispers. A name that sent the people he was supposed to protect fleeing for the safety of their homes.

A name they feared.

When he couldn't be Reyna's hero, Ronan turned to the darkness and became a monster instead.

And now it was time for the Butcher to go to work.

～

RONAN DIDN'T BOTHER with the matte black armor he'd commissioned specially for these nightly escapades. Tonight's mission was about stealth, and he wanted nothing that would give him away.

Just because he didn't expect to live long enough to see the sunrise didn't mean he was planning on rolling over and making it easy. He'd always known he'd go out in battle. Such was the way for a warrior born and bred like him. His final battlefield just looked a little different than he'd envisioned.

But if death was coming for him, he was damn well taking Nightshade out with him. Consider it a parting gift. One final act of heroism.

That had to count for something.

With that sunny thought in mind, he strapped every possible weapon to his body. As always, his Fire would be his greatest asset, but the Butcher didn't use anything that could be traced back to the Shield. Especially his Mother-gifted magic.

He'd gone this long without anyone connecting him to his alter ego, and he intended to take the secret to the grave. It was the least he could do for the woman he considered a sister. He made a vow to protect her with his life, and he *would* protect Helena's legacy, even in death. It was his duty as her Shield. Though after tonight, the title would no longer be his.

Ronan did a final sweep of his one-room safe house to make sure he wasn't forgetting anything. He'd purchased the sorry excuse of a house under a false name, selecting it for its isolation and placement on the outskirts of the city. The shanty was hardly fit for inhabitants; even the furry critters nesting in the walls deserved far better. Considering how often he found himself here, the realization should have been depressing, but since it was little more than a glorified armory, it suited his purposes just fine.

Given the location and lack of security system, he was actually surprised he'd gone this long without being robbed. Perhaps even the most desperate thief didn't believe there to be anything of value in the dilapidated dwelling. There was likely a metaphor there if he cared to think on it. Something about the broken man whose ramshackle house mirrored the barren state of his soul.

He squeezed the bridge of his nose and sighed at the maudlin and wholly uncharacteristic thought. What a pitiful wretch he'd become. He hadn't waxed poetic like that in years. Had his current and former selves found themselves face-to-face, the old Ronan would have laughed at the pathetic sack of shit staring back at him. Right before punching the bloody daylights out of him and tossing his sorry arse outside to sleep off the black mood.

He missed old Ronan.

In a hurry to distance himself from the tragedy of his thoughts, he turned to leave, freezing when a flash of silver on the crumbling stone mantle caught his eye. His heart lurched in panic.

Ronan, you rutting bastard. Don't get careless now. You have one last job to finish.

Stumbling in his haste, he half fell, half ran over to it. Ignoring the burst of pain as his ribs connected with the stone, he cradled the dagger in his calloused palm. He couldn't believe he'd almost left it behind.

Far more ornate than anything he'd choose for himself, the weapon had become his most prized possession. It belonged to Reyna, the elaborate swirls she used to paint on her face etched into its hilt. Now, it was all he had left of her.

How fitting it would be with him tonight.

Recalling the day he acquired it, Ronan let out a harsh exhale that might have been a laugh were he anyone else.

Reyna hadn't gifted it to him. Far from it. The assassin queen had practically buried it in his throat, hurling the blade before he could finish whatever silky insult he'd been uttering. She hadn't spoken a word, though her message had been received loud and clear as the wickedly sharp metal trembled a mere hairsbreadth away from his neck: tread *very* carefully.

Though the warning didn't have the effect she'd anticipated. Instead of being cowed, he'd been painfully aroused. But that had always been the nature of their relationship. A careful dance of danger and seduction.

Pressing his lips to the cool blade, he breathed, "Save me a seat, killer. I'm on my way."

Palming the dagger, Ronan left the safe house without a backward glance.

Less than an hour later, he dropped into the sewers considering the fifty gold he'd parted with money well spent as he made his way to Lukas's hideout. Just because the man had managed not to be gutted in his sleep didn't mean no one knew his whereabouts. Business wouldn't be nearly as lucrative for him if that was the case. After a few strategic inquiries, greased palms, and just as many untimely deaths later—to cover his tracks, of course, no need to be sloppy—Ronan possessed the Bargainer's most recent address.

Anticipation ignited in his veins, suffusing him with dark pleasure. Or as close to pleasure as he was capable these days. This was the part he'd always loved. When a chase neared the end and success was finally within reach.

Ironically, this was the most alive he'd felt in weeks. Perhaps longer.

Not lingering to dwell on it, Ronan ducked his head and followed the serpentine tunnels until they circled back up and he approached the remains of the original city. Instead of leveling the prior iteration, the Chosen had simply built on top of it, meaning that there was an entire network of forgotten chambers and crumbling passageways right beneath their feet. The fact that these ruins were situated between the city and the sewer, well . . . what better place was there for filth to hide?

The low murmur of voices reached him, and Ronan allowed himself a curl of his lips so filled with malice it couldn't be misinterpreted as anything other than the promise of violence.

Keeping his steps slow and unhurried, he pulled down his mask. The black leather would keep all but the bottom half of his face concealed, and he'd already dealt with the beard that would have given him away. Confident in his anonymity, he began to whistle, the haunting melody bouncing off the walls and creating an eerie echo.

The voices fell silent for a beat, and then there was a whispered, "Oi, wot's that?"

"Dinner," a second, meaner voice replied.

Ronan dropped all pretense as he turned the corner and spotted two men guarding a door. "Well then, lads, come and get it."

They rushed him, but he was ready, sweeping the legs out from the first man and knocking him flat on his back while gutting the second. By the time the first thug recovered, Ronan had already wiped Reyna's blade clean and was right there to drive the deadly metal into his windpipe.

"Sorry about your free meal. Guess you'll have to make do choking on your blood."

Pulling the dagger free, Ronan let the man slump to the ground with a gurgled moan.

The door at the other end of the passage creaked open.

"Atticus? Mouse? Yous twos all right?" A set of dark eyes leveled on Ronan, widening in surprise as he took in the two dispatched corpses at his feet. "You're gonna pay for that, gobshite."

Ronan held out his arms. "Always happy to pay my debts."

The thug whistled over his shoulder, and Ronan knew he was about to be vastly outnumbered. So much for stealth. He supposed there wasn't much reason to play it safe then.

"Do me a favor, puppy, and call out your boss for me, yeah? I have something for him."

Pushing open the door to reveal four new companions, the other guy grinned. "Nah, I don't think I will. How's abouts you do me a favor and get fucked?"

"Clever. You stay up all night working on that line?"

The man opened a switchblade, tapping his forehead with the end while giving a little bow. "Just came to me."

Ronan was about to fire back another smart-ass retort when the woman behind his new friend gave him a hard shove. "Shut yer gob, Ned. He's fuckin' with yous."

Ned scowled. "Ain't no one asked you, Linda."

Ronan mentally shook his head, having absolutely no clue how Nightshade had managed to last this long surrounded by a clusterfuck of incompetent idiots. Truth be told, it was almost *more* impressive.

"Well maybe they should've." She put her hands on her hips, glowering. "Who's idea wos it to let those twos stand guard tonight anyway? You knows we has a shipment."

No one was paying any attention to Ronan as he crept closer. He was content to let them bicker amongst themselves and save him the hassle of distracting them himself.

"Listen, Linda—"

It was the last thing Ned said before Ronan slit his throat. "Who's next?"

Linda spun and ran while the other three lunged at him. He was soon lost to the familiar rhythm of brawling and bloodshed. Three on one was nothing new, not even much of a challenge, really, without any of them using magic. But three soon became six, and six quickly turned to more than he could easily count. One after another, they came at him until his vision was tinged red and his palms were slick with blood and sweat. Still, it would take a lot more than that to take him down.

"Nightshade!" he bellowed, wanting this over with. He could fight all night if he had to, but that's not what he was here for.

Low chuckles met his call. They thought him a fool, coming into their den. Alone. Calling out their boss.

As if he gave one single fuck what any of these lowlifes thought of him.

Breathing hard, head swimming, Ronan continued to pummel his way through the wall of bodies, turning to his fists when he ran out of weapons. Bones snapped and cartilage caved in beneath his ruthless blows. They weren't laughing now. Nightshade's army was growing restless. None of them considered him a threat. But as more and more of their brethren joined the corpses on the floor, the more furious and volatile they became.

Two men came for him at once, one trying to tackle him, the

other's hands glowing a familiar green. Ah, they were bringing out the magic users. Things were about to get interesting.

"Nightshade!" he roared. "Come out and face me, you swine!"

As Ronan dodged the first attack, the second man's fist connected with his rib cage. There was a sickening crack as the Earth-enhanced blow broke at least two of the slender bones. Gritting his teeth, he pulled back his arm to return the strike when the voice he'd been waiting for rang out.

"What's all this then?"

CHAPTER 2

RONAN

Finally.

Ronan glanced up, spotting the elegantly dressed man standing on a makeshift scaffold against the far wall. There was a darkened archway just behind him, which Ronan assumed led to his office. The man's black and silver hair was pulled back in a queue, his eyes a tepid brown and the rest of his features and build utterly nondescript. He'd bet Reyna's dagger that wasn't the man's true face. If Nightshade truly possessed four of the five branches, he could easily use his magic to modify his appearance.

Lukas's thin lips curled in a sneer. "A visitor. How lovely."

He somehow made the words sound as if he'd just discovered shit on the bottom of his boot.

The feeling was mutual. Though for Ronan, there was a definite undercurrent of relief at the sight of his mark. He was ready for this to be over, weary down to the tattered remains of his soul.

The crowd backed away as their boss called on his magic and floated down from the metal structure. While their lust for blood—namely Ronan's—was as potent as ever, it was clear this was now Nightshade's show. And they wanted front row seats.

"Well, you went to all this trouble to find me. Might as well tell me what you want. I can't promise you'll get it, of course, but I do find myself wildly curious."

Never taking his gaze off the man stalking toward him, Ronan tipped his chin to the side and spat. Lukas eyed the pink-tinged spittle with a grimace.

"Not much of a talker, are you? That's all right."

"He was mouthy 'nuff before."

Ronan's eyes found Linda hovering to the left of the crowd. She took two scuttling steps back as he pinned her with his gaze.

"Perhaps he's regretting his decision to come poking around where he wasn't invited. Fear has a tendency to make one lose their words. Its sister, pain, however, tends to do the opposite. Shall we test the theory?"

Snickers rang out.

Ronan snorted. "There's not much I'm afraid of, but I assure you, a rat doesn't make the list."

"Oh? Is that so? Then why the mask, friend? If you're so unafraid, show us who you really are." Lukas's smug smile was telling. The prick was showboating. He intended to draw this out and make it a real spectacle.

Ronan inwardly sighed and suppressed the urge to call on his power. The arse wouldn't be nearly so smug with a broken jaw. Or if he was on fire.

His voice was a bored drawl when the throng of onlookers quieted enough for him to speak. "The mask is for your protection."

"*My* protection?" Nightshade laughed, drawing out several others all around them. "Sir, I don't think you realize just what a world of shit you've found yourself in. Do you have any idea who I am?"

It was on the tip of his tongue to say it . . .

You know what? Fuck it. If ever there was a time.

"I think the more pertinent question, Nightshade, is do you have any idea who *I* am?"

Lukas raked his cool gaze over Ronan's form. "I know everyone worth knowing. You don't rank among them."

Ronan's lips twitched. "You've heard of me. I guaran-fucking-tee it."

Little gasps sounded throughout the room. These people weren't used to someone openly confronting their boss. They likely couldn't wait to see what would happen next. Frankly, neither could Ronan. He just wanted to get on with it.

Nightshade stiffened, his smile a frozen, brittle thing. It hadn't ever been friendly, but his voice was icy with anger as he snapped, "There's no one more notorious than me."

"Wanna bet?"

"The Kiri herself could walk that sweet arse of hers in here, and not even she could claim the same. She may be known throughout Elysia, but my name is a thing of legends. It's whispered about in lands you've probably never even heard of."

Ronan laughed at that, his first genuine laugh in months. "More famous than Helena? The goddess of all creation's divine vessel? Next you're going to try to convince me you're Luna herself." Tears blurred his eyes by the time he managed to control himself. "Mother's tits, I needed that. Go on, tell me another. I haven't been this entertained in years."

Nightshade wasn't smiling any longer. "I grow tired of your games."

"Games? Who's playing?"

A muscle twitched in his jaw. "Tell me who you are. I want to make sure we know what name to etch on your grave after I make your insides your outsides."

"Eh, you're going to have to do better than that."

"Excuse me?"

"That's not even the best threat I've heard this week. If you're trying to intimidate me, Nightshade, you'll have to try a whole hell of a lot harder."

Lukas's eyes narrowed, but he didn't act.

Ronan silently groaned. If he'd realized it was going to take this much effort to get the man to attack him, he wouldn't have bothered with stealth in the first place. He could think of a dozen men, his best

13

friend among them, who would have had a blade to his throat by now. What the hell was Lukas waiting for? He had the upper hand. There was no way Ronan was getting out of this. So why the hesitation?

Realizing he would have to take matters into his own hands, Ronan stepped forward and slammed his forehead into the other man's face. Shouts rang out as blood sprayed from his nose.

"You're going to die for that."

"Finally, you're getting the idea."

"Who are you?" Lukas growled, a flickering ball of Fire in his hand.

"They call me the Butcher."

A vein spasmed in the other man's throat. "Liar."

"Am I? You sure about that, Nightshade? Willing to bet your life on it?"

People were openly trying to flee. He may not be wearing the famed armor or carrying the sword they'd heard so much about, but they weren't going to take a chance Ronan was telling the truth either. Smart.

"I don't have to. I'll take yours instead."

Ronan grinned. "You can certainly try."

Chaos erupted all around him. Four of Lukas's most loyal followers darted forward to restrain Ronan as Lukas shouted, "Seal the room! No one leaves until this fucker is dead."

Wind whipped through the underground chamber as the ball of molten flame swelled in Lukas's hand.

"You really going to throw that at me with so many of your people around?"

Flames danced in the other man's eyes, making him appear absolutely unhinged. Ronan felt his own power begging to be unleashed, but he tamped it down.

"Oh, I'm not going to throw it at you. I'm going to melt you from the inside out."

Ronan swallowed, knowing just how literal the threat could be. Depending on the strength of his gifts, Lukas could suck the air from Ronan's lungs. Or make the blood boil in his veins. He could even take that ball of Fire and find a way to shove it into his body while leaving his flesh intact. Such was the power of the Chosen.

Bracing himself for the worst, Ronan shuddered as Lukas inhaled, sucking the swirling ball of red, orange, and purple flame into his lungs. As a master of multiple elements, he must be immune to the burn. Lucky bastard, even he could admit it was a cool trick.

Then Lukas stepped forward, death shining in his eyes.

This was it, the moment he'd been waiting for. There was no escape.

His final battle had begun.

But now that it was here, Ronan didn't feel quite so willing. Nothing had changed, yet . . . something in him rebelled at the thought of this being the end. He struggled against the men holding him but couldn't shake them off. He tried again, this time calling on his Earth magic to give him a boost. It didn't help.

Ronan was well and truly fucked.

Lukas took the final step and grasped Ronan by the jaw, forcing his mouth open. Knowing that this was the end, that it was really over, he allowed his eyelids to fall closed, picturing a raven-haired beauty with forest-colored eyes just as Lukas blew a jet of flame straight into his mouth.

Reyna . . . I'm sorry.

CHAPTER 3

RONAN

"Ronan!"

Before the sound of his name registered, two thoughts occurred to him almost simultaneously. *Isn't dying supposed to hurt* and *shouldn't death be quieter?* Then the shout came again, this time tinged with a mix of fury and exasperation.

"Ronan, *move!*"

His mind must be going. Instead of his life flashing before his eyes, he was hearing people he loved yell at him. Or perhaps that *was* his life flashing through his mind. It was certainly a common enough occurrence. He'd been known to piss the people he loved off at every turn. Most of the time on purpose. If the Mother intended on taking him to task for it, he'd simply explain aggravation was the best form of motivation, and he was all about results. Surely, she couldn't argue with that.

Pleased with his logic—especially during what he assumed was a glorious death—he was only vaguely aware of the third shout.

"Elder's weeping dick, Ronan. Are you deaf? I said MOVE!"

Ah, Effie. She always had been filled with fire. She'd tried to dull her flame, but it had always been there, shining—

Something collided with his side, sending him toppling over. Ronan finally risked opening his eyes, blinking a few times as he tried to make sense of the world around him.

It was not all gossamer clouds and ethereal music as he'd expected. But it didn't resemble the underground cavern he'd spent his last waking moments in either. Somewhere between Lukas's attack and his heart's final prayer, reality shifted.

Surely *this* wasn't the afterlife.

He must have spoken aloud because a flushed and very irritated Effie barked, "It isn't. Because you're not dead, Ronan. Give me and my gift some credit."

Ronan lifted a hand to his throbbing temple. He would have sworn he'd faced his final moment, that he'd slipped away with the tickle of the fire's heat blazing in his lungs, his nose filled with the acrid tang of burnt flesh. He gave a cursory sniff. All he scented now was a hint of the sewers still clinging to his clothing.

Huh.

His poor overwhelmed mind simply could not make sense of this unexpected turn of events. He'd never considered a rescue. That his spur-of-the-moment decision would register as an important enough event to catapult one of the Keepers—the most renowned Keeper—into a vision.

But that's what happened because Effie wasn't just here—she'd been prepared for battle. And she wasn't alone. Her mate, Lucian, was mercilessly cutting down those stupid enough to get in range of his sword. Anytime someone stepped too close, a tendril of smoke would whip out and slice them in two. An oval of displaced air that could only be a portal shimmered beside him, explaining how he, Effie, and several others Ronan didn't recognize had made it here in the nick of time.

All of this Ronan took in in a matter of seconds. Glancing to his left, where he'd been standing before Effie so unceremoniously shoved him out of the way, stood an irate Lukas. Whatever Fire he'd been channeling was no longer in his control. Rather, it seemed to have turned against him. Now it ringed him, locking him in a fiery cage. The shackles at his wrists explained the expression on his face. Nullifiers. Without access to his gifts, he was at the mercy of the flames just as much as the next person. He wasn't going anywhere.

"Are you just going to stand there, or are you planning on participating in your rescue?" She tossed him a double-headed axe only years of reflex helped him catch.

"Who says I wanted to be rescued?"

Something dark flashed in Effie's sapphire gaze, but there wasn't time to explore it before a woman flung herself at him, clawing him with her nails as she attempted to climb him like he was a fucking tree. Ronan twisted, throwing her off and adjusting his hold on the weapon in preparation for the next attacker.

Things had definitely not gone to plan, but he was nothing if not adaptable. And Ronan—whether acting as Shield or Butcher—was always up for a fight.

He began fighting in earnest then, experiencing a sort of relieved euphoria that was at complete odds with what he'd been feeling at the start of the evening. But now was not the time to entertain questions such as: *why do I feel relieved at all when I'd failed in my mission?* Ronan was hardly inclined to decipher his feelings on an ordinary day, let alone amidst battle, so he didn't. Instead, he fought until only Night-shade remained.

Wiping his blade clean, he rounded on the man, smirking as he drawled, "Guess you're really regretting your life's decisions right about now."

Lukas sneered. "I regret nothing, *Shield.*"

"And yet you hide here in the shadows like a coward."

"Hide? I consider it surviving, but then I suppose you would see it that way. At least, I've never had to lie about who I am."

"I didn't take you for a hypocrite, Nightshade."

"Hypocrite? That's rich coming from you."

"What else would you call wearing a false face?"

"A false face is hardly the same as a false name. Wouldn't you agree?"

"Two sides of the same coin."

Lukas shook his head, disgust etched on his features. "My men would have never let you through the door if they'd known who you really were."

Ronan glanced at the bodies littering the ground. "What men? And as I recall, I'd made it through the door without ever having to introduce myself, so your argument is flawed."

Effie stepped forward then, her voice gentle but firm. "There will be time to goad him later, Ro. Time is of the essence." She shifted slightly, her expression softening as her gaze landed on her mate. "Luc, can you escort our new friend back to the Palace? Helena's expecting him—"

Guilt clawed its way through Ronan at the mention of the woman he'd vowed to serve. "How does Helena already know about this?"

Effie shot him a look he had no trouble interpreting. *Are you really interrupting me to ask me* that?

He supposed it was among the more stupid questions he'd asked. As the Mother's Vessel and Voice, respectively, the two women were in near-constant contact. If Effie wanted to send Helena a message, it would be done as easily as a Guardian opening a portal. Feeling foolish, Ronan wisely shut up and waited his turn.

Lucian sheathed his sword and came to join them, pressing a quick kiss to Effie's forehead. "Well done, fledgling. Your casting is nearly seamless."

"Nearly?" she scoffed. "Did you see how quickly I transformed that fireball into a cage? The poor bastard never saw me coming."

Lucian's expression was tender, his voice soft as he ran a hand down Effie's spine. "No one ever does, love." Then he looked to Ronan, dipping his chin in greeting. "I'd say it was nice to see you again, Shield, but . . ."

Something that felt a lot like shame swirled beneath Ronan's ribs. It was an unfamiliar sensation, one he did not remotely enjoy. It sent him instantly on the defensive. "If you're expecting gratitude—"

Lucian held up a hand. "I wouldn't waste my breath or my time. You and I both know I'd long be dead before such words ever passed your lips."

"Funny, considering you're an immortal."

"That was the point."

Ronan grunted. "Glad you're finally starting to understand me. Only took you, what, five years?"

Instead of rising to the bait, the look Lucian shot his way was brimming with understanding. Taking a step closer, he wrapped Ronan in a one-armed hug, his voice pitched low. "I know what it is to feel that you've lost everything. Do not lose hope, Shield. It's not too late."

Ronan stiffened, wondering what the hell *that* was supposed to mean. With his ties to the Keepers, surely Lucian had already heard the news about Reyna? So why would he urge him to cling to futile hope?

Before he could ask, Lucian turned to face the cage of dancing flame, his eyes glowing a blinding bronze as the fire surrounding Lukas was extinguished. Then he stepped forward, grabbed the prisoner by the wrist, and opened another portal. The fluidity and ease with which he executed the maneuvers spoke to his centuries of experience.

"This will only take a minute. I'll be right back."

Effie nodded, her and Lucian sharing a meaningful look before he yanked his prisoner through the glimmering air. The others who had come through the original portal left with him, leaving Ronan and Effie alone in the now silent chamber.

Not sure what to say or what her vision had already shown her, Ronan scrubbed a hand down his neck. "It's been a while, Efs."

"Don't. Not with me."

The gentle chastisement had him feeling like a boy caught stealing sweets. It had been a long time since he'd had a reason to feel small in the face of a loved one's disappointment. Ronan glanced away, his earlier misery and grief cresting like a wave at the reminder of why he —and consequently *she*—were both here.

"Well, let's get it over with then," he said gruffly, unable to meet her gaze as he crossed his arms over his chest.

"Get what over with?"

"The tongue lashing."

"Is that what you think I'm after?"

"Isn't it? Why else get me alone if not to scold me?"

"*Ronan.*"

He stubbornly refused to look at her.

"Ro, I know why you came here."

There was no judgment in her voice, and yet he felt all of two inches tall. Ronan gritted his teeth, his shoulders so tight the muscles felt like boulders embedded in his skin.

"I understand, truly, I do. I wish—" She broke off with a sigh. "It doesn't matter now. We got here in time to relay the message."

That . . . was not what he'd expected her to say.

Ronan blinked, his head shooting up. "What message?"

"She isn't dead."

He blinked again, a loud ringing sounding in his ears.

"Did you hear me?"

He couldn't move. Couldn't breathe.

"Ronan?"

His heart thundered as his head swam. He couldn't feel his legs. Was he still standing?

"Oh no, you don't," she growled, her eyes blazing sapphire. Her palm cracked against his cheek, clearing his head of its mental fog. "Focus, big guy. I didn't come all this way for you to faint before you heard what I have to say."

"Sorry." He swallowed, his voice hoarse as he whispered, "C-can you repeat that? I'm not sure I heard you correctly. I . . . I thought you said . . ." He couldn't even get himself to repeat the words, his poor, fragile heart terrified to believe in the possibility only for it to be wrenched away from him again.

Her expression softened for a second, the empathy he found shining in her eyes stinging almost as much as the imprint of her hand on his face. As if she could sense he would need her strength to keep him upright, Effie dug her fingers into his biceps, gripping him tight as she stared him straight in the eye. And then, with two fiercely whispered words, she sent his world careening off its axis for the second time that day.

"Reyna's alive."

EFFIE

"ALIVE?"

Her friend's voice was so broken, so scared to hope, that it hardly sounded like the playful and protective warrior she considered an annoying but much-loved older brother. She barely recognized the man standing in front of her.

Oh, he was still undeniably handsome, with that same tangle of rust-colored braids running down his back. But not in the playful, roguish way he used to be. He towered over her, but the muscles that had once been perfect for bear hugs were more pronounced, as if they'd crush rather than comfort. And he'd shaved his beard. In and of itself, not a damning act, but certainly one he'd never done so long as she'd known him. The newly exposed angles of his cheeks and jaw lent his face an even harsher cast. Instead of charming, he was . . . intimidating. Even when she was a nothing girl who hid behind her hair, he'd never given her a reason to fear him. Despite his size and penchant for violence, he'd always been kind. Gentle. Now there wasn't an ounce of softness left in him.

But the part that truly worried her was the bleak and lifeless quality of his gaze.

Ronan had long been known for the mischievous twinkle in his ice-blue eyes. It was an unspoken invitation to play and be in on the joke. But now there was . . . nothing. That spark was gone. And Effie knew, even without the aid of her visions, it had guttered out the second he'd stopped believing he could save Reyna.

She moved to take one of his massive hands in hers, squeezing it tight. "Yes, Ro. Alive."

"But . . . they found her body."

"No, they didn't. It was a false rumor."

His brows furrowed. "But why? Why now, after so many years?"

"They meant to draw out the last of the Night Stalkers from hiding." The famed assassins who called the Forest of Whispers their home had been under attack ever since their queen went missing. Although attack felt like too kind a word for it. They'd simply gone missing. Disappearing in the night or while on patrol, never to be seen or heard from again. Just like Reyna. Whoever had been hunting them was clever, covering their tracks and not leaving a single clue.

Until now.

"They who?" The words were bitten off, savage.

"My vision didn't say."

"Vision?"

"Yes, Ronan. Has it been so long since we've seen each other you've already forgotten how the Mother likes to visit me from time to time? That she gifted me with prophecy?" He snarled, which she took as a good sign, so she kept on with her sisterly ribbing. "How else do you think I learned the rumors were false?"

His gaze sharpened, zeroing in on what she'd left unsaid. "You know where she is."

"I do."

"Tell me."

"That's why I'm here."

"Stop fucking around and tell me." Each word bitten off and dripping with impatience.

There you are, big guy.

Ronan hadn't so much as blinked since she confirmed she knew Reyna's whereabouts. With each growled word, she could practically see the warrior waking up and breaking free of the metaphorical prison his despair had trapped him within. He positively radiated tension, his big hands curling and uncurling at his sides, his nostrils flared, jaw clenched, and chest rising and falling with every rapid breath. He was no longer a man ready for death, but one preparing to go to war.

One he had no intention of losing.

Nearly giddy with relief at the proof her friend wasn't beyond saving, Effie smiled.

"I thought you'd never ask."

CHAPTER 4

RONAN

"*I*t is the height of impropriety—"

"Not sure Ronan gives a Talyrian's teat about being appropriate, Tims."

The Kiri's Advisor glanced sharply up at her Sword. Shoulders drooping, he let out a disgruntled huff. "No one in this blasted Circle does. But the point stands, *I* am the one who calls the meetings. Any matter important enough to require a formal gathering of the Circle—"

"Yeah, yeah. We heard you the first seven hundred times." Kragen rested a meaty palm on the older man's shoulder. "You can get the next one, buddy."

"Do. You. Mind?" Timmins shrugged him off, taking a moment to smooth down his jacket and adjust his cuffs, as if the Sword's two-second touch had somehow rumpled him beyond repair.

Laughing, Kragen scrubbed his palm over the other man's hair, which had gone more salt than pepper at the temples. "Not as much as you, Tims."

Timmins slapped his hand away with a beleaguered, "Why am I the only one who treats my position with the deference it deserves?"

"Because you're the best of us, Timmins. We've always said so,"

Joquil answered, finally interceding. Helena's Master had always been better than the rest of them at soothing the Advisor's easily ruffled feathers.

The announcement seemed to have caught the older man off guard. Cheeks tinged pink, he cleared his throat before feigning indifference. "Yes, well. It is nice to hear it acknowledged on occasion."

Ronan watched all of this play out with the barely suppressed aggravation of a man desperate to be elsewhere. After Effie's revelation, the two of them returned to the palace, where Ronan called an emergency meeting, and Effie went in search of Lucian and the prisoner. That had been well over an hour ago. It took every ounce of his control not to storm up to the Kiri's private rooms and forcibly carry Helena down here and toss her in her damned throne so they could have this farce of a tribunal and be done with it.

But he didn't.

The small part of him still thinking logically knew she'd be far less agreeable to his plan if he attempted to run off and do it without her blessing. Just as she had to know his 'request' was a way for her to publicly save face. Helena knew him too well to believe he was actually asking for permission. He'd already made up his mind and would be leaving, blessing or no, but it would make things so much easier on them both if it appeared she willingly freed him of his vow.

When he'd pledged to be her Shield, it had been for life. Same as the rest of the Circle. His leaving without her consent would be deemed an act of outright treason. Meaning he'd never be able to set foot on Elysian soil as a free man again. Given their history, Ronan doubted Helena would go to such extremes, but sometimes the queen was required to do things the woman would rather not. And Helena was every inch a queen.

Ronan inwardly shrugged. Whatever the outcome, his path was set. He'd started over more than once before. He wasn't afraid of doing so again. Though he *would* miss these arseholes if that was the case.

The arseholes in question still hadn't ceased their senseless bickering.

"You have something, just here," Kragen said, pointing at an invisible speck of dirt on the Advisor's jacket.

"Where?" Timmins asked, eyes widening in horror as he dipped his chin to inspect the aforementioned area. Kragen was already quaking with laughter as he quickly moved his hand and smacked Timmins in the nose. Realizing he'd fallen for what was quite possibly the oldest trick in the book, Timmins flushed with anger. "So help me, Sword, if you so much as twitch another eyelash in my direction—"

"How exactly am I supposed to control my eyelashes?"

"Figure it out," he growled.

The door opened, and Ronan didn't even realize he'd stopped breathing until Effie's blonde curls appeared instead of Helena's chestnut waves.

What in the Mother's name is keeping her?

Effie spotted him and beelined in his direction, Lucian right behind her.

"My, how you've perfected that glower, Ro."

He spared Effie a side-eyed glance but didn't comment.

"You know, for a man who was just given what could arguably be described as the best news of his life, you're acting quite pissy."

"Pissy?"

"Oh dear, is your hearing failing you?" Effie tutted softly. "Poor lamb. I've been told it's the first to go. Right after the hair."

He raised a brow, knowing exactly what she was up to. It may have been a while since they'd played the game, but not so long that he couldn't recognize the opening salvo. They'd done it often enough, taking jabs at one another until one or both would break. Break, in this case, meaning burst into laughter. It had been their way of bringing one another back into the light after a particularly difficult day. He didn't think anything short of holding Reyna in his arms would pull him out of the darkness he'd been living in these last years, but he appreciated Effie's attempt all the same.

"My hearing and hair are perfect, thank you very much."

She reached out, curling her small hand around his. "Peace, Ronan.

I know you are chomping at the bit to go to her, but we have time enough for this. I promise you."

"That's not what you said before. I believe your exact words were 'time is of the essence.'"

"And it is, but another few hours will not affect the outcome."

"How can you be so sure?"

Her eyes flashed with blue fire, and though pitched low and only for him, her voice was brimming with power. "I have Seen it. You have many trials ahead of you, Butcher. But you are finally on the path you've been seeking. Stay the course."

Ronan stiffened, making note of her word choice. Butcher, *not* Shield. No one in this room knew of his dark persona, but he should have guessed nothing would remain a secret from Effie.

But that wasn't what concerned him right now.

If she was referring to him as the Butcher, it meant he would need to play the monster in order to succeed. In many ways, that was a relief. Ronan wasn't sure he knew how to be a hero anymore.

As far as hints went, it was a mere breadcrumb, but he wasn't thickheaded enough to ignore it. Effie had been annoyingly tight-lipped on the details of her vision. Other than assuring him Reyna was very much alive and that they'd yet to find her because she was no longer on this continent, she refused to say anything else.

When he'd pushed the issue, she'd given him an infuriatingly calm response.

"To tell you more is to risk the outcome. I will give you what you need to begin your journey. The rest is up to you."

"What good are you and your fucking visions if you're not going to share anything of actual use?"

Effie had laughed at him then. He'd heard her shout similar words at her mate when she'd undergone trials of her own, so he took her laughter to mean she appreciated his exasperation rather than it being at his expense. Ronan also understood she'd share more if she could, but he still resented her withholding details that could potentially aid his quest.

This journey, as she called it, had already lasted five years. How much fucking longer did he have to wait?

She must have sensed his mounting frustration because her hand tightened around his. "Take it from me. Specifics impede the true message. I once knew two men who received similar visions. The first was fed nothing but details, but they were out of context and ultimately misinterpreted. He went mad obsessing over what he'd Seen. While the other man, the one who knew next to nothing and only had a mere possibility to guide him, ultimately succeeded in getting everything he yearned for."

"It wasn't possibility driving him," Lucian corrected.

Effie raised an eyebrow. "Oh?"

"It was hope."

The lovers shared a look so filled with tender devotion that Ronan's chest ached. He had to look away, their happiness too painful to bear. When he finally dared to glance back at them, Lucian's eyes were locked on his. The Guardian didn't say a thing, and yet Ronan knew he was relaying a message. A second later, the man's earlier words echoed in his mind.

"Do not lose hope."

On the heels of Effie's story, the encouragement took on new meaning. Once upon a time, Lucian had found himself in a position similar to Ronan, armed with nothing *but* hope to guide his way. He'd had no way of knowing whether it would pay off in the end, but he'd believed anyway. Faced with nothing but adversity, Lucian believed he would succeed.

And he did.

Ronan appreciated their warnings, but he couldn't help but wonder why they were so insistent he'd need hope in the coming days. Effie already assured him that Reyna was alive. He had cold hard fact to keep him motivated. No blind faith required.

Frowning, he started to ask when the doors to the throne room opened once more. This time, Helena swept in, a red-faced angel in her arms and her Mate hot on her heels.

"Sorry we're late. Stella absolutely refused to go down for her nap.

Every time we tried to set her in her crib, her screams would either send something up in flames or shatter the windows." Helena rolled her eyes. "Who knew a child with such a sunny disposition could turn into an absolute banshee over a couple of new teeth?"

"Do you need me to make you a concoction?" Joquil offered. "Something to help with the pain?"

Helena sighed, somehow still managing to look regal despite the toddler drooling down the front of her dress. "I think so. The only thing that seems to soothe her these days is being held." She paused and rubbed her nose against Stella's, making the little girl giggle as she cooed, "And Mommy cannot run a realm with a sweet nymph who feels like a two-ton monkey constantly in her arms. No, she cannot."

Von laughed. "Let me take her."

"No," the little girl whined, surprising them all when she held her arms out and made grabby hands in Ronan's direction. "Wo-Wo."

What was left of the blackened stump Ronan called a heart cracked wide open. The day Stella had been born had been one of the few bright spots in an otherwise miserable couple of years. Watching his best friend finally find peace and how the little mite had wrapped everyone around her tiny fingers in a matter of seconds had been a thing of absolute beauty. She was so little he'd been afraid to touch her. All he'd been willing to risk was the lightest brush of his finger over the downy softness of her cheek, and when she'd grabbed his finger and held him there, staring up at him with such absolute love and trust shining in her eyes, he'd been a goner.

It frightened him, that trust. He didn't deserve it.

Afraid he was too broken to be around someone so pure, he'd kept his distance ever since, finding more and more excuses to be away from the happy family. And despite all of it, little Stella still seemed to have a preference for her Uncle Wo-Wo above all others.

He may be a sorry bastard, but not even he was immune to the request or the glint of tears still shimmering in those big blue eyes.

He could feel the gaze of every person in the room trained on him, waiting to see what he would do. Ignoring all of them, Ronan crossed the mosaic floor and plucked his niece from her mother's arms.

"Come here then, mite."

Stella let out a happy gurgle and snuggled into him immediately, making his own eyes burn and his throat tighten. "Ella wuv Wo-Wo."

It was hard to swallow past the ball that seemed to be lodged in his throat, but he curled his hand over the back of her head and brushed his lips to her forehead. "I love you too, wildheart."

Stella cooed and wrapped surprisingly strong arms around his neck, hugging him tightly. Happy and content, her breaths evened out, and she seemed to drift off in his hold almost between one breath and the next. Clearing his throat a few times, Ronan forced himself to meet Helena's gaze, trying not to flinch at the emotion reflected at him.

He knew she was worried about him. Everyone in this room had expressed their concern in some fashion or another. Timmins admonished and Kragen goaded, while Joquil offered a non-judgmental ear. Helena had tried to get him to open up about his feelings. When that hadn't worked, Von offered to be his punching bag so he could purge the heartache in his native tongue. Lucian and Effie's two-pronged approach today was hardly the first time the Guardians had broached the subject either. Everyone was doing their best to help him stay afloat, but none of them seemed to realize it was too late. He'd already drowned.

"You're leaving," Helena said without preamble.

Timmins's shocked inhale told Ronan Effie hadn't looped the others in on her vision.

"I have to."

Helena nodded. "Of course. We'll go with you."

The offer felt like the twist of a dagger. Her immediate willingness to drop everything to assist him was a reminder of how little he deserved her loyalty. He'd been a shite friend these last few years, physically present but more absent than not. Too consumed by his own grief to have space left for anyone else.

He could make up for that now.

"No."

She flinched, a furrow working its way between her brows. "But Ronan—"

There was no denying Helena's considerable power would make short work of whatever waited for him, but Ronan wouldn't allow her to uproot her life and put herself at risk for him. Not when so many, including the softly snoring babe in his arms, needed her safe and whole right here. She'd fought too damn hard for her happily ever after. She should enjoy it.

"You can't, Hellion," he whispered. She flinched at her old nickname, her expression crumpling as he gently continued, "And you know it. Stella needs her mother. Elysia needs their queen."

"And *you* need *me*."

"Always, but this is something I can do on my own."

"Just because you can doesn't mean you should."

That fucking ball was back. "Helena . . ."

"Ronan . . ."

"Let me go." The plea was a ragged whisper. "She needs me more than you do."

"I know." Tears swam in Helena's aqua eyes.

"If there was another way—"

"I know," she repeated, her voice steadier this time. "It's okay. It would be selfish of me to force you to stay when your heart is so clearly elsewhere. I will not be your jailer, Ronan. You made your vow to me before Reyna was ever in the picture. You may not have had the chance to voice them yet, but the unspoken promises of your heart supersede any you gave to me."

Relief rolled through him. He closed his eyes, sucking in a shuddering breath. He'd known she would consent, but hearing it affected him far more than he thought it would. Helena was the final tether keeping him in Elysia. Without the shackles of duty to bind him, he felt unmoored.

Weightless.

Free.

"Thank you."

"It is the least I can do for the brother of my heart."

Ronan didn't bother wiping away the tear that slipped free. His hands were full, holding on to the child in his arms anyway. "You've always been the sister of my soul."

"Hey," Effie protested softly, breaking the tension in the room and making the others laugh.

Ronan used the moment to catch Von's eye. A lifetime of memories passed between them. Ronan couldn't think of a single milestone in his life that didn't include the silver-eyed warrior. This would be the first time since childhood they'd be apart. When Von had set off to face his destiny, Ronan had been right there at his side. It had always been that way between them. Where one went, the other followed.

But not this time.

This time Ronan had to walk alone.

Von's eyes darkened, and his voice was gruffer than usual when he spoke. "Find her, Ronan."

"I will."

"Find her, and then *come home*."

Ronan didn't answer that time. Not because he didn't want to, he was simply too overwhelmed by all he was feeling. And after feeling nothing but anger for so long, he couldn't seem to remember how to function any other way.

"Kiri, who will you name in his place?" Timmins asked.

Ronan almost smiled. Fucking Timmins. Of course the Advisor would be more worried about following protocol than anything else. Some things never change.

"No one."

"But Helena, the Circle . . . you cannot—"

Her eyes turned a sparkling iridescent. "*I* can do whatever I want, Advisor. Ronan is my Shield. Though he must leave me, he will return, and on that day—no matter how far away it might be—the position will be waiting for him. Until then, we will find someone to stand in during his well-deserved vacation."

"Since when do we get to take vacations?" Kragen grumbled.

Ronan wanted to point out that he didn't anticipate there would be much in the way of relaxing in his future, but that wasn't the purpose of Helena's proclamation. Her message was clear. As far as the Chosen were concerned, the Shield was taking an extended trip but would return. His position would be filled by another in his absence. It might seem a small distinction, but her version of events would raise fewer eyebrows than the truth.

It also had the added benefit of ensuring word didn't reach the Night Stalkers' assailants—whoever or wherever they were—that their days were numbered.

"But who is even worthy of such a post?" Timmins argued.

"Kael," Effie answered, referring to the third Guardian who protected the Keepers alongside her and Lucian. The certainty in her voice left little doubt in Ronan's mind that this must have been part of her vision.

"Can you spare him?" Helena asked.

"Lucian and I are more than capable of carrying out the Triumvirate's duties on our own, but perhaps it is time for a new Guardian to join our ranks."

"Making decisions on behalf of all of us now, are you fledgling?" Lucian asked, amusement quirking his lips.

"Someone has to," she said with a slight shrug. "Might as well be the woman blessed with knowledge of the future by the Mother."

"Convenient excuse," Lucian murmured, making the others in the room chuckle.

"I'll leave the Guardian matters up to the two of you," Helena said, biting back her own smile. "As for my interim Shield, it shall be as Effie says. So long as he is not opposed, Kael will take over in Ronan's absence." Her smile faded, and her gaze returned to him. "When do you leave?"

"Now."

The slight tremor of her hand was the only hint as to what the knowledge did to her. "I . . . *we* will miss you."

Ronan couldn't quite find the words to tell her it would be the same for him.

Von saved him the trouble, stepping forward to collect his daughter. "Happy hunting, brother." They exchanged dark smiles before

Von's voice dipped low. "And when you find the fuckers who took her, make it hurt."

"You know I will."

They shared another long look before Von stepped away. Helena was in Ronan's arms almost immediately. "Safe travels, Ro."

"Be well, Hellion. You've earned your happiness."

Her answering chuckle was watery. "If any of us deserves to find happiness, it's you. I hope you find whatever it is you've been searching for all these years."

He pulled back to look at her. "You know what I've been searching for. Or rather who I've been searching for."

Helena shook her head. "Reyna is only part of the puzzle. You were restless long before she was taken."

Ronan wasn't sure what to do with that truth, so he gave her a soft kiss on the cheek. "Take care of him for me."

She pressed a palm to her chest. "With my life."

Unable to draw this out any longer, Ronan turned and gave Effie a slight nod. Her eyes glimmered with power as she summoned the portal that would take him to Reyna. His eyes fluttered closed as another wave of relief crashed over him.

Finally.

"Where's he going?" Timmins whispered.

Home. Ronan wasn't sure where the thought came from, but before he could dwell on it, Lucian provided the others with his actual destination.

"Empyria."

Stunned silence met the revelation. Empyria was a place of legend. A fabled land whispered about but never seen. A place of monsters and magic and dreams.

And soon, Ronan vowed, a reckoning.

Pausing only long enough to glance over his shoulder, Ronan drank in the sight of his friends. It may be the last time he ever saw them. He wanted to make it count. As he stood there, poised between his past and his future, Kragen offered a wave, Timmins a nod. Helena's lips wobbled, and Effie took her hand. Von helped Stella blow him a kiss, and Joquil simply stared.

That's when Ronan remembered the Master shared Reyna's homeland.

"Save her," he mouthed.

Throat tight, Ronan nodded as he stepped through the portal, a promise simmering in his veins.

I will not rest until I find her. Mother save the man who dares stand in my way, for he will find no mercy with me. I almost gave up once. I will not quit again.

One way or another, Reyna will be mine.

~

HELENA

"Do you think he's going to be okay?" she whispered as the others slowly filtered out of the room.

Her Mate studied her with stormy silver eyes. *"Mira,* you know I cannot lie to you."

"I didn't ask you to."

He quirked a dark brow. "Didn't you? You seek reassurance, but I can offer none. I've known Ronan since we were boys. He's the brother of my soul, if not my blood. I do not know what awaits him at the end of his journey. But I pray he finds peace."

"Me too."

As they had so many times in the last handful of years, Helena's fingertips blindly traced the lines of her Jaka, the Daejaran warrior's mark running down the length of her rib cage. Ronan had gifted her with it during one of her darkest times. Even though the iridescent tattoo was currently concealed by her dress, she instinctively sought out the hidden symbol he'd worked into the design. The one he bashfully informed her represented his undying loyalty. It felt like a lifetime ago that they'd been those people. Her the one falling apart without the other half of her soul, and he the pillar of strength and hope holding her together when it felt like nothing else would.

When she'd had a chance to do the same, to repay the debt, she'd failed. Ronan hadn't simply cracked; he'd shattered. And not even their bond had been enough to piece him back together.

Helena barely recognized the man who'd just stood before them. Sure, he looked and talked the same. He even managed to smile once or twice. But Ronan, *her* Ronan, was gone. Even gifted with Effie's vision, he was only a shadow of his former self. A creature composed of darkness instead of light.

She knew it wasn't by choice. He'd simply lost too much, had his faith tested one too many times. No one could be expected to face such trials and remain unchanged. It was a truth she understood better than most. Not everyone survived meeting the darkest parts of their soul. Mother knows she barely did.

Fear skittered across Helena's spine and dread pooled low in her stomach. She couldn't shake the feeling that when Ronan stepped through that portal he suspected he wouldn't return. That even though the words hadn't crossed his lips, his last look over his shoulder had been goodbye.

Blinking away tears, she whispered, "I already miss him."

"So do I, love." Reaching out, Von tangled his fingers with hers, their daughter already fast asleep. Her thumb tucked sweetly in her mouth as she cuddled into the safety of her daddy's arms. "So do I."

CHAPTER 5

RONAN

"This is where I leave you."

Ronan glanced back at Lucian, who remained beside the flickering portal. "Are you sure there's nothing else you can share with me? An address, perhaps?"

Lucian offered a sympathetic smile. "I know as much as you."

"So fuck all then."

"At least you know she's here somewhere."

"I've learned when it comes to the Keepers 'here' could as easily mean the whole damned continent as the city itself."

Lucian's lips twitched. "Here, meaning Glimmermere"—he waved a hand to indicate the bustling port town in the distance—"Empyria's capital. Chin up, Shield. Your journey nears its end."

"Effie said it was just beginning."

"I suppose it's a matter of perspective, then."

Ronan growled. "Fucking Keepers and their word games."

"Comes with the territory, I'm afraid. Take care of yourself, Ronan. My woman will be devastated if anything happens to you. Don't give her a reason to cry."

Realizing that this was the point of no return, Ronan cleared his throat. "Make sure to tell her—"

"She already knows."

Ronan sighed. "I suppose she does. If this is the last time . . ."

"Don't you dare finish that sentence. I've only barely begun tolerating you. I'm not ready to actively like you."

He barked out a laugh. "That's fair. Never did care for you much either."

"Good. Let's keep it that way, shall we? Some traditions are sacred." Despite the words, there was genuine affection in the other man's gaze. "Best of luck to you, Ronan."

"Farewell, Luc."

With a slight tip of his chin, the Guardian took his leave.

Palming Reyna's dagger, which he'd sheathed in his belt, Ronan set off the well-worn path, estimating it would be full dark by the time he reached the city gates. He hadn't had time to grab much between Effie's arrival and leaving. Luckily, his travel bag, magicked by Helena a few years ago, was always packed. Thanks to her, no matter what he placed inside it, it never grew heavy or changed its shape. So while it appeared to be an empty coin purse, hidden within was his best sword, the Butcher's armor, a significant amount of coin, a couple cloaks—one fur-lined, one travel-stained—a set of court attire, his camping equipment, and a few other essentials. It should serve until he got a lay of the land.

Although he wasn't sure he'd be needing the fur cloak.

The weather, so far at least, seemed moderate. A bit warmer than Elysia, but nothing like the sweltering temperatures he'd suffered in the Vale. He supposed that could change once the sun was at its zenith. But that was tomorrow's problem. For the moment, the sky was painted in shades of orange, the sun hanging low over the horizon while a light sea breeze salted the air. It had been a fair while since he'd had to make do with a bedroll and the dirt, but if he had to rough it tonight, at least he'd be comfortable enough.

Ronan tried not to think too far past that. His plan for the moment was to make his way to town and find food and hopefully lodging for the night. Depending on how that went, he'd also put feelers out on potential work so he could buy whatever he might need at the market if the coin he had was not viable here. That was assuming these people even had some version of a merchant's square where he could acquire such goods. He was well traveled, but Empyria was an unknown entity. The only thing he could count on was running into the unexpected.

The sound of crashing waves grew louder as he neared the town, and soon he could make out the familiar calls of a working port. That small dose of his homeland was enough to ease his nerves. The particulars might vary, but people were ultimately the same wherever you went. He'd find his footing soon enough.

Wiping sweat from his brow, Ronan counted several spires jutting up from the city's center, all topped with blinding gold onion-shaped domes. The towers, as far as he could tell, were a mix of blood-red and black with some sort of scrolling ornamentation running along their lengths. He couldn't quite make out the details from here, but the overall effect was striking.

Something about the structure called to him, so he paused, squinting as he tried to get a better sense of what was catching his attention. *There.* The easternmost tower. A series of balconies jutted out, spiraling upward. And standing on one of the upper balconies was a woman. At least, he assumed it was a woman due to her willowy build and the way her moonlight-colored hair blew in the breeze. For a second, he would have sworn she was staring straight at him. A little shiver worked its way down his spine, but he couldn't pinpoint why something so innocuous would affect him.

Ronan amended his earlier assessment of the building, blaming it for his uncharacteristic response. Striking, yet foreboding. A warning for citizens and visitors alike to tread carefully. They were being watched.

Taking the warning to heart, he quickened his steps and made his way to the main gates. After his reaction to what he'd decided must be the palace, he expected more fanfare at the gates but passed through without so much as a sideways glance from the guards posted on either side.

Once inside the city proper, the road turned from dirt to stone.

Following it until it branched off at the end, he found himself in front of a sign he had absolutely no trouble deciphering. A board hung from the center of the thatched-roof structure, depicting cold drinks and hot food. That could only mean one thing.

A tavern.

"Now that's a sight for sore eyes."

"Talking about me, handsome?" a pretty wench with a gap-toothed grin asked. Once she had his full attention, she leaned forward to better showcase her assets. "Looking for some company?"

He offered her a polite smile in return and a quick shake of his head, happy that despite her unfamiliar and somewhat lyrical accent, it didn't seem like there would be a language barrier to contend with.

She gave him a disappointed pout as he made his way to the tavern's green door. "Pity. If you change your mind, you know where to find me! Or just ask for Camille!"

Before he could push it open, a couple of patrons tumbled out, along with the welcome sound of raucous laughter, men and women well in their cups, and lively gambling. Taking this for the boon it was, Ronan walked in and straight up to the bar.

Perfect.

Seemed like the Mother might be on his side after all.

For what better place was there for a weary traveler to find some respite . . . or for a hunter to collect a bit of town gossip regarding his target?

ANY LINGERING concerns Ronan had about blending in were long gone a few hours later. Glimmermere, as it turns out, was a breeding ground for all sorts. Nearly everyone he'd interacted with had a different accent, and it didn't take long to realize that travelers were not only common in the city, they were welcome. No one had given him a second glance when he approached one of the back tables and asked to join their game, which he'd since learned was called Diamonds.

The men and women seated at the table seemed eager enough to teach him the rules—likely because they saw him as an easy mark—but that was all right with him. If he could get some information out of them, it was a fair trade in his eyes. Not that being good at the game seemed to be a requirement anyway. The man seated next to him had been losing steadily for the past hour.

"Your move," he said, nudging Ronan with his elbow.

A quick check of the cards in his hands and the ones on the table proved he had nothing to gain staying in the round. "I'm out."

Picking up the stein of house brew that one of the tavern's servers had kept filled for him, he drained it and allowed his eyes to roam around the room, picking up snippets of conversation as he did.

"Do you think the High Lord will make an appearance?"

"At the champion selection?"

"No, at the bleeding races. Of course, I'm referring to the selection."

Ronan discreetly turned his ear in their direction. This was the fourth time he'd heard mention of the High Lord and his contest. Whatever it was, it seemed important.

"The whole point of the games is to determine who his champion will be, can't imagine he won't want to attend."

"I thought he was off hunting one of his monsters," a third voice interrupted.

"He and that shadow of his just returned," the first speaker answered.

Ronan stiffened at the mention of a shadow, then reminded himself these people weren't referring to the walking corpses he'd spent the better part of two years fighting back home.

"Do you think she'll enter the competition?" the second asked, sounding hopeful.

"It's game over for everyone else if she does, isn't it? Don't see why the High Lord wouldn't just hand her the title straight away if that's the case. Would save a lot of needless death."

"Where's the fun in that?"

The three patrons laughed.

The man beside him elbowed him again. "Are you playing or no?"

Realizing a new hand had been dealt while he'd been eavesdropping, Ronan quickly picked up his cards and dropped a couple coins in the center pile. "Apologies. I'm in."

His neighbor gave him a cursory once-over. "For someone interested in learning the game, you don't seem to be paying attention."

"For someone familiar with the game, you don't seem to know how to win."

The man feigned affront and then laughed. "Touché. I do appear to be paying for the privilege of sitting beside you. A kind man would at least buy me a drink to ease the sting."

Ronan raised a brow. "I never claimed to be kind."

The blond man played his next cards and then swept his gray eyes over Ronan, lingering on his face. "You seem a gentleman of good breeding all the same."

"What gave me away?" Ronan asked, making his own selection.

"The truth?"

"I didn't realize we've been trading falsehoods up until now."

Grinning, his tablemate declared, "You don't stink." Then he leaned forward and sniffed. "Not much anyway."

Ronan slowly turned his head to gaze down at him, noting the care with which the blond man had styled his hair, his ostentatious silver-embroidered tunic and matching turquoise breeches, and the slight smattering of freckles across the bridge of his aquiline nose. The fact that he could count the specks if he so chose meant the fop was entirely too close.

"If you want to keep your teeth, I suggest you move your fucking face."

Completely unfazed, his neighbor held out his hand. "Allow me to introduce myself—"

"I'd really rather you didn't."

When it was clear Ronan wasn't about to take his hand, he rested it over his heart, dipping his head in the slightest bow. "I'm Sebastian Jean-Rene Villehardouin, but you may call me Bast. All my friends do."

"I'm not your friend." Though that name was a fucking mouthful, so he could see why they shortened it.

"You will be."

"You court disappointment."

"Ah, but you are wrong, *friend*. I court pleasure, and pleasure never disappoints."

"If that's a come-on, you are seriously barking up the wrong tree."

Sebastian laughed. "You're pretty, but not my type."

"No," one of their other table mates agreed. "He prefers his bedmates married."

"And stupid," another added.

"I think the words you were looking for were 'willing' and 'talented,'" Sebastian corrected haughtily, playing his next card. "And if they're already married, I don't have to worry about them growing attached. It's a win-win."

"Seems like you have a reputation, *Bast*," Ronan said.

"It's nice to be known for something."

"And being an adulterer is what you want to be known for? Seems like a quick way to end up dead."

"That's what makes it so exciting. Where's your sense of adventure?"

"You're an idiot."

"At least I'm famous."

Ronan shook his head. He'd spent more than half his life with a reputation and name that preceded him everywhere he went. He'd take anonymity any day.

"So what about you, friend. Do you have a name?"

"Yes."

"Are you going to give it to me?"

"No."

Sebastian laughed. "*Mon ami* it is."

The rogue looked entirely too pleased with himself. Ronan didn't trust it. The foreign words didn't sound like an insult, but on the off chance they were, he'd really rather not walk around the butt of some unknown joke.

Sighing, he gave in. "Ronan."

"What was that?"

"My name. It's Ronan."

"*Enchanté*, Ronan."

Laughter danced in Sebastian's gray eyes, making Ronan's shoulders knot with tension. "No."

"No?"

"Whatever you're doing. No."

Sebastian pressed his lips together. "I'm not doing anything, Ronan. Except losing all my money."

Ronan scowled, already regretting his decision to cave. The night had been so much more enjoyable before this fucker opened his mouth. Shaking his head, he returned his attention to his cards. An hour later, the game came to an end with Ronan winning the pot.

"Beginner's luck," one of his tablemates muttered with a good-natured scowl.

Since a couple of the gamblers had plans elsewhere for the evening, further play was suspended while the rest got up to stretch their legs or grab a refill before the next round began, providing Ronan with another opportunity to eavesdrop.

Once again, conversation centered on the High Lord and his tourney. Although this time he seemed to be listening to a husband and wife.

"You should really stop referring to it as the Tournament of Death, dearest. The High Lord's Raven has ears everywhere."

Raven?

"But that's what it is. Only one will survive. What do you think happens to the rest? They float off into the sunset? Be reasonable, love. This is blood sport."

"What better way to test the mettle of his champion?"

"Any other way. There is no honor in mindless slaughter."

"The contestants know what they're signing up for."

"I'm glad our Gregor is too young to enter. What a waste, all those lives lost. And for what?"

"A chance at honor, dearest. Men have lost their lives over less."

"It's not right."

"Hush, darling. The High Lord is fair, but he does not tolerate dissent."

"I'm speaking the truth. That's hardly dissension . . . "

The voices trailed away, leaving Ronan with more questions than answers. This was the first time any of the patrons had spoken of their High Lord with anything other than approval or outright awe. From what he'd gathered from the various snippets of conversation he'd collected, their ruler was newly appointed, having made a name for himself after saving the prior High Lord's life from some sort of attack. The city had been nearly razed to the ground, but he, along with his army, had arrived in the nick of time—though not before the man's wife and daughter were lost. When his predecessor died a couple of months later—many claim from a broken heart—the citizens of Glimmermere overwhelmingly showed up in support of the hero taking his place.

Sebastian returned to the table a moment later. "What did I miss?"

"What's raven?"

He froze in the act of taking his seat. "I think you mean, *who's* Raven. And that's a bold question for a man newly arrived in town."

"Why, is it a secret or something?"

Sebastian looked around, dropping his voice. "The Raven is the High Lord's chief spy. Very few know their exact identity, though it is widely assumed Lady Dovina holds the title. More importantly, and perhaps more relevant to you, *mon ami*, is that she has many in her employ. One never knows to whom they are speaking, so it is best to watch what you say, *oui*?"

Ronan wasn't sure what the word meant but took it as some sort of affirmation check, so he nodded. Head swimming with all he learned, he decided to forgo another round of Diamonds and call it a night.

"I'm going to pack it in." He did a swift calculation in his head. "You owe me seventy starling." Ronan hadn't quite gotten a handle on the various coins, but he knew the sum was no small fee.

"About that . . ." Sebastian's throat bobbed, and he paled.

Ronan narrowed his eyes. "You better not be about to tell me you cannot make good on your debt." The other gamblers had winnings enough to cover their bets, but Sebastian had started using badges, or what amounted to an IOU, about an hour prior.

"If you stay a while longer, I'm sure I'll make back what I owe you with interest."

"You haven't won a game all night."

"So my luck is about to turn."

"Spoken like a true addict. I want my money."

"Please, I'll—" Sebastian licked his lips, his eyes darting around nervously. "I'll make it up to you. It just . . . it cannot get out around town that I am . . . *without means.*"

"You mean broke."

"Hush, I'm begging you." Genuine fear lightened the other man's eyes, telling Ronan everything he needed to know about his new friend's current financial situation.

"Oh no," Ronan said, sensing the trap a mile away. He wanted nothing to do with it. He had more than enough trouble of his own.

Sebastian gripped his shirt, stopping him before he could stand and walk away. "Please, Ronan. I beg of you. As a man of honor. I will repay my debt, if not in coin, then in deed. Let me work it off."

Crossing his arms, Ronan drawled, "And how do you propose to do that?"

"I could be your valet."

"I have no need of a valet."

"Your guide, then? You are new to town. Surely that will be of use to you?"

"You are as much a foreigner here as I am."

"True, but I know my way about the city and have contacts that could prove useful. I also have a place where you can sleep tonight or for as long as you need."

He knew he was seven shades of a fool for trusting the adulterous gambler—two activities centered heavily around deceit—but Bast did raise an excellent point. Ronan would absolutely benefit from a guide. Though to be fair, it was the offer of a room that truly swayed him, even if it came equipped with a degenerate for a roommate. At least there would be one less thing for him to worry about until he located Reyna and determined his next steps.

Groaning, he squeezed the bridge of his nose. "Fine. Lead the way."

"You won't regret this."

"I already do."

CHAPTER 6

SHADOW

The sun sank into the ocean the same way humans wake, little by little and all at once. With every fiery sliver that disappeared into the navy depths, her grip tightened on the balcony's railing until her knuckles were bleached and her fingers cramped.

You're running out of time.

And right on the heels of that thought came a flood of guilt. Just as it always did.

Shadow bit back a growl of frustration. Every day that passed allowed the invisible noose to tighten further around her neck. Erebos wanted an answer.

Tonight.

A vehement 'No!' bled across her mind, but she silenced it. As much as the word begged to be freed, she knew she couldn't give it wings.

Not without dire consequence.

She had no excuse. None. Well, none that she could voice.

Shadow simply had no ambition to be the High Lord's wife. She enjoyed the relative freedom of her current position too much. For all that she was chained to the man, she could mostly come and go as she pleased. She spent as much time alone as she did at his side, if not more. If—when—she became his wife, all that would go away. Any autonomy she had over her own destiny would be a thing of the past the second the vows were spoken.

So really, he could have been any man, and her answer would be the same.

But Erebos wasn't just any man. In so many ways, he was her savior. Taking her out of the gutter, giving her life meaning. He was wonderful. Handsome. Brave. Unfailingly selfless. Everything she was not.

Any other woman would be in absolute rapture to find out he wanted her as his bride. They likely stayed up at night praying for that very thing, hoping he'd spot them in a crowd and be consumed by his need for them. But not her. For all that she could admit to his desirability—at least in theory—she didn't yearn to be his. Not in *that* way. Shadow didn't think she was capable of loving anybody in a romantic capacity. She'd never been in a position to try.

Raised on the streets, she'd grown too reliant on herself to fully let anyone else in. Partnerships required trust, and she didn't trust anybody. Not after what she'd seen. It's what made her so good at her job.

An assassin could hardly be a bleeding heart.

She wasn't completely without morals. She had rules. No innocents. No children. No animals. The exception always being when death would be a mercy compared to the alternative. She'd had more than one brutalized woman beg to be put out of her misery. Shadow knew she'd made the right decision the first time she witnessed peace wash across the woman's face. Death was a comfort. A father's warm embrace and promise of eternal safety. It was the least she could offer to those who had suffered so much under the watch of an indifferent mother.

The door opened with a click.

"There you are, my sweet Shadow. Will you not come down to join the festivities?"

Ah yes. The festivities.

Sign-ups for the High Lord's contest officially opened tomorrow.

For weeks people had been flooding into town, eager to either be among the ranks or watch those who entered fight to the death for the final position in the High Lord's formal court.

His champion.

A harbinger of justice or a weapon in the dark. Two sides of the same blade, both equally effective and utterly lethal.

It was essentially the same role she filled now, but with more fanfare and better pay. It was a sore spot between them that he hadn't simply granted the title to her after their years together. But the conversation was the same every time she broached the subject.

"Is it to be the silent treatment again?" Erebos sighed, his footsteps growing louder as he moved across the room to stand just behind her. "I thought we'd finally put this to bed."

You did, perhaps.

He rested his hands on her shoulders. "We've been over this, Moonbeam. I have a more important role in mind for you."

She inwardly gagged at the nickname and then silently mouthed the next words with him.

"Don't you want to be my Lady?"

No!

When she still didn't answer, he spun her around, curling his finger to lift her chin until she met his gaze. His golden hair was swept back, though the ends fell over his shoulders like a silky water-fall. The sharp aristocratic angles of his face were bathed in the last rays of the sunset, illuminating his jade green eyes. The only outward sign of his frustration was the slight tightening around his full lips.

"Why do you continue to put this off when we both know how it could be between us? We're *good* together, Shadow. We make sense. And there's no one I trust to stand at my side more than you. You've been my loyal supporter since day one." He frowned when she still didn't speak. "You've never had trouble saying yes to me before."

Because you've never asked me for something I wasn't willing to give.

Reaching out, he took a strand of her white-gold hair, rubbing it between his fingers before tucking it behind her ear. "Is there someone else?"

"What? Of course not."

She was so caught off guard by the question that she hadn't realized she'd spoken aloud until he grinned.

"I must admit. I'm relieved."

"With as busy as you keep me, when would I have had time to meet someone, let alone fall in love?" she asked dryly, crossing her arms to force a little more distance between them.

"I don't know. It's the only reason I could think of why you've yet to accept my offer."

Because the possibility a woman might not want to get married and be shackled to a man for all eternity is such a novel concept?

Not every woman dreams of becoming a wife and mother. Shadow was certain she wasn't fit to be either. Not with all the blood on her hands. How could she possibly care for anyone, let alone keep something so fragile alive when she'd made a living out of ending them?

It was probably for the best she couldn't conceive. She'd been stabbed through the abdomen some years ago. They'd stitched her back together, but the damage was so absolute the healer had tearfully informed her she'd never be with child. And on the off chance she did manage to get pregnant, it was likely neither she nor the child would survive the experience.

She hadn't understood the other woman's tears. To her, with the kind of life she led, it was a relief. But she quickly learned people didn't like when she said that aloud, so she'd never spoken of her condition again.

Blinking, Shadow mentally slapped herself upside the head.

No one else knew. Meaning Erebos didn't know. Perhaps if he did, he'd finally let the matter drop. Certainly the ability to bear him an heir would be a nonnegotiable requirement when selecting his future wife?

"Erebos, there's something I need to tell you."

"Sounds serious. Should I be sitting down?"

She shook her head. The only place to sit in her room was on the bed, and she didn't think that would set the right tone for this conversation.

"Well then, I guess I'll risk staying on the balcony, but I expect you to catch me if shock sends me over the side."

She laughed despite herself. "You're putting an awful lot of faith in my reflexes."

"No," he murmured, his voice soft and expression warm. "Just in you. As I have since the day we first met."

She shifted uncomfortably, not sure how to broach the subject other than just blurting it out. "I . . . that is I cannot . . ."

Erebos blinked. "I did not think I'd ever see the day my Moonbeam was actually flustered. Whatever it is, darling, you can tell me. We will deal with it together."

"I cannot bear you a child."

He stiffened for a second before his shoulders sagged and he blew out a heavy breath. "Is that it? Stars, you really had me going for a minute."

"Perhaps you didn't hear me—"

He squeezed her shoulders. "I apologize for what might seem an insensitive reaction. You were just so serious. I assumed the worst. My relief it was simply that—"

"Simply that?" Confusion clouded her mind. This was not remotely the reaction she expected. He didn't seem surprised at all. Suspicion took root. "You already knew."

"Of course I did."

"But how? I never told a soul."

He remained silent.

"The healer . . ."

"You nearly died, Shadow. I was worried. You can't expect me not to follow up. Especially when it was my fault you'd been so grievously injured in the first place."

"I don't see how my reproductive system is any of your business."

"I didn't pry. It was in the report. No one betrayed your confidence."

That was a matter of opinion, but she wasn't going to debate the point. "Well, surely you must agree I'm hardly fit to be a High Lord's Lady."

57

He cupped her face and skimmed his thumb over her cheekbone. "Of course you are. As for children, we will find you a healer. In case you forgot, I do rule practically all of Empyria. I have a far reach. I'm sure there is someone out there who will be able to fully repair any damage you sustained. There's no price I won't pay to see you whole. "

Of course he assumes he can fix me. That I'm broken because I cannot conceive. What a typical reaction. He didn't even stop to consider I might not require saving. Or want it, for that matter.

Shadow shook her head, watching the last of her hope fade away. Erebos would have his way. Nothing she said would dissuade him. It's why she stopped saying anything at all. What was the point when no one was listening?

He mistook the sheen of frustrated tears in her eyes. Tilting her face up, he leaned down to ghost his lips over hers. "I will always take care of you."

For a second, Shadow leaned into the kiss, closing her eyes and hoping maybe this time she'd feel something besides flickers of annoyance. Things would be so much easier if she could simply make herself want him. But no. The only desire she felt was the desire for him to leave her alone.

"It pleases me I was able to put your mind at ease."

Is that what you think you did?

"If I'd known that was what was worrying you, I would have spoken up far sooner."

Do you even know me at all?

"I will give you some space to collect yourself. Then I expect you to come down and greet our guests. So many have come so far to meet you and show their support."

Shadow heard the steel beneath the velvety voice. This was not a request. Erebos loved to show off his favorite toy.

He released her and turned to head into her room. He paused just before crossing the threshold. "And make sure you wear the dress I like. The silver one I purchased in Brillergarde. You look like a fallen star when you wear it. A piece of the heavens gracing us mere mortals."

She knew many women would swoon at the words, but they had her barely suppressing the urge to roll her eyes. She saw straight through his courtly lies. What he really meant was the dress—if you could call it that—made her look like one of Dovina's whores. The gown in question was little more than a glittering scrap of fabric that was so sheer it was practically see-through. He couldn't seem to remember where her eyes were when she wore it.

Not that she blamed him. She had an excellent set of breasts; they were one of her best weapons. Many were the men—and quite a few women—lured to their deaths by a pair of great tits.

Without waiting for her to agree, Erebos left, simply expecting it would be done.

And it would.

He was the High Lord. She'd taken the knee and sworn herself into his service years ago. In all things, his word was law.

Stepping back to the railing, Shadow allowed her eyes to roam over the city below. The waves of newcomers had slowed to a trickle, but even now, people continued to flock to the city. One such person paused just outside the gates. His hood slipped free and revealed a thick fall of rust-colored hair. Redheads were rare in these parts. She couldn't help but admire the fiery shade, so different from her icy locks. What a sight they would be side by side. Fire and ice.

Shadow shook her head at the folly of her thoughts. The only way she'd ever find out if her theory was correct was if he entered the competition. But the poor bastard would likely die before getting far enough to be recognized by her or the High Lord.

Pity.

Leaning over the railing, she clasped her hands and thought about who might become Erebos's champion. Calix, perhaps. Or maybe Bannock. They were lucky they didn't have to go up against her. She'd wipe the floor with both their sorry asses. In fact, there wasn't a person in all of Empyria that would beat her if she entered the contest. And then Erebos would have no choice but to name her as his champion. Those were the rules, and not even the High Lord himself would dare break them. He'd be forced to give up his foolish notion to wed her.

If.

What a wonderful, terrible word.

Erebos would never allow it.

He hasn't expressly forbidden it either.

Because you knew better than to ask.

Oh, but if . . .

If she could.

If she dared.

If she won.

Her eyes trailed the redheaded man as he made his way through the gates, those two little letters taking root. By the time he slipped into the tavern and out of sight, they'd become a full-fledged plan. And when she finally straightened to go inside, she was no longer thinking in *ifs* but *whens*.

CHAPTER 7

RONAN

"Mother's tits, do you ever stop talking?"

Bast tossed him a cheeky grin. "Not usually, no. Why would I when people are so fond of—"

"Do I look remotely fond of you?"

Waving a dismissive hand, he shrugged. "Who's to say what you're feeling? I've known you less than twenty-four hours and have only seen you wear the one expression."

Ronan hated himself for having to ask. "And what expression is that?"

"Like someone shit in your boots."

Old Ronan would have laughed, but the Butcher had a point to make. Taking hold of Bast's tunic, he lifted him onto his toes. "I have quite literally killed men for less, so if you value your tongue, I suggest you shut the fuck up, or I will rid you of it."

Sebastian opened his mouth, but Ronan silenced him with a challenging lift of his brow. Pulling free of his hold, his guide huffed but didn't say anything further. Which was a miracle, frankly. The man hadn't shut up since they'd woken up that morning. Actually, there had been about an hour of blessed silence before Bast stumbled out of his room, bleary-eyed and still reeking of ale. The second he saw he had a captive audience, he'd started talking and hadn't stopped.

Ronan now knew far more than he ever intended to about his guide—home realm: Colvers, age: twenty-seven, star sign: the lumineer, longest relationship: two weeks, shortest relationship: two hours, life's mission: fuck and drink his way across Empyria. From the sound of it, he'd nearly completed his goal.

As for new information about Glimmermere or Reyna's location? He had none.

The few times he'd managed to slip Sebastian long enough to ask a townsperson if they'd seen a woman matching Reyna's description, they shook their heads and offered apologies that ranged in sincerity. Many were too distracted by the High Lord's competition to spare him more than a passing second, so he couldn't be certain they'd given his request the attention it deserved.

As they'd neared the heart of the city, the crowd had only grown, to the point it was impossible to walk down the street without squeezing past another person.

Bast eyed the throng and then looked across the street to a busty wench blowing him kisses. "This is where I leave you, *ami.*"

"What happened to being my guide?"

He gestured vaguely around him. "Welcome to Glimmermere. You aren't going to get far with these crowds. Besides, you made it clear you do not value my company, so I will spend time with someone who does."

"It's not your company she values, and you're fresh out of coin. Remember?"

Bast rolled his fingers, making something round and golden glint in the sunlight.

"You little shit," Ronan growled. "If I find out that you stole from me, I will break every single bone in your hand. One at a time. And I will take great pleasure in it."

"Relax, Ronan. It's not your purse you need to worry about. Find me when it's time to eat. In the meantime, I will see about satisfying my other appetites."

Ronan watched the blond man saunter away with a wry shake of his head. That bastard may not know his way around town, but he certainly knew his way around women. Within seconds, one hand was tangled in the wench's hair while the other slid beneath the back of her skirt.

"Good riddance."

Relieved of one burden, Ronan spotted a fishwife making use of the influx of visitors.

"Silverjacks and flippered-eels, two motes each!" she crowed, a dead fish raised high above her head. "Caught fresh this morning!"

Dusting off his most courteous and charming voice, Ronan stepped up to the side of her booth. "Excuse me, madam."

Judging by the glare she sent his way, he was more out of practice than he thought. Usually a smile was enough to charm any woman regardless of age or marital status, but unlike the fish at her stall, she wasn't biting.

"Buy something or get out of my way. You're scaring off my patrons."

He raised a brow and did a pointed scan of the complete lack of customers. "I think the smell of your wares is doing that all on its own."

She glowered. "This is prime product. You can fuck straight off, you foul-mouthed shite."

Well that escalated quickly.

Ronan's brows flew up. "Foul-mouthed? I was being polite. You're the one hurling profanities."

"That's not all I'll be hurling if you don't pay up or get lost."

I should be taking notes.

Ronan pulled out two of the starlings he'd won the night before. As far as he could tell, that was enough to pay for everything she had on ice and then some.

For the first time, the woman looked at him with something other than annoyance. Genuine interest shimmered in her eyes. She reached out to snag the coins, but he held them high over his head. "Ah-ah-ah. Answer my questions, harpy, then I'll pay."

"Half up front or no deal."

"Are you always this delightful, or are you making a special effort with me?"

"Only my customers get my smiles."

He tossed her one of the coins. "That right there makes me the best damn customer of the week."

She grinned, revealing a surprisingly sweet smile despite her several missing teeth. "So you are. How can I help you, dove?"

"Oh, so it's dove now? What happened to 'foul-mouthed shite'?"

She shrugged. "I wouldn't press my luck if I were you."

Ronan found himself oddly fond of the cranky bitch. She reminded him of his mother, what little he remembered of her. "Do you have a name, harpy?"

"Glinta the Good."

"Good? At what, exactly?" He asked the question because, with a title like that, he knew it was expected.

She didn't disappoint him.

Tossing him a saucy wink, she purred, "I wasn't always old, dove. I still know my way around a meat pole, if you catch my drift."

He wheezed from the effort of swallowing down the roar of laughter threatening to escape. He barely managed to let out a choked, "Noted."

Her brows slashed down in a deep scowl. "Don't hurt yourself. I'm not about to waste my breath or my voice calling for a healer to save you, you miserable cur."

"I thought I was your dove?"

"Best start talking or I'm as liable to stab you as I am answer your questions."

"You're a bloodthirsty bitch, aren't you?"

"Smart of you to remember that when you get the itch to piss me off."

Ronan couldn't help but smile. It felt as if he'd discovered a kindred spirit. How refreshing. "I'm looking for a woman."

"Of course you are." She eyed him up and down. "A big fella like you shouldn't have trouble in that regard, but I guess once you open your mouth, the appeal is lost." She waved a hand. "No matter. For the right price, you can have any lady you want. Surely you noticed there's pleasure dens aplenty."

"No, not that kind of woman. This one has the same fondness for a blade as you. Goes by the name Reyna."

Glinta frowned. "Can't recall hearing of a woman who goes by such a name. And many in these parts know how to weld a knife. You have anything else for me to go by?"

"She's tall, comes to about here"—he held a hand up to his sternum —"with hair the color of an oil slick, falls nearly all the way down her back. Green eyes, but not regular green, multihued, a bit like staring up into a tree while the sun shines through its branches."

"Right poet, aren't you?" she asked with a smirk.

Ronan scowled. "Have you seen her or not?"

"No, dove. Sorry. A woman like that would stand out."

Yeah. She sure as shit did.

Frustration churned in his gut, chasing away any lingering amusement he'd experienced while on the receiving end of Glinta's callous tongue. Reyna was one in a million. It's why he hadn't been able to let her go. After nothing but false leads for years, it had been a relief to set aside the despair he'd worn like a mantle after Effie gave him her promise. But running into the same dead ends here brought it all roaring back. His next breath didn't come as easy as the last.

Don't give up now. She's here somewhere. Try another tactic. Effie wouldn't lead you astray.

"You mentioned women here were skilled with blades. Is there one who stands out amongst the rest? Perhaps one who's made a name for herself because of it?"

Glinta chewed on her lower lip. "There's a few. Blood sports aren't just a man's game these days. Women can get in and out where they cannot, you feel me?"

Ronan nodded. Sex workers made excellent assassins for that reason. No one ever suspected their lover. Especially not the one they paid. One day people would start realizing money couldn't buy loyalty.

"Who holds the number one spot?"

"You ain't from around here, are you, dove? No . . . you'd have to have been living under a rock not to know about Shadow."

"Shadow?" Ronan repeated, the name tickling the back of his mind, though he couldn't remember why.

"She belongs to the High Lord." Glinta frowned when it was clear Ronan had no clue what she was talking about. Holding her hand up to her eyes, she scanned the crowd. "Bet you my week's catch she's around here somewhere. Can't imagine she won't want to check out her replacement."

Ronan tucked that nugget of information away. If she was the reigning champion, why was the High Lord replacing her? He wasn't sure why it was important, only that instinct warned him it was.

Glinta rose onto her toes, craning her neck from side to side. "You can't miss her. She has the face of an angel and hair the color of stardust."

Ronan frowned at the detail. He knew it was a longshot, but part of him had hoped, by some turn of fate, it would end up being his lost Night Stalker. He sighed but tried not to let himself get too discouraged. It was only his first full day here. Surely this Shadow had to be aware of a woman whose skill with a knife rivaled her own.

"There, that looks like her. The one in the hood." The fishwife pointed to a cloaked woman standing near the front of the sign-up line. "Mind your manners, dove. She makes me look like a peach."

Ronan tossed Glinta the second coin. "Don't be so sure you're not."

"Come visit me anytime!"

Though he doubted he'd stick around long enough to become a regular, he knew he wouldn't leave town without at least trying to see her again. She was a prickly bitch, but he loved how she owned it. So few people were that unapologetically honest. It was the mark of a person worth knowing, in his opinion.

Shuffling through the mass of bodies, grunting as elbows dug into his stomach and numerous feet stomped over his boots, he finally reached the front of the line.

"Hey, arsehole! You can't cut. Line starts back there."

Ronan gave the man his middle finger, not sure if the insult was known here but certain he got his point across regardless.

"Pardon me, I'm hoping you can help me find someone," he said, tapping the woman in the cloak on the shoulder.

She turned, peering at him with curious green eyes. But not just a standard shade of green. A green so multihued and prismatic, he'd only ever seen its like on one woman.

He gasped, his vision going spotty, and the breath knocked from his lungs as he reached for her.

"R-Reyna."

CHAPTER 8

SHADOW

How hard is it to write your night-damned name?

Shadow couldn't remember the last time nerves got the best of her. The consummate professional, anxiety or self-doubt were rarely an issue she had to contend with. But the sign-up line had slowed to a crawl, and with each passing heartbeat, she feared discovery. Moving about unseen was as natural for her as breathing. It was standing still that was the problem. With her unique look and reputation, it was only a matter of time before someone recognized her. And then she would be well and truly lost.

The longer she was out here in the open, the more on edge she became. That blasted piece of parchment was her ticket to freedom. If only the line would move so she could secure her spot.

Sweat rolled down her spine as she adjusted the hood of her cloak to ensure her hair was still concealed. People had to be wondering why she'd opted for such a garment in this heat. She prayed the nature of the contest excused her odd choice instead of drawing more eyes to her.

Either way, it was a risk that would eventually bite her in the ass, because if Erebos didn't sniff her out, her competition might just get curious enough to see who was hiding beneath the hood. Another bead of sweat trickled down her back at the thought.

Stars, if they don't hurry up, I'm going to start stabbing people just to get them out of my fucking way.

A tap came on her shoulder, and Shadow's weapon was in her hand before she turned around. The only thing keeping her blade from finding a new sheath was the fact she didn't recognize the man's voice.

"Pardon me—"

Static filled her ears, drowning out the rest of whatever was being said. Schooling her expression into a polite but disinterested mask, she lifted her eyes to his. The sun glinted off his fiery tresses, and she recognized him immediately as the man she'd watched from the balcony the night before.

He'd been too far for her to see much in the way of detail last night, but she had no such trouble now. He loomed over her, which was saying something because she could look most men straight in the eye without lifting her chin. But the stranger had at least a head on her, if not more. And that said nothing of his sheer bulk. Even fully clothed, she could make out the definition of his muscles beneath the tight fit of his tunic and leather pants.

His hair had been tamed into a series of twists and braids, revealing the sides of his head, which were shaved down to the skin. From the sun-darkened state of his scalp, it was his preferred look. The rest of his body, so far as she could tell, was much the same shade, speaking to many hours spent outside. Faint lines feathered the area around his eyes, but she couldn't tell if they were from laughter or something fiercer. Given the way he currently frowned at her, she assumed the latter.

For such a large man, he was oddly pretty. The angles and proportions of his face were perfect in their symmetry and placement. If his hair was the color of flame, his eyes were shards of ice. A flinty shade somewhere between blue and gray, they brought to mind the sky in winter. And his lips were full, if not a touch pouty. For the first time in her life, she had the impulse to lean forward and steal a kiss. Just to see if he was real.

He was so handsome. In fact, he reminded her of a sculpture she'd seen once. A depiction of a celestial come to life. Something more than human, rivaling the perfection of the heavens themselves.

The color bled from his sun-kissed skin, and the man staggered, reaching out as if to touch her. "R-Reyna?"

She jerked her head back on instinct, knocking her hood free. Shocked gasps rang out as whispers of her name exploded up from the crowd like kernels of roasted corn.

For fuck's sake.

"It's her, the High Lord's Shadow."

"Shadow is entering the contest!"

"Stars above, it's really her!"

"Do you think she'll autograph my sword?"

"Put that away, Gary. She's not interested in signing your wee willy."

She squeezed her eyes shut and swallowed back a howl of frustration as panic began to claw at her. Time was up. She needed to get her name on that list before it was too late.

"You've got the wrong person," she informed him, taking a step back and forcing the people around her to get out of her way. It didn't take much effort on her part now that everyone knew who she was.

The handsome stranger put his hand on her shoulder, tugging her back. Panic morphed into icy anger, and this time, she moved in close, pressing the tip of her dagger in just hard enough there was no mistaking her intent.

"Mister, you do not want to fuck with me," she growled.

Something like nostalgia washed through his expression. "That's not the first time you've held a blade to my groin."

He was mad. Moon-touched. She didn't have the patience or restraint to deal with this.

"Oh? Perhaps you didn't learn your lesson. Shall I remove the appendage this time to make it stick?"

"You always were overly interested in my cock."

"Now I know you've got me confused with someone else. I couldn't give two shits about the dangling bit of meat between your legs."

She rolled her eyes, her lip curled in disgust. Men were so damn predictable. They thought everything was about their dick. As if anyone was impressed by a cock and balls. What was so special about it? Dogs had them. Horses too, and they were a fair bit more impressive. The first lesson any woman learned when fighting off a man was to aim for his crotch. Surely they had to realize those balls they were so proud of were a weakness, not a treasure?

"It's more than a bit," he said with a cocksure grin.

Shadow sighed, disappointed he went with such a typical reply. Elbowing people to the side, she started forcing her way to the front of the line. When she realized he was keeping pace with her, she snapped, "And for the record, size says nothing of skill. If I've learned anything about men, it's that the more one has to say about the subject, the more unimpressive they are. In *all* regards."

He shook his head, his lips twisted in a confused smile. "You really don't remember. I'd wondered . . . It was the only thing that made sense, assuming you weren't imprisoned."

She paused long enough to blink at him, his words not making sense. Even though a panicked voice in her mind screamed for her to shove everyone aside and get her name on that damn list, she couldn't help but ask, "What are you going on about?"

"Why you didn't come back. It never made sense to me. You're too skilled not to evade your kidnappers. Eventually I started to wonder if you'd taken a blow to the head and lost your memories. It happens sometimes."

"That's a lovely story, but I assure you I know exactly who I am, as all these people can attest."

"Reyna—" he tried again.

"That's not my name. It never has been."

Instead of shutting him down, her brush-off seemed to infuriate him.

"Yes, it is. *You* may not remember who you are, but I do."

A somewhat hysterical laugh crawled up her throat. "Ask anyone here. They'll vouch for me. My name is Shadow, has been since the day I was born." Well, that wasn't strictly true, but it was the only name she remembered. The brothel owner who'd taken her in, the only mother figure she'd ever known, had taken to calling her Shadow because of the way she'd followed her around those first few weeks. In the years after, Shadow suited her for other, less innocent reasons.

When there was only one more person between her and the man with the list, Shadow grasped them by their shirt and tugged them back.

"Hey!" he protested, until he realized who she was. "Lady Shadow, I-I . . . please, after you."

"See."

The redhead crossed his arms over his chest. "That proves nothing."

She huffed, done with his nonsense, as she turned to the man with the list. He gaped at her, having to clear his throat a few times before he could speak. "Lady Shadow, what an honor. Are you here to inspect the troops?"

"I'm here to sign up."

"Sign up?"

"Did I stutter?"

"No. I just didn't expect to see you." She glared at the scribe until his ears turned pink and he held out a quill dribbling ink. "Just sign your name on the next available line."

Her heart finally returned to a somewhat normal rhythm as she scrawled her mark across the page with a flourish.

She'd done it.

Shadow shoved the document back at him, a giddy smile curling her lips.

"Lady Shadow, you're not done."

"What?"

His hands trembled as he pushed two more forms in front of her. "You need to sign these waivers."

"Darkness above, why?"

"In-in case of injury. O-or death. It says that your next of kin will receive a small sum and that no action will be taken against the High Lord for your untimely demise."

"Oh, for the love of—" Needing this to be over, she snatched the quill back up and signed her name so forcefully the parchment ripped beneath the sharp nib. "That better be it, or the next thing I start ripping is you."

"That's i-it, m-my lady. You're all set. Welcome to the Contest of Champions, and may the stars bless you with good fortune."

She had only enough time to suck in her first full breath of the day when she felt it. A shift in the air, like a ripple in water.

He'd found her.

But it was too late. She'd already done it. Not even he, the High Lord, could stop what she'd just set in motion.

The crowd parted as Erebos stalked straight for her. "Moonbeam," he growled, taking her elbow in a painful grip, "what have you done?"

Before she could answer, the redhead shoved her to the side, his face twisted in fury. "Get your fucking hands off her." Then he blinked, his body going still. But not with calm; her stranger was the very picture of rage about to bubble over. Even she shivered at the violence shimmering in his eyes. His voice turned ugly as he sneered, "Kieran."

Something about the barely masked threat in his voice had her snapping into action. She may have her own issues with the High Lord, but she was still his faithful servant.

Her dagger was pressed to his neck before he sucked in his next breath. "Think very carefully about what you do next, stranger. I will bleed you dry and not lose a moment's sleep over it."

"You'd defend him? After everything he's done?"

"I defend him *because* of everything he's done. The High Lord is a hero. I would give my life to spare his. So would everyone else in this city."

The stranger looked as though he was about to be sick. "What has he done to you?"

CHAPTER 9

RONAN

"Saved me. Gave me a home, a purpose, a future. That man is the only reason I am standing here now."

Lies. All of it.

It had to be.

There was no universe where *Kieran* was the fucking hero of any story but his own. It had been nearly five years since he'd heard the other man speak, so he couldn't trust his memories of his voice, but he'd recognize that face anywhere. It was definitely him. He must have brainwashed her somehow. Convinced her the lies were fact. It was the only explanation for this travesty unfolding in front of him.

"How did you even escape?" he asked, his eyes boring into the other man's. He had to find a way to get word to Helena. She needed to know her prisoner was missing.

Reyna pressed her dagger in deeper, a trickle of blood gliding down his throat. "Watch your tone."

Kieran raised a brow and gave him a considering look. "Is it safe for you to wander these streets alone, friend? You seem confused, dare I say lost. Is there someone we can send for? Someone to see you safely home?"

Ronan bared his teeth, swallowing back every insult that begged to be unleashed. He may be hotheaded, but he recognized when he was outnumbered. Between her weapon, the guards standing en masse behind their High Lord, and the crowd waiting to see what he'd do next, there was no way to proceed but to retreat and reassess.

It took everything in him not to grab Reyna, toss her over his shoulder, and bolt. She may go by a different name and have done something to her hair, but there was no doubt in his mind it was her. He'd risk a few nicks of her blade to get her far away from the spineless serpent she'd bound herself to.

"My mistake," he gritted out. "You look exactly like someone I used to know."

"A handsome one, from the sounds of it."

"No. A criminal imprisoned for treason."

Kieran tilted his head, and those familiar green eyes crackled with an energy so potent it had the hair on the back of Ronan's neck standing on end. "Pity. Come, Shadow. There's much to do before tomorrow's ceremony."

"Do *not* follow us," she hissed, kissing his neck with the blade a final time before pulling back and spinning away.

He watched them disappear down the street, the onlookers filling the now empty space where they'd just been and creating a barricade of sorts between Ronan and the woman he'd spent years searching for.

"This isn't over," he growled beneath his breath. Now that he had proof that she was here, that she was *alive,* there wasn't a force on this earth that would stop him from bringing her home. Given enough time, he was certain he could help her remember who she was, what they'd been to each other.

Don't get ahead of yourself. The voice of reason was immediately hushed.

He knew all too well that they'd never made promises to one another. Never had the chance to explore what existed between them. That didn't diminish the truth of it. He just needed to help her see it. That was going to require two things he didn't currently have. Time and proximity.

"Who's next?"

Ronan's head snapped around, spotting the scribe collecting signatures for the contest.

"Me."

The word left his lips before a plan could fully form in his mind. He knew next to nothing about the details surrounding the competition, but the one thing he did know was that Shadow was participating. As a fellow contestant, he'd have nearly unrestricted access to her.

The part where one of them had to die was an undeniable hiccup, but they'd deal with that when the time came. Nothing said they both had to see this farce through; the contest was simply his means to an end. The sooner he could help her remember who she was, the sooner they could both get the hell out of here. No death required.

Save perhaps Kieran's—but that would be a bonus. Reyna was his priority.

Those who had been standing near enough to hear the altercation murmured excitedly as Ronan continued to entertain them with his unpredictable behavior. This time no one raised a brow when he stepped to the front of the line.

"You're a big one," the scribe said, craning his neck back to meet Ronan's gaze.

He snatched the quill out of the man's hand, quickly jotting his name below Shadow's. The scribe twisted the page around, his eyes skimming Ronan's signature.

"Butcher . . . I do not believe I've heard of you. Where are you from?"

"Colvers." Ronan mentally thanked Bast for his incessant rambling. Outsiders might be welcome here, but he didn't need to draw any more attention to himself than he already had by claiming to be from Elysia.

The other man's brows disappeared into his hairline. "You do not have their accent. Or their coloring."

Ronan grunted. "My mother was a whore. We traveled a lot."

That much was true, and he'd learned early on people didn't ask too many questions when confronted with an answer as uncomfortably blunt as that.

"Right." Clearing his throat, the scribe shuffled some papers. "I just need you to sign the waivers."

"Death, maiming, bodily harm, yes, I was here for your last explanation," Ronan muttered, snatching the stack of papers and getting to work signing them. As he did, the scribe continued prattling on.

"There will be an opening ceremony tomorrow night at sundown to introduce all the participants to the High Lord and go over the specifics of the first trial. There will be five trials total, each separated by a day of rest. If you do not have accommodations in the city, they will be provided for you for the duration of the contest. Any living expenses will likewise be covered during this time, including any special attire that might be required. You are, of course, responsible for your own armor and weapons. The winner will be determined at the final trial and will be granted a single boon in addition to the position of the High Lord's Champion and all the benefits that come with such a title."

Ronan nodded along, barely listening to a word. He was eager to find Sebastian and prepare for his next run-in with the High Lord's Shadow.

"Any questions?"

"No."

"Excellent. May the stars—"

"I don't rely on luck."

He turned and stalked away before he had to do more than note the flush of outrage his dismissal caused. Unless it was about Reyna—Shadow—he wasn't interested in anything the man had to say. Least of all his insincere offers of goodwill. He'd been killing men since he'd been old enough to hold a blade. His rivals didn't have a fucking prayer of taking him out.

Nothing would get between him and the woman he'd come so far to save. Not a few burly men with swords. Not a madman's contest. Not even the woman in question herself.

If that meant he had to win the whole damn thing, so be it. He hadn't come this far to return home empty-handed.

More than a few curious stares followed him as he stormed back through the marketplace in search of Bast, but Ronan didn't care. He was single-minded in his focus. He and his guide had work to do.

There were a number of things he intended to uncover before tomorrow's ceremony, namely the ins and outs of the High Lord's court. He had a feeling Bast would be a veritable treasure trove of knowledge in that regard. If the man hadn't already fucked his way through at least half of them, Ronan would be shocked, but he'd also bet Sebastian's entire debt that the man already had a plan in place to rectify that as soon as possible. Which meant he had all sorts of sordid details locked up in that pretty head of his.

Details Ronan intended to learn and use to his advantage.

Sebastian might be a shit tour guide, but his penchant for courtly gossip was about to make him worth his weight in gold.

Spying the red door he'd watched the blond man disappear through earlier, Ronan followed suit. After a somewhat uncomfortable conversation convincing the procuress he was not a prospective client but rather in search of one, he followed the woman's directions to the room at the very back.

Ignoring the vigorous thumping and exaggerated moans, he kicked the door open. Three women squealed and grabbed for anything to help conceal their nudity. Bast, however, continued to pump away, his bare arse on full display.

"Give me five more minutes, then they're all yours," he panted without turning around. The woman beneath him looked torn between pushing him off and letting him finish as she shyly met Ronan's gaze over Bast's shoulder.

"He could join us," she offered.

Ronan shook his head and stepped aside as the other two women not currently being serviced rushed out of the room.

"Am I not doing enough for you on my own, *mon trésor?*"

She squealed as he leaned forward and bit her breast, showing Ronan entirely too much ball sack for his liking.

"Sebastian, get your fucking pants on." He scooped them off the floor and flung them at the other man's head. "We have a tournament to win."

Bast finally glanced behind him, face flushed, eyes wide. "What have you done?"

"Let's go. I'll tell you all about it."

"Not before I finish."

"Well, I'm not leaving."

Sebastian's lips curled up. "I don't mind an audience."

Ronan groaned, staring at the ceiling as he debated his next move. "Five. Minutes. Then I'm coming back in here, and I don't care if you're in the middle of spurting down her throat, I will bodily remove you from this room. You owe me a debt. I intend to make you pay it." He turned and slammed the door behind him, Sebastian's words floating after him.

"You heard the brute, *trésor*. Hold on to the headboard. Looks like this is going to be fast and dirty."

CHAPTER 10

EREBOS

Five Years Earlier

𝓘t's been said that dreams are a devil's playground. An in-between realm where what's true and what's fantasy become not only possible but undeniably real. Anyone who's woken up with their heart in their throat, breath shallow, limbs trembling, can speak to the accuracy of the claim. As can the ones who find themselves on the cusp of release only to have it slip through their fingers as reality crashes back through.

Fear and pleasure . . . the reactions may seem diametrically opposed, but they are more connected than one might think. For what else is the journey to a climax but the fear you will not reach your destination and the unmistakable relief when you finally do?

The little death, they call it.

His lips curled up into a cruel smile. *Yes . . . that tracks.*

Dreamscapes contain the most fertile soil, which is why they have always been his preferred hunting ground. His wife had always been concerned with the creatures of Earth, but he found them boring and predictable. There was a natural order to the universe that left no room for surprise or creativity. Not like the land of dreams. There, anything was possible. It was a world where phantoms became real, wishes given wings, monsters granted life.

And it was *his* domain.

Once upon a time, he was known as the Father of Dreams. Now those who still remembered called him the Lord of Death . . . if they called him anything at all.

Fools. All of them.

But they would pay for their oversight. No one could run from a god. No one was immune to dreams.

For that was the problem with the natural order. Mortals had to sleep, and sleep begets dreams. Which meant he would always find them. There was no way to hide from the dream world's one true king.

Soon, far sooner than anyone realized, their waking hours wouldn't be safe either. Because he wasn't content ruling the dream world any longer. Not after his wife and her treacherous children tried to lock him away.

They thought they'd outsmarted him. They thought they'd won. But he'd bided his time. Made his moves in the dark where they couldn't see. It had taken centuries, but he'd found his way back.

Oh, was he back.

Erebos tilted his neck from side to side, appreciating the glide of hair across his back, the rapid flutter of his heartbeat, the deep pull of air into his lungs. He stood and stretched, flexing his arms and testing his strength. Every sensation was a wonder, but also a reminder of the limitations of his newly acquired human body. The vessel would do.

For now.

He glanced around his cell, smirking. The damp stone may imprison a mortal, but never him. Any minute now, those he'd summoned would arrive and free him. And once he was out, once he was free, he was coming after all of it.

Every.

Fucking.

Piece.

And he wouldn't stop until he destroyed them all.

Deep within the bowels of the Kiri's Palace, the Dreamer grinned.

Long live the king.

~

THREE WEEKS LATER

"THIS IS HER?" He gave the pile of dingy rags and wild hair a tentative kick. A mild pang of disappointment settled in his chest. He'd expected more of the leader of his progeny.

"She's not much to look at, I know. But she took out half her guards before we were able to sedate her. We haven't allowed her to be fully lucid since."

Erebos eyed the Night Stalker's queen with greater appreciation. "I should be able to help with that." Kneeling beside her in the dirt, he took one of her limp hands in his and pressed his lips to her temple. "Hello, dearest one. Do you have any idea how long I've waited to meet you? You have such an important part to play, but first, I need to borrow a little something of yours. Just until I get my own back, you see, and in return, I shall give you everything."

With every word, Erebos latched onto her consciousness, tying his will to hers, twisting her dreams until they became the memories of a life that had never been. A past that would inform her future at his side.

He watched her eyes dance behind their lids, chasing the dreams he wove as they became her reality. Only once they fell still did he allow himself to press his lips to hers and inhale. With each lungful, he leached away her power, reclaiming it as his own. He'd created the Night Stalkers, forming them from whispers and mist and tethering them to this world with threads of his magic. But in order to see his plans to fruition, he needed to take those threads back. As their queen, this one's power was the purest source, a font that would never run dry. It wasn't enough to get him to the finish line, not remotely, but it was a start. And until each thread was returned, she would be his personal well, keeping him topped up until they arrived at the endgame.

When he'd drank his fill, the raven-haired queen was no more, and the only testament to what he'd taken was the now pearlescent strands of her hair. They reminded him of beams of moonlight filtering through the clouds. He took a few pieces and rubbed them between his fingers, unable to resist the urge to touch them. The slight tug was enough to pull her from her sleep.

She blinked up at him, a small frown marring her brow. "I'm sorry, my lord. I must have drifted off."

He pressed a kiss to the center of her forehead. "It's quite all right, my darling one. You needed your rest."

"I did?"

"Oh yes, we have work to do, you and I. Are you ready?" He held out a hand to her. Without hesitation, she placed her hand in his and allowed him to help her up.

"Of course. Wherever you go, I will follow. I am yours, my lord. Your faithful shadow."

PRESENT DAY

"I'M surprised you didn't slit his throat."

Shadow's steps didn't falter, but the muscles beside her eyes tightened ever so slightly. She didn't appreciate the subtle chastisement. Considering he didn't appreciate her outright betrayal, he deemed the blow not only fair, but necessary. She needed to remember who served whom.

"There was a crowd, my lord."

"Since when has the public ever minded a little bloodshed? You do realize these people are hungry for it, don't you? Why else would they come to watch my games?"

She tipped her head to the side, conceding the point. "Do you want me to go back and finish the job?"

"No. Any change of course now will appear as weakness. You spared him, so now the redheaded bastard gets to live."

He had no doubt the reprieve would be temporary. That stubborn arse had a history of popping up where he wasn't wanted. Erebos knew it was only a matter of time before his wife's playthings showed themselves. He just hadn't expected to discover them on the other side of the world.

No matter.

He hadn't come this far to fumble now. Not this close to the finish line. The endgame was nearly upon him; he *would* see this through.

The Shield's—the title tasted like ash on his tongue—days were numbered.

For the first time in a long while, Erebos was pleased with his choice of vessel. The man's memories and intimate knowledge of the Kiri and her Circle would come in handy in the days to come. Perhaps even sooner, given their unexpected visitor.

As for his rebellious little shadow, well, he had other ways of keeping her in line.

He'd grown too lax with her since he'd ascended as High Lord. His daily duties had kept him occupied and given her too much room to roam. Pets needed a firm hand, or their feral natures started to reveal themselves.

And he couldn't have that now, could he?

Slowly, subtly, like one might approach a street cat, he lifted his hand and rested it along the back of her neck. He felt the involuntary shiver roll down her spine. Could sense the tension coiled in her muscles as she realized her mistake. With every step, his grip tightened, and his will asserted itself over hers.

"Please, High Lord . . . this isn't necessary. I-I'll behave."

"But that's the problem, isn't it, darling one? You've already misbehaved, and now you must be punished."

It was only because he knew her so well that he could sense the riot those words unleashed in her. For everyone else passing them on the busy street, it would seem as though the High Lord and his right hand were deep in conversation.

She swallowed, but her voice betrayed nothing of her thoughts. "Yes, High Lord. Of course."

As soon as they cleared the palace gates, he tugged her into the courtyard, shifting his hold so that he now collared her throat. His grip was tight enough to bruise, but not to cut off her air as he pushed her up against one of the vine-covered walls.

"I thought we rid you of this rebellious streak of yours years ago."

She held his gaze without flinching. "Apparently not, my lord."

He brushed his knuckles over her cheek. "Apparently not, indeed. But I must admit, I do so look forward to taming you."

Her eyes widened.

"Oh, yes, Shadow. I do mean to tame you. One way or another, you will be my lady. This game you're playing? It's done nothing but delay the inevitable. You want to prove that you are the realm's fiercest blade? Fine. Kill them all, and then, once it is done and you are named my champion, you will cede the title and accept one far grander. And do you know why that is, Shadow, darling?"

"Because I live to serve you," she bit out, the barest hint of temper leaking into the words.

His hand spasmed around her throat, making her gasp. "Try again."

She tipped her chin up, still holding his gaze. "Because I am yours."

"There it is." He leaned down until his nose grazed hers. "You are *mine*, Shadow. I found you. I gave you purpose. I. Created. You. You will always belong to me."

With every affirmation, his eyes bore into hers, cementing the words into her psyche, burying them deep.

"I belong to you," she whispered.

"Good girl."

And then he sealed his lips over hers and breathed in every drop of her power, draining her nearly dry. He hadn't fed so deeply on her since their early days together, but it was time his faithful servant was brought back to heel. She slumped against him, the drain on her essence rendering her unconscious.

He caught her easily, sweeping her into his arms and resuming his walk up the palace steps as if nothing out of place had happened.

A servant rushed forward, concern etched on their face, but Erebos waved them off.

"It is nothing. She's been working too hard. I'm taking her upstairs so that she may rest."

He infused the words with compulsion, and the servant gave a relieved smile as they backed away.

Once he reached Shadow's room, he laid her gently down upon her bed. To anyone else, the way he ran his fingers down her face might have appeared tender. In reality, he was twisting her dreams, giving the nightmares a little more bite. He had a point to make. He intended to ensure she didn't forget it.

Her soft whimper told him it was working.

If he'd been the sort of man to feel guilt, he might have experienced some now at weakening her so thoroughly a mere day before she was to enter a battle to the death against fifty or so others. But he wasn't a man. He was a god.

Gods didn't apologize for anything, least of all for getting what they wanted.

Right now, this god wanted her.

So have her, he would.

CHAPTER 11

RONAN

Torches lit the winding path leading through the palace gates, around a greenery-filled courtyard, and into a glittering ballroom. Music and laughter spilled into the night, setting the tone for what the guests would discover inside. Though the sheer number of lavishly attired people pouring through the open French doors was clue enough to that.

Opulence was the word of the evening, though another came to mind.

Spectacle.

Ronan was no stranger to a courtly lifestyle, but even he was not immune to his surroundings. Massive chandeliers hung from the mural-painted ceiling, and the white and gold marble floors twinkled with reflected light and created the sense of walking across the surface of the moon. Especially with the night sky displayed so prominently through the wall of glass along the back of the room. He couldn't quite make out the crashing waves in the inky depths, but they were an unexpected accompaniment to the orchestra's sweeping melodies.

Everywhere he looked, there were tables laden with food and

drink. The guests were in the hundreds, some dancing, most clustering in small groups to gossip or enjoy the High Lord's hospitality.

Does no one else find it unnerving that we're all here to celebrate the future slaughter of their heroes?

"I told you you were underdressed," Bast hissed as they joined the throng of people already gathered in the ballroom, taking up a spot in one of the far back corners.

"And I told you I didn't care."

Ronan glared at his guide from beneath the hood of his cloak, taking in his turquoise and gold tunic with a slightly darker blue pair of leggings and a matching ostrich feather adorning his cap. He'd told Sebastian to dress for discretion, and this was what he'd come up with. As for himself, he'd opted for all black, though he was currently concealed by his cloak. He wanted to remain undetected for as long as possible. After the impression he'd made the other day, he wasn't in a hurry to be singled out by the High Lord or his staff.

"You should. These people will be rooting for you. Rooting requires supporters. Supporters mean funds. No one wants to root for the dirty street urchin."

So that's how they planned to finance the competitors' room, board, and extras—through donations made by public supporters. Ronan sighed. He really wasn't in the mood for schmoozing.

"First, you tell me I smell, and now I'm dirty too? Do I have no redeeming qualities, Bast?"

"Your face is tolerable. And you showered today."

"Remind me again why I haven't rid myself of you yet?"

Ronan waved away a server with a tray of sparkling alcohol, but Bast reeled him back in and plucked two glasses from the offering. Neither of which he shared with Ronan.

"You need me," he answered, draining the first of his two flutes.

"That can't possibly be true."

"Oh? And do you suddenly know who the High Lord's closest advisors are? How to spot them? Because I assure you, there are far more pleasurable ways I can spend my evening than playing your escort."

"You are not my escort, Bast."

"I am here *escorting* you, am I not?"

"What you are is a pain in my arse."

"Not yet, but you keep giving me those eyes and I can be." He winked and made short work of his second drink.

"Bast," Ronan said with an annoyed growl.

Sebastian laughed. "You're far too uptight. We would never work out, *mon ami*."

"It's a miracle you've lived this long."

"I was going to say the same of you."

A begrudging laugh rumbled in his chest. "In that, you're probably right. Now come do your job and point out the people of note to me."

Sebastian heaved a weary sigh but obediently scanned the crowd. He'd been horrified when he'd heard Ronan had signed up for the contest, but after Ronan had explained about Reyna and why he was here in the first place—an admission he still wasn't certain wouldn't come back to bite him in the arse—Bast had gotten on board with helping him. Ronan had asked about the sudden change of heart, only for the blond man to clutch his chest and give a dramatic sigh.

"I am a disciple of true love."

"Is that why you find yourself jumping into every bed—and beneath every skirt—you come across?"

"But of course."

And that had been it. They'd spent the rest of the night reviewing every bit of knowledge Sebastian had acquired about the High Lord and his court since coming to Glimmermere nearly a month prior.

Now it was time to put faces to the names.

"There. That's the Lady Dovina, the High Lord's Raven."

Ronan followed his gaze and spotted the woman whose black hair was pulled back in a severe bun. She appeared deceptively serene, her expression wiped clean, her hands gathered loosely in front of her. But her dark eyes scanned the room, noting every detail. It was easy to see how she'd come to earn her title, both as a raven and as the High Lord's spy. It was clear nothing went beneath her notice.

"And that man there, that's her twin, the Lord Dominic." There was a slight edge to Sebastian's voice that hadn't been there prior. Apparently he didn't think too highly of the man he'd dubbed the Vulture.

Ronan shifted his attention to the man Bast indicated. He matched his sister in height and build, both regal in bearing with an innate grace that spoke to their upbringing. These two had been born for court. According to Sebastian, they'd served the prior High Lord but had been so taken by Erebos's heroics that they'd devoted themselves to his reign. As had many who served alongside them. After what he'd witnessed with Reyna in the marketplace yesterday, Ronan was willing to bet there was more to the story than that.

Whereas Dovina seemed calm, Dominic had the coiled energy of a loaded gun. He was ready to spring into action at any second, which made sense given that he was the head of Erebos's military. The scar running along the left side of his face from temple to jaw was a testament to just how hands-on he could be.

The twins were definitely two people to watch out for.

"There was a third bird you mentioned yesterday," Ronan murmured, offering bland smiles to passersby as he continued to study the crowd.

"Bird?"

"Raven, Vulture . . ."

"Ah, yes. The High Lord's flock. Dovina, Dominic, and Dmitri. Those three make up his inner circle, along with the Lady Shadow, of course."

At her name, Ronan had to force himself not to immediately search for her. He knew she was here somewhere. His entire body vibrated with the need to go to her. To speak with her. To help her remember who she was. But this was a recon mission, not a social visit. He wasn't here to see her. He needed to focus.

"Dmitri. Right, and he was what, The Rooster?"

"The Peacock."

Well, he'd gotten the cock part right.

Ronan shook his head. He much preferred the simplicity of Helena's Circle. That naming convention at least made sense. A circle surrounded and protected. No explanation necessary. But a flock?

What message did that send? That they were a squawking nuisance liable to shit all over you?

"And what does he do?"

"He's the Master of Ceremonies. You'll meet him soon enough. He's overseeing the tournament."

"And how does Rey—Shadow fit into the flock?" He barely suppressed an eye roll.

"She's the High Lord's most loyal supporter."

Ronan clenched his jaw. If ever there was proof of foul play, that statement was it.

"There's your bird now."

He should have known from the phrasing that Bast wasn't talking about Shadow, but his body braced in anticipation of seeing her anyway. At least there wasn't anyone to notice his exhale of disappointment as he watched a reed-thin man with pale blond hair and dark eyes ascend a set of stairs onto a raised platform on the other side of the room. Despite his moniker, he was plainly dressed in a pair of fitted black trousers and a matching jacket. Sebastian looked like more of a peacock than him.

As he took center stage, the orchestra fell silent, drawing the notice of the other guests, who began to clap and cheer as they recognized him.

"Welcome, welcome." Dmitri held up his hand, quieting the applause. "Tonight marks the official beginning of a historic event. It has been decades since a Contest of Champions has been held, and I am humbled to bear the supreme honor of overseeing it." He bowed to more enthusiastic applause, which he again silenced, this time by holding up both his hands. Beaming, he then said, "We will open, as always, with the Parade of Honors."

There was a trumpet flourish, and a set of doors opened, but Ronan was still stuck on what the man had just said. His entire body stiffened. "Did he just say parade?" Beside him Sebastian snickered, causing Ronan to grasp the other man by his shirt and pull him in close so he could bite out, "What parade?"

"Oh, didn't I mention it?"

"No, Bast, you definitely did not mention anything about a fucking parade."

"It's less of a parade and more of a presentation. You'll just walk across the stage, stop in the center to honor the High Lord, and be formally recognized as a contestant."

"What happens if I don't?"

"Don't what?"

"*Parade.*"

"Then you are disqualified."

Ronan's pulse roared in his ears. So much for not drawing any attention to himself tonight.

"Fuck."

"I believe in you, *mon ami*. I'm sure even you can manage to walk without preparation."

Ronan was about to curse him further when the Master of Ceremonies spoke again. "Contestants, if you would please line up along the far side of the stage so we may begin."

Bast gave him a cheeky grin, crossing his arms over his chest. "I'll wait for you here, shall I?"

"Oh no, you're going to wait in the queue with me."

"Why? Do you need me to hold your hand?"

"You are enjoying this entirely too much, Bast," he ground out, following the fifty or so others making their way to the front of the room.

"Not nearly enough, I assure you."

Ronan groaned, taking in the sea of faces, wondering who among them would be his biggest competition. "See anyone you recognize?" he asked under his breath.

"A few," Bast said as they took their spot near the back of the line. "The tall woman at the front, with the braid and the muscles? That's Marin."

"Her specialty?"

"She's an expert marksman and highly skilled in hand-to-hand combat."

"Who else?"

"There, the woman in the black veil, see her?"

"She's hard to miss."

Bast snickered. "Only because she's not trying. That's Dichen. The things she can do with her blades. Legendary. Before your Shadow arrived, she was the most infamous rogue in the realm."

Ronan tucked the information away. If she was anywhere near as skilled as Reyna, she was one to keep an eye on for sure.

"What about the men?"

Bast hummed and pointed two men out in quick succession. "The mountain of a man is Bannock, and the misshapen lump to his right is Calix."

"Specialties?"

"Isn't it obvious?"

"Would I waste my breath asking you if it was?"

For a second he contemplated whether he could get away with grasping Sebastian by the neck and smashing his face into the wall, but ultimately decided against it. Despite the amusement it would bring him to force Bast to walk around with a broken nose for the rest of the night, the move would also garner too much attention. He settled for imagining it instead.

Bast must have known something was up because his smile slipped. "Well, the wall of muscle is a brawler who tends to pummel his opponents into a pulp. And the ugly sonofabitch beside him is a master poisoner."

Ronan immediately discounted the fighter. He wasn't worried about overcoming brawn. The poisoner, however, would be crafty. That bore remembering. People would dismiss him because of his size, which he would use to his advantage to slip by unnoticed. He was willing to stake both his reputations that the man would be a finalist.

Before he could quiz Bast further, the crowd erupted into cheers. The High Lord had arrived, but Ronan only had eyes for the light-haired woman at his side.

Just like the first time his eyes landed on her, everything around him fell silent. She was as beautiful as ever, her sharp edges softer somehow. He'd seen her in gowns plenty of times before, but not like this. Tonight she wore a dress the color of starlight. It hugged her curves, and one side bore a slit that exposed her from hip to ankle with every step. Her hair was a waterfall of curls down her back, and something shimmery had been dusted across her cheeks and eyes, the effect meaning she positively sparkled.

For a woman who'd risen to fame as an assassin, she didn't look dangerous, but Ronan knew with absolute certainty she was the biggest threat in the room. The one who, with a single look, could absolutely destroy him.

"What I wouldn't give to have someone look at me the way you look at her," Bast murmured.

Ronan jerked to attention, clearing his throat and running a shaking hand along his neck. "I don't know what you mean."

Sebastian patted his shoulder. "Of course you do, for you are also one of true love's warriors. That makes us brothers, don't you see?"

"No."

"Ronan, deny it all you want, but we are the same."

His lip curled as he eyed the popinjay beaming up at him. "We absolutely are not."

Bast rolled his eyes at Ronan's vehement denial. "Lie to yourself then, if it pleases you."

As they watched, the High Lord and Shadow took their seats in the center of the room, Dovina and Dominic poised protectively just behind them. The Reyna he remembered would have been insulted that someone felt she required additional protection, but Shadow seemed used to the twins' presence. The High Lord smiled and waved while she stared straight ahead, looking bored but sexy as hell as she crossed her legs. Ronan drank in the sight of all that exposed flesh and swallowed. Hard.

"Down, boy," Bast whispered as Ronan clenched and unclenched his hands at his sides. "She is not yours. Not yet, and certainly not here."

"I know that."

"Do you? Because your face says otherwise."

"My face?"

"It's promising death to the High Lord if he so much as breathes in her direction."

That sounded about right.

"It does not."

"Doesn't seem like the appropriate expression for a champion to wear while gazing upon his future master."

Ronan glowered at his guide.

"Better. At least now you aren't staring daggers at *him*."

The wall plan was sounding better by the second.

"Now that the guests of honor have arrived, we may begin."

The crowd fell silent again, and the Parade of Fools—sorry, honors—officially commenced. One by one, men's and women's names were announced. From there it was much as Bast said; the contestant would walk across the stage to differing amounts of applause and 'honor' the High Lord with a bow, curtsy, or some other display of fealty.

Besides the handful of people Bast had already pointed out, there were two more in the procession Ronan took note of. The first stood out because he was the oldest and most grizzled in the lot. According to the announcer, he was a blood mage named Cedric Aldair. He'd never come across the man's like, but thanks to Bast's voice in his ear, he now knew the man used his blood to perform incredible feats of magic. As the only other magic user—not that anyone here knew about his skill with Fire—the mage was a wild card, much like the poisoner. Ronan immediately marked him as someone to watch out for.

The second was a man named Loren. He was clearly a crowd favorite. The moment the gilded warrior set foot on stage, they let loose a cheer rivaled only by the one given to the High Lord himself.

"What's his specialty?" Ronan asked, eyeing the man's robes, which perfectly matched his golden hair and amber eyes. He exuded a charisma that spoke to great familiarity with winning over crowds. The wink he tossed as he finished a sequence of acrobatic flips and spins said he enjoyed it too.

"Everything," Bast said, doing nothing to hide the appreciation shining in his gaze.

"Don't forget whose team you're on, *brother.*"

Sebastian actually blushed. "Never."

Despite the number of contestants, it wasn't long at all before Ronan found himself at the front of the line.

"Name?" the scribe from the day before asked.

"Butcher."

The man looked up from his scroll. "I remember you."

"I get that a lot."

When his name was announced, the room buzzed with whispers but none of the excited applause the better-known contestants received.

Bast clapped him on the back. "Enjoy your big moment. Don't trip."

"Why would you say that?"

Sebastian's only answer was a shit-eating grin. Knowing he didn't have time to waste, he shook his head and started to ascend the small flight of stairs, but when he took his step forward, Bast held fast to his cloak, pulling it off.

Every eye in the ballroom was aimed his way as he moved across the stage. He'd never felt more exposed in his life. Usually the looks were filled with awe or a little fear. This time, most were openly hostile. He didn't have the benefit of his name and reputation to do the heavy lifting for him. If he wanted to make a statement, if he wanted to set himself apart as a real contender and secure the support of a few big spenders, he needed to do something significant.

His original plan had been to do the opposite, to lie low and do the bare minimum to get to the next round, but it was clear that wouldn't be enough.

Bast was right—not that he'd ever tell him so—he needed the support of the crowd.

Ronan stopped when he reached the center of the stage, lifting his gaze until he stared not at the High Lord, but his Shadow. He knew her well enough to read the interest hidden in her expression. To most she would appear mildly curious, but she hadn't blinked once since his identity had been revealed. Her full attention was locked on him.

It wasn't exactly a declaration of love, but it was a start.

Beside her, the High Lord silently fumed. Ronan could read it in the slight curl of his upper lip and the whitening of his knuckles on the arms of his chair. He wasn't pleased to see him again.

The feeling is mutual, you rutting gobshite.

More whispers broke out when Ronan continued to stand there. On the far end of the stage, Dmitri cleared his throat, discreetly prompting him into action.

It's now or never. You want to make a statement? Do it.

Without stopping to think about the consequences, Ronan slowly raised his right hand, palm up. Then, for the first time since arriving in Empyria, he called on his Fire. Shocked gasps rang out as the orb swelled, and those gasps turned to cries as he hurled the ball directly at the High Lord's head.

He caught the scrape of metal being pulled free of scabbards and the hiss of boots rushing across the marble to intercept him. Ronan bit back a laugh. Did they really think they could get to him in time if his intention was to cause harm?

The High Lord and Shadow hadn't managed to do more than rise from their seats when Ronan twisted his hand and snuffed all the air out of the molten ball of flame, extinguishing it a split second before it would have connected with Erebos's face.

Stunned silence met the display before the entire room broke into shaky applause. The High Lord had no choice but to follow suit in order to save face.

Ronan smirked, giving the barest inclination of his head in the place of any sort of bow and then lazily strolled off the stage.

Bast was already waiting for him, his face pale and eyes wide. "Do you have any idea what you just did?"

"Aye, do you?"

"Put an even bigger target on your back?" he hissed. "Because if that was your intention, mission accomplished."

"No, Bast. I just secured our supporters."

"How?"

"By ensuring not a single person in that room will ever forget my name. Watch, by tomorrow, everyone in Glimmermere will know it."

"You're a brave bastard, I'll give you that."

Ronan clapped him on the shoulder and risked a glance back into the crowd, where a pair of multihued green eyes were still trained on him.

He'd made a splash all right.

One not even she could forget.

CHAPTER 12

SHADOW

*P*eople were still talking about him an hour later. She'd never seen anything like it, flames dancing in his hands. Called there and controlled by him. Could everybody do that where he was from? Or was he special? His hair had reminded her of fire, and now she wondered if it was somehow related to his gift or simply a coincidence.

Realizing she was obsessing over him, Shadow scowled. She'd come out to the garden to get away from talk of the contest. Okay, fine—of him.

Not that it worked on either account.

What she should be thinking about was the fact that there was a threat to her lord she had been ill-equipped to meet. That fireball had been lobbed through the air before she even registered what was happening. But even if she had, what good were her daggers against a ball of molten fire? The simple truth was, if the Butcher hadn't extinguished it, Erebos would have gone up in flames. She would have failed her most sacred duty.

More troubling—and perhaps more selfish—than that, there was a very good chance she'd have to go up against him in the days to come.

She could very easily be on the other side of that fiery orb. What had seemed so simple, so straightforward, a mere two nights ago suddenly seemed like a far bigger challenge.

"Starling for your thoughts?"

For a second, Shadow allowed his deep growl of a voice to wash over her, basking in its warmth as a little shiver raced down her spine before steeling herself against it. And him. She'd be lying if she said she hadn't been thinking of him nearly nonstop since the day before. And not because he was a threat to the High Lord.

His fascination with her. His insistence that he knew her, that she was someone else. It should have her running the other way. Instead, she felt a slight pang that she wasn't the woman who had him looking like he'd been twisted into knots.

He must care about her very deeply.

"They aren't worth that much," she finally said, turning to face him.

Clearly, he hadn't gotten the message about tonight's gala being a formal event. His clothes were clean, but nothing like the lavish fashions back in the ballroom. She wondered if that was because they didn't make such elaborate garments in his size. He was quite . . . large. Still, she found his fitted black leather breeches and simple black shirt he'd left unfastened at the throat and rolled up over his forearms uncommonly attractive. As was the lone decoration he wore strapped to his wrist. The simple leather cuff had some sort of sigil pressed into its smooth surface, but the lanterns were too few and far between for her to make out any further detail from here.

And his hair . . . he'd worn the silky mane down tonight, with a few strands pulled back and tied into an elaborate knot. Her fingers itched with the desire to run through it and see if it was as warm as it looked.

Everything about him fascinated her. Drew her in. Seduced her senses.

Especially the potently male scent of him. The men of court practically bathed themselves in colognes, but not this one. He smelled of sunshine and embers and leather. He called to mind images of a campfire after a long day's ride. A place she could curl up and find peace.

Instead of endearing her to him, it had the opposite effect. She grew suspicious, her every instinct on high alert. She couldn't relax around him, or worse, grow attached to him. He was an opponent. If someone else didn't kill him, she'd eventually have to.

That a girl, Shadow. Nothing like impending death to put things back into perspective.

"Let me be the judge of that," he said belatedly, making her realize he'd been sizing her up just as thoroughly as she had him.

Since she couldn't exactly admit her every thought recently had been consumed by him, she asked a question of her own instead. "What are you doing out here?"

"I wanted some fresh air."

"So you didn't follow me?" she asked, cocking her brow and crossing her arms around her waist.

"If I promise I didn't, will you stop fingering the blade hidden along your side?"

Her lips parted in a surprised huff of laughter and then curled up in a rare, genuine smile. "No, but don't be offended because of it. One of my weapons is always within reach when I find myself cornered in the dark by a stranger."

His lips twitched. "You're hardly cornered." He gestured to the maze of plants stretching out in every direction and the palace looming behind him. "You are free to leave whenever you'd like."

"I'll amend. One of my weapons is always within reach. Full stop."

"Fair enough." He tilted his head forward, lowering his voice, "You should know it's the same for me."

"Well, you should probably know that I *am* a weapon."

"I've been told the same."

"About me?"

"About myself."

"After what I saw tonight, I'm inclined to agree."

"That? Parlor tricks."

She snorted. "Conjuring fire is a parlor trick? Stars, the High Lord should just hand you the title and spare the rest of us."

His open, easy expression hardened, and his gaze, which had grown playful during their back and forth, shuttered. He stared at her intently, his eyes raking over her face.

"How?" he asked, his voice tortured.

Some inexplicable emotion twisted in her chest. "How what?"

"How did you come to be here? With him? Working for him? Bound to *him*?"

"I told you yesterday, he saved me."

"Saved you? Reyna, you were kidnapped."

It was her turn to drain of all lighthearted playfulness. *This again.*

"And as I also explained to you yesterday, I am not Reyna. I'm Shadow. You have me confused with someone else."

A muscle feathered in his jaw, and his hands curled into fists. "One of us is confused, but it's not me."

She shook her head, feeling completely out of sorts. Nothing about this interaction was normal for her. It was rare that anyone willingly sought her out—they were too afraid of her to dare. It was rarer still that she deigned to engage in small talk with them when they did. Especially someone outside of the High Lord's flock.

Unless they were an assignment, of course, but that was different.

This was unfamiliar territory.

For a few seconds, it had been easy; the words had flowed between them as effortlessly as breathing. For once she hadn't been thinking in moves like 'if he goes for my wrist, I'll drop him with a knee to the groin or a blade through the ribs.' She'd simply existed in the moment, enjoying the banter, eager to hear what came out of his mouth next. But then he'd called her by that other woman's name, and her walls slammed back into place.

Not sure where to go from here, she opted for a tactical retreat. "If you'll excuse me, I should probably get back inside."

"Rey—Sh-Shadow, wait." He fumbled over her name, his expression pained as he took a step toward her. "Please, will you just stay out here and talk with me for a while?" It looked like there was more he wanted to say, and she sensed the fists at his side weren't threatening violence but were his attempt to keep from touching her.

A part of her wanted him to lose the battle just so she could know what it would be like. His hands on her skin. His lips against hers. She mentally slapped herself.

Bad, Shadow. Very, very bad.

When she didn't immediately respond or make any move to leave, he took another tentative step, this time lifting his hand. He moved so slowly, giving her every opportunity to stop him.

She didn't.

Reaching for her, he brushed a strand of her hair behind her ear. Then he trailed the tips of his fingers along her jaw. As his fingers skated over her skin, she forgot how to breathe. The act was so simple, yet it left her craving so much more as a wave of goosebumps rushed down her neck and arms.

"I've missed you," he whispered.

"You don't even know me."

He glanced down at her lips, his eyes hooded. "I know you better than you think."

She'd never been this aware of her pulse. How it fluttered at the side of her neck, how it buzzed in her veins and roared in her ears. She barely even recognized her voice when a reply slipped from her, completely unbidden.

"Impossible."

His soft laugh was a gentle breeze ghosting over her. "What is?"

"You . . . knowing me."

He gently skimmed her bottom lip with the pad of his thumb. "I'm coming to learn that nothing is impossible."

His head dipped.

Her heart stopped.

"Ronan? Where did you go? It's rude to leave your date—oh!" A blond man in a silly feathered cap came around one of the hedges that had blocked them from view of the ballroom. He smiled, looking much like the cat who just ate the canary. "Do carry on, don't let me stop you. I love a good tryst."

Shadow jumped away so fast she nearly tripped over her dress in her haste.

"Sebastian," the Butcher growled. "Fuck off."

"I don't think I will. Seems like the two of you were just getting to the good part."

He finally looked away from her to pin the other man with his stare. "Leave. Now."

"No, it's okay. He can stay. I'm going," she said, heat suffusing her cheeks as she tried to slip away.

He gripped her elbow, his touch gentle but unyielding. "Don't. Stay with me. Let me help you remember."

The earnestness of his plea had her considering it for all of a heart-beat. Then she remembered where she was—*who* she was—and the growing list of reasons the thing she'd just been wishing for with every fiber of her being could never happen. She needed to put an end to whatever *this* was. Right now.

Stupid full moon making me act like a complete and utter tit.

What the hell had she been thinking? If the High Lord had discovered them . . . Her eyes darted around the garden, all its secret corners now seeming ominous. Was that a flash of dark hair?

The possibility that Dovina or one of her spies might be lurking nearby was enough to put the steel back in Shadow's spine. Her voice was notably cooler when she snapped, "The only thing I have to remember, Butcher, is that you're the enemy."

His face fell, only for a second, but it was all she needed to see that she'd cut him deeply. Good. Maybe if she reestablished the line between them, he'd finally stay on his side. She felt a pang of regret at the thought, but it was short-lived.

Schooling his expression, Ronan straightened. "Then I guess there's only one thing left to say."

"Good riddance?"

He held out his hand. "May the best man win."

She rolled her eyes and brushed past him. "The best *woman* shall."

The man in the feathered cap howled with laughter. "Well said, Lady Shadow," he murmured, holding up a hand for her to slap.

"Bast, you have an annoying habit of forgetting whose side you're on."

"I may be on your team, Ronan, but you know I'm a sucker for a beautiful woman. Especially one who can put your grumpy arse in place."

Shadow had to bite back a smile at the snarl of exasperation those words caused, giving Bast his high five as she sauntered past.

"See you around, *Ronan.*"

"Not if I see you first."

The rumble of words caressed her ears, causing another involuntary shiver to roll down her spine. As she turned to duck around the hedge, she couldn't resist a final parting shot.

"You will never see me coming."

EREBOS

THE WHISPER of the hidden door sliding open was the only hint he was no longer alone. His hands tightened on the railing, the waves a dull roar below him. The salty breeze a welcome assault against his anger-flushed cheeks. The party ended hours ago, but he'd only just been left to his own devices ten minutes prior.

"Did you find her?"

"Of course."

When Dovina's husky rasp with its clipped consonants and lyrical vowels offered nothing further, he pried his fingers free and spun around to face her.

"And?"

The single word was dripping in warning. It was a demand for information wrapped in the frayed edges of his patience.

"It was as you'd suspected."

He swallowed back a snarl, fighting hard to keep his expression wiped clean. After the procession, Shadow had slipped away. That wasn't uncommon at these sorts of events; she was always running off seeking calmer waters. The difference tonight was that *he* was here. The man from her past. The one bump in an otherwise smooth road to success.

Ronan of Daejara, Shield and Butcher. A mage gifted in three of the five branches: Fire, Earth, and Air. A mercenary whose hands were so stained with blood they nearly rivaled his own. A man who'd just made himself a very powerful nemesis.

"I see." He worked his jaw, one of his muscles ticking. "Did anything *untoward* occur?"

Dovina seemed to be choosing her words with care.

"Spit it out," he snapped.

"She was chaste, High Lord."

Erebos jumped on the distinction. "But he wasn't?"

"He touched her, but . . ."

"But what?" he snarled, already imagining breaking each and every finger on the man's hands. Shadow was his pet, and his alone. No one touched what was his.

"He didn't cross any lines."

"He touched her. That is line enough."

Dovina inclined her head. "That is, of course, for you to decide, my liege."

Erebos ground his teeth together, more than ready to be rid of this threat to his future. "You and your brother know what to do?"

She dipped into a shallow curtsey. "Consider it handled."

"I expect reports. Daily."

"Of course. And shall we make a move if the opportunity presents itself?"

Erebos considered it. "No. I want to handle this myself. Intel only for now."

"It will be as you say, my lord."

"Leave me."

She slipped away without a word, and he turned back to the ocean, releasing his first easy breath since he'd spotted the redheaded bastard crossing his stage in that mockery of a display. As if he'd ever allow one of Luna's Chosen to serve him. The only service he'd provide would be to send a message.

A bloody one.

CHAPTER 13

RONAN

"Are you sure you're prepared for this?" Ronan kept his eyes on the other contestants, drawling, "I'm always prepared."

Bast chuckled.

"Why's that funny?"

"I've used that line a time or two myself, but in a very different context."

Ronan rolled his eyes. "Why doesn't that surprise me?"

Instead of answering, Sebastian asked another question of his own. "Do you know what today's trial is going to be?"

"No. I thought they might give us a heads-up last night, but all they said was for us to be here by dawn. I guess they wanted to save the surprise."

"No unfair advantages that way."

"I suppose."

They both looked around the mostly empty field. Other than the contestants and a few annoyed cows, no one was here. That was surprising only because of the interest in the competition. Since his first night in Glimmermere, he couldn't set foot anywhere in town without overhearing someone talking about it. And at every contest-related event he'd attended, there'd been a horde of rubberneckers on the sidelines eager for a crumb of gossip. But today, at the first official trial, nothing. Not a single supporter.

"Where is everybody?" he asked with a frown.

"Your guess is as good as mine," Bast said, sounding just as troubled by the lack of onlookers as he was.

The others seemed to share in the restlessness. No one was talking outside of a few hushed conversations. Mostly it was lots of suspicious looks and foot tapping.

Just as the sun peeked over the top of the palace's many domed towers, a carriage rolled down a dirt path from the north.

"Showtime," Ronan muttered.

"Do you want me to stay?" Sebastian asked, uncharacteristically serious.

"No. Head back to town and see what you can find out. I'll touch base with you once we're done with this farce."

Bast looked conflicted.

"What?"

"Don't die, okay? I've grown rather fond of you."

"I should have warned you against forming attachments."

Sebastian laughed. "Is that your way of saying I should know better than to fall in love with you?"

"Something like that."

"How many times do I have to tell you? You're not my type, and even if you were, we would never work."

"Why's that?"

"You're a nightmare, and likely a terrible lay."

It was his turn to bark out a laugh. "I'll see you tonight, Sebastian."

"Until then, *mon ami.*"

Sebastian peeled away, leaving Ronan surrounded by those who would prefer if he were dead. Instead of unnerving him, it was surprisingly calming. This he was used to. No courtly games of intrigue required, simple battle strategy. In a lot of ways, it felt like coming home.

The carriage rolled to a stop, and even the hushed conversations ceased. The door opened, and three familiar faces poured out. Dmitri was the first to appear, followed by the High Lord, who offered a hand to the final occupant, a leather-clad Shadow.

If she was stunning in a gown, she was breathtaking in the skin-tight leathers with her hair pulled back in a sleek ponytail high atop her head. Ronan's mouth went dry. Her outfit left nothing to the imagination, but provided plenty of inspiration for a whole slew of other things. From the rumbles of appreciation around him, he wasn't the only one to notice.

"Damned shame she has to die," a man grunted to his left.

Ronan shot him a dark glare.

Bannock.

You just found yourself at the top of my list, brawler.

Shadow might be the only one here with a target on her back larger than his. He'd have his hands full ensuring she made it through these trials alongside him. The knowledge was enough to dampen his ardor.

"Gather round," Dmitri called, waving the crowd of competitors in.

Ronan hung back, allowing the others to press in so he could observe them while listening to the details of the day's task.

"In just a few minutes, the sun will have fully risen. The trial begins as soon as the field is completely illuminated."

He glanced to his left, watching the last sliver of darkness melt away from the knee-high field of stocks they were standing in.

Dmitri continued with his speech. "There are thirty tokens hidden around this field."

"What are the boundaries?" Marin called. Like him, she stood near the back, her arms crossed casually over her chest.

"If you can see it from here, it's in bounds."

Ronan heard a few whistles. That was quite a bit of ground to cover.

"So that's it? We find a token and we're done?" Loren asked from his place front and center.

Kiss arse.

"Not quite," Dmitri said with a smirk. "The token is only half of the task. You cannot cross the finish line without one, but between recovering it and getting to the end, you'll also have to swim across the bay, climb up the eastern cliffs, and then sprint through town until you reach the palace steps. Besides the marked-off section of the bay, there's no set course you must run. You may reach the steps however you see fit. Between here and there, there are a number of traps you might encounter. There's also nothing in the rules stating that you must find a token *before* making your way back to town."

Meaning the contestants could procure their tokens through any means necessary, chief among them outright thievery.

"Not very sportsmanlike, is it?"

This was from Bannock again, whose shit-eating grin clearly conveyed his approval of the fact. The snickers in the crowd said most of them agreed.

Only Ronan, Calix the poisoner, and the veiled maiden Dichen seemed not to share the other's amusement at the endorsement of underhanded tactics.

Interesting.

"The High Lord is not interested in your morals, only your ability to get the job done."

"I look forward to your creativity in accomplishing today's task," Erebos said, his silky voice rubbing against Ronan's ears like the scratch of sand in a wound.

"It's nearly time. Are there any questions?" Dmitri asked, rubbing his hands together in anticipation.

"How do we know she won't receive special treatment?" Cedric called, jerking his chin in Shadow's direction.

"I'm assuming you mean how can you be sure she hasn't been given any privileged information?" Dmitri asked, his expression thunderous.

To his credit, Cedric didn't shrink away. "Exactly."

Shadow rolled her eyes. "Perhaps you should worry about your own performance, Aldair."

There were a few derisive snorts as Cedric shot back, "Anything that unfairly benefits my opponents and hurts my chances *does* affect my performance."

"Need I remind you that a slight against Shadow is a slight against me?" the High Lord drawled dangerously. "I am just as vested—if not more—in the outcome of this contest than you. I wouldn't risk my reputation, let alone that of my future champion, by tampering with the outcome of these trials."

Liar.

Shadow didn't seem to appreciate his coming to her defense. She adopted her most unaffected mask, though her voice was sharp enough to cut. "I'd take offense to the implication I can only win through duplicitous means, but then I've never shied away from doing whatever it takes to win. So believe whatever you want, Aldair, but I will be crossing that finish line. Not just today, but every single time. Can you say the same?"

Ronan's lips curled up in a proud smile. Mother, but he loved watching her set arseholes in their place. For the second time since her arrival, he found himself discreetly adjusting his pants.

Before Cedric could do something foolish, like goad her further, the last of the darkness vanished, putting an end to the verbal sparring match.

Dmitri's voice boomed like thunder across the seemingly empty field. "Contestants, begin!"

CHAPTER 14

SHADOW

*C*ontestants scattered before Dmitri finished speaking. It was immediately clear that well over a quarter of the participants wouldn't bother searching for their tokens in the field.

Strategic? Certainly. Fair? Perhaps not, but morals had no place in a game where lives were on the line. It was a kill or be killed kind of crowd because that's what the prize demanded. It wouldn't do Erebos any good to have a weak-willed shrinking violet as his champion. He required someone who wouldn't be afraid to get their hands dirty.

Someone like her.

Shadow wasn't surprised so many would prefer to rely on their more nefarious skills rather than luck. Choosing to steal from a competitor and rob them of their chance to cross the finish line was a good way to cull the herd. Not to mention target those you considered a threat. She might have done the same had she no firsthand knowledge of how the High Lord's mind worked.

It was true, what she'd told Cedric. She hadn't been given any special treatment, but that didn't mean she didn't have the upper hand. After spending the better part of the last five years by his side, she knew Erebos better than anyone. Finding where he hid one of his silly tokens should be easy.

It was really just a question of what would Erebos do?

Scary question, that. Because really, what *wouldn't* he do? There was no doubt in her mind that he was one of the good guys, but she'd also seen firsthand how far he'd go to succeed. A man like him would stack the odds in his favor. He'd also want to weed out anyone seeking the easy path, preferring those who thought outside of the box. In fact, he'd likely go so far as to punish those who didn't.

Intuition crooned so loudly in her ear that a sense of certainty buzzed all the way down to her marrow. She'd bet everything those traps Dmitri mentioned were attached to the tokens hidden in obvious places. Same for any that might be located in the area immediately surrounding them.

With those bits of insight firmly in mind, Shadow sprinted to the west, not caring that several sets of eyes were fixed on her, tracking her every move. They could copy her all they wanted, but they still didn't know what she did, which meant taking their cues from her wasn't going to help them.

There was one set of eyes in particular she sensed more keenly than others. She'd felt his gaze land on her the second she stepped free of the carriage. It had taken all of her considerable restraint not to look over and lock eyes with Ronan. The man muddled her mind, and right now, she couldn't afford the distraction.

Focused on the task at hand, she mentally discounted any tokens that might be lying somewhere obvious, like out in the open or along one of the wooden beams surrounding the outskirts of the mostly barren land. Her eyes scanned instead for markers others may overlook, like a pile of rocks or freshly tilled soil. She was on the hunt for anything that *could* be natural but was just a touch out of place. She had a hunch they might actually indicate the place where a token had been buried.

Spying a flash of color in the periphery, she spun around. There was a barely audible click and a whoosh of air a split second before a wall of muscle collided with her and knocked her to the ground. Her ears rang, but not from smacking her head. There'd been an explosion.

Looks like I was right about the traps.

It took a second for her eyes to clear enough to make out Ronan hovering just above her. The bastard had tackled her and used his body to shield hers from the blast.

"What are you doing?"

His worried gaze swept across her face, though it lingered on her lips for a second before returning to her eyes. "I saw the brunette hit the trip wire, and I just . . . reacted."

She eyed him wearily as his warm body pressed against hers. "They did warn us about traps."

"Yes, but I couldn't be sure we were free of the blast area." He shifted slightly on top of her, causing his hips to roll against her.

It was harder than she cared to admit to ignore what that did to her. It took her a few tries to get her words out. "Well, as you can see, I'm perfectly fine." If her voice was a little more breathless than usual, she blamed it on him forcing the air from her lungs with his weight.

"Yes, thanks to my quick thinking."

Shadow peered over his shoulder at the smoldering crater. It was right where the competitors had been gathered minutes earlier. Now there were only the remains of those who hadn't sensed the danger.

Better them than you, Shadow.

All around the field, those who'd been out of range stood back up on shaky legs and resumed their search.

Shadow slapped at Ronan's shoulder. "Get off me."

"What? Oh." He blushed and pushed off her, holding out a hand to help her up. "Sorry."

She begrudgingly accepted it but dropped his hand as soon as she was upright so she could resume searching. To her ever-growing annoyance, he trailed along beside her. It was impossible to focus with him standing so close to her. There was something magnetic about his presence. It tugged at her, forcing her to sneak looks out of the corner of her eye. When she found him looking back, she snapped, "What?"

"I was just thinking, we should work together on this one. You know, I watch your back . . . you watch mine."

"Absolutely not." She scowled at him. "You're the enemy. Why would I help you?"

"I just helped you," he pointed out.

"You did not."

He squinted, his expression lined with genuine concern. "Did you hit your head? I literally just used my body to save your life."

"Please, all you did was throw your body on mine. Without my consent, I might add."

"Since when do life-saving heroics require consent? Most people would say thank you."

"Yeah, well, I'm not most people."

"I'm well aware of that," he muttered.

He sounded so put out, she had to bite back a laugh. She couldn't help but be amused by his annoyance, but she knew better than to show it. If she gave him an inch, he'd take a whole damn mile, and then she'd never get rid of him. The last thing she needed was for him to become more entrenched in her life than he already had.

With a slight shake of her head, she turned away from him. "We may not have to face each other until the final trial, but that doesn't make you any less of an enemy. Only one of us can win."

"True, but as you've just seen, one false step could be your undoing." He whispered a soft "boom" while his hands mimed an explosion.

"Luckily for you—or perhaps *unluckily*—I don't intend to make any 'false steps.' I am exceedingly good at what I do."

"Still, it never hurts to have allies."

"We will never be allies, Ronan."

"We already are. As I proved just a moment ago when I saved your neck."

She rounded on him. "Stars, you are a stubborn bastard. Don't you know when to quit?"

He grinned at her. "Nope, don't have it in me. I always have to see a task successfully completed." Then he winked.

An unexpected wave of heat crept into her cheeks, followed by a flurry of frustration. *Who in the darkness's name is this guy, and why won't he leave me alone?* A little growl escaped as she stormed off. Once again Ronan dogged her steps. Determined to ignore him, she squatted down to inspect a stack of rocks. He copied her.

"What the hell do you think you're doing now?"

"Making sure you don't get killed."

"Well, I didn't ask for your help. Nor do I want it. Go. Away."

He shrugged, standing as she did, entirely unfazed by her scathing tone and matching glare. "Doesn't matter. It's a service I'm providing free of charge. That's quite a boon. You should consider yourself lucky."

She fought the urge to knock him over. "I'm really starting to loathe you."

"You wouldn't be the first."

"I don't think you realize who you're picking a fight with. The people I hate have a tendency to end up dead."

His lips curled up. "I've dealt with worse. And far scarier, I might add."

Oh, the gall of this man.

She had half a mind to show him that no one was scarier than her, but she was in the middle of something far more important. Something that could cost her her freedom. Shaking her head, she decided he wasn't worth the time or effort. Ronan might annoy her, but she'd be far more upset with herself if she allowed him to distract her from her goal.

As if underscoring the point, there were a few victorious cries as competitors began to locate tokens. Shadow clenched her fists, furious with herself for taking so long to find hers. Just as she had the thought, her eyes landed on a bit of disrupted shrubbery. Upon closer inspection, she saw the betraying glint of a coin nestled in a tangle of thorny roots.

Knowing Ronan was watching her every step, she tried to move stealthily. But as her hand snaked out, his was already there, stealing her prize.

"You bastard, that's mine."

"Is it? Since I'm the one in possession of it, I'm pretty sure it's mine. Especially given the rules of this little contest." He shot her a cocky grin as he dropped the coin down the front of his pants. "But please do feel free to go digging for it, if you really want to press the point."

"If you think something as unimpressive as your balls will prevent me from taking back that which you stole, you're in for a rude awakening."

He snickered. "Is that your way of saying you want to play with my balls, Shadow?"

"Ugh. No."

"Pity." He winked at her.

"Stars, you're so deluded you can't even react to an insult properly."

"I think you have me confused with Bast."

"Who?"

"Sebastian, my guide. He's the one who so rudely interrupted us last night."

"And how is your appalling decorum his fault?"

"I've spent too much time in his company."

A disbelieving laugh escaped before she could stop it. "You are ridiculous. Blaming your poor friend for your own failings. I shall advise him of your disloyalty if I ever cross paths with him again."

"He'd be the first to agree with me. He's entirely unrepentant."

"As are you."

"What's there to apologize for?"

Realizing he'd sucked her back into yet another fruitless conversation, she huffed and stomped away, muttering about egotistical men whose heads were shoved up their own asses.

"Sounds painful."

"You got what you came for, so do us both a favor and fuck off."

"I told you—"

Temper beyond frayed, she spun and shoved him as hard as she could. Surprise knotted his features as he fell back, landing on his ass in the weeds.

"Now be a good boy and stay." She growled the words, lacing them with as much violence as she could muster, considering his absolute shock had her wanting to laugh.

Maybe now you will finally stop underestimating me.

But instead of being cowed, his expression shifted, turning almost . . . admiring. "I'll just maintain a healthy distance, then, shall I?"

"That would be wise."

This time, thank the stars, he stayed put, allowing her to creep along the edge of the field without issue. It wasn't long before she spied a sapling with a broken branch. It didn't appear to be a natural break, but an intentional one. Like an X on a treasure map, marking the secret spot.

Gotcha.

Using that as her guide, she sank her hands into the earth just beneath it. The soil gave way easily, unlike the nearby dirt, which was hard and packed, so it was no surprise when her fingers brushed against something metallic after only a few seconds of digging. Making a point to keep her face free of expression, she palmed the coin and stood. Then she continued to wander about the field, moving as aimlessly as she could manage while still cutting a path that would lead her toward the bay and the next part of the trial.

It didn't take very long to realize her movements hadn't gone unnoticed. Once again, Ronan trailed behind her like a stray searching for a meal. Shadow sighed, mentally kicking herself. She'd unintentionally fed him by engaging in conversation, and now she'd never rid herself of the pest.

Instead of trying to shake him now, she gave up all pretense and took off at a dead sprint. He caught up easily, and she comforted herself with the knowledge he'd likely fall behind during the swim. She was familiar with the bay and its currents since she swam them weekly, but he was an outsider. There was little doubt in her mind she could lose him in the water.

Still, it rankled how easily he kept pace with her, and she debated more than once whether she should stick her foot out to trip him.

When they finally reached the shore nearly half an hour later, there were a series of red balls bobbing in the sea, marking the path that would lead them to the cliffs. There were also a handful of smoking craters along the beach. The twisted limbs and splatters of blood around them spoke to the fates of several unlucky contestants. Not everyone who thought they'd have an easier time stealing made it very far.

Poor bastards.

She wished she knew how many competitors had already been taken out, but given that only thirty of them would move on to the next round, it didn't really matter. All she needed to do was hang onto her token and cross the finish line.

Easy.

When she reached the water's edge, she didn't stop, not even to remove anything she was wearing. She chose this set of clothes intentionally, knowing it would see her through all possibilities. Not only was it waterproof, but it was also lightweight and bent easily with her form, meaning it wouldn't slow her down in the water. Unlike the idiots who'd opted for full suits of metal armor.

As she started to swim, she looked back at the shore, catching sight of Ronan as he peeled off his shirt and tucked it into a small bag hanging from his belt. She wasn't prepared for the sight of his well-muscled torso and the intricate black tattoo climbing up the left side of his rib cage, up over his pec and onto his shoulder. *Stars, he was beautiful.* Her smooth movements turned jerky, and she accidentally sucked in a mouthful of salt water.

Focus, Shadow! A couple of muscles aren't worth drowning over.

She resumed her efforts, executing a couple of flawless strokes before risking a second glance back, even though she knew she shouldn't. This time she spotted Ronan pulling off his boots and shoving them into the same bag. Her third check caught him completing an expert dive into an oncoming wave. It was then she realized her miscalculation. He was no novice swimmer. In fact, despite her significant head start, it wasn't long before he was gaining on her.

He may not swim these waters like she did, but he was clearly no stranger to the sea. Given his form and the easy way he cut through the current, he'd spent a significant amount of time in the ocean.

Shadow gritted her teeth and kicked even harder as she fought to stay ahead. Logically she knew she didn't have to fight so hard. All she had to do was get to the finish. No one said she had to be first, but it was a matter of pride to her. She was supposed to be the High Lord's ringer. She couldn't let this *outsider* beat her.

There was a panicked cry and then a, "Please!" Shadow spotted the floundering swimmer a ways ahead of her; her head popped up long enough for her to shout a frantic, "I'm drowning!" before slipping back beneath the unforgiving waves.

A better person might have stopped to save the woman. But not her.

She didn't even pause to consider it.

Rather she continued to swim to the rocky cliffs she still had to climb, mentally calculating how much longer it would take her to reach them. Experience told her the looming rocks appeared far closer than they actually were. In the end, it took almost thirty minutes before she finally pulled her shaking limbs onto the wet sand.

As always, the first few seconds after leaving the sea were an adjustment, requiring Shadow to relearn how to move without the weightless buoyancy the salt water granted her. Though she was used to it, she couldn't deny it took even more effort than usual to lift her arms as she wrung the water from her hair and shook droplets from her skin. So much, in fact, that she was still working on it when Ronan joined her.

"Would you like some help drying off?"

"No," she growled. "How many times do I have to tell you? We"— she pointed between them—"are not partners."

With an amused lift of his brow, he stared at her as his hands began to glow, calling on his magic as he dried himself. "You sure?"

Damned convenient skill.

It was almost on the tip of her tongue to take back her denial, but watching the way he moved his hands over his body, she knew she couldn't. He was distracting enough from a distance. She didn't need firsthand knowledge of how much worse it would be if she allowed him to invade her personal space.

Turning her back on him, she began mapping out her path up, using the time to strategize and catch her breath. There were a few people climbing, giving her a pretty good idea of where the best hand and footholds might be. Some had opted for ropes, others going free hand, but no one seemed to be having an easy time of it. That didn't surprise her. With the rocks slick with sea spray, it would be treacherous going no matter what.

"Last chance . . ."

"You put those hands anywhere near me, and I will gnaw them off."

His chuckle followed her as she strode to the cliff and tested her grip. Satisfied she wouldn't immediately drop, she started to climb.

The danger of the climb didn't allow her mind to wander, but there was a sort of meditative state that came with being utterly focused and in the moment. There wasn't room to worry about her competitors or how many people would be waiting for her at the top. So far no one had made a move for her token, but that would all change once she got into town. Thankfully, few knew their way around better than her. She was confident that as long as she could get off the cliff without setting off any sort of trap, she'd be in the clear.

When Ronan's voice, strong and clear, sounded just to her left, she wasn't even surprised.

"I once worked with a man with the gift of transmutation. He could turn anything he could touch into whatever he wanted. Such a power would sure come in handy right now, don't you think?"

"Don't."

"Don't what?"

"Distract me."

"I'm just trying to find an enjoyable way to pass the time."

"Well, stop."

"You're right. Conversation is overrated. There are so many better things we could be doing."

She fought against a smile, charmed by him despite herself. There was something about a confident man who refused to give up that had to be admired. Shaking her head, she selected her next hold and propelled herself upward.

They were just over halfway up when she felt the tremor beneath her fingers.

No.

The tremor was quickly followed by the telltale rattle of a stone breaking free.

Oh, shit.

Heart in her throat, Shadow looked up. She didn't even realize she was holding her breath until she determined the fall of rocks was not directly above them as she feared. There wasn't time for her to wonder why she'd also made a point to ensure Ronan was in the clear.

To the right of them, a tiny woman whose name she couldn't remember flattened herself against the wall of rock she'd been gracefully scaling seconds earlier. But it was too late. There was no hope for her as more deadly stones slid to the ground, taking the climber with them and crushing her beneath their weight.

"Mother's tits."

"That was close," Shadow agreed.

"It could have been worse."

"But it wasn't, not for us anyway."

"Does nothing faze you?"

She didn't bother answering since the last of the quaking faded, allowing her to continue with her ascent. Thankfully, there were no other traps or natural disasters, and they—the prick was still keeping up with her—made it to the top unscathed.

Flopping over onto her back, she panted as she stared at the shifting wisps of clouds drifting across the sky. Rolling to her side, she forced herself up, her breath sawing in and out of her through a throat that burned. Her arms and legs visibly shook from the exertion of her climb and swim as she stood there desperately trying to catch her breath.

She was more out of shape than she'd realized, having grown soft during the relative peace of last year, but now was hardly the time to slow down.

"This is where I leave you," she panted as soon as Ronan's red hair appeared, not waiting for him to fully clear the wall before she took off toward the city gates.

Knowing many would use the alleys and various dark corners to lie in wait, Shadow had already decided she would be going up instead of through. The best way to do that would be from the East, where the roofs were flat, rather than the more direct path from the West. She angled right, heading in that direction and hoping the longer route would keep others from following her.

She knew she'd made the right choice when she slipped through the gate and was met with a wink from one of the guards.

"Only two have come this way so far," he murmured. "But I believe you're about to take the lead."

She grinned at the man before offering a nod and then used one of the merchant stalls to jump up and grasp the metal rod just above it, using it to pull herself up and then over onto the shop's balcony. From there, she climbed the wrought iron and jumped up onto the roof. With nothing but the buildings between her and the palace steps, she took off in a dead run.

It was a careful dance, jumping from roof to roof while keeping an eye trained on the streets below to see who might be watching her. She could probably move faster if she didn't look down, but there were too many places for people to hide, too many dark alleys and side streets where one of her competitors could be lying in wait for her to disregard them. Thankfully, so far as she could tell, no one was paying any attention to her.

That changed the second she jumped down to the street.

She'd barely made it four steps when a meaty palm slammed into her chest, halting her forward momentum.

Bannock.

The meat shield's brown eyes gleamed with wicked intent as he peered down at her. "Now now, little Shadow. Where do you think you're going in such a hurry?"

"You don't want to fuck with me, Bannock."

"I wouldn't be so sure about that. A pretty girl like you . . ." His trailed-off words left little doubt as to his intention.

She and the brawler had never been friends, but they'd always been friendly. There was mutual respect among the people in their circle. He'd broken it the second he laid a finger on her.

"Bannock, you don't want to do this," she cautioned, panting a little as she lifted an arm to wipe the sweat off her brow.

"Sure I do. Just give me what I want, and you can be on your way. Plenty more folks will be coming this way. You can take one of theirs or go back and grab another if you're that afraid of a little confrontation."

"I got mine fair and square. I suggest you do the same."

He threw his head back and laughed. "Didn't you hear, sweetheart? Nothing's off limits. I'm in the clear so long as I walk up there with a coin in my hand. Aw, what's this face?" He reached out as if to touch her, and she jerked her head back out of his reach. "Don't be mad I outsmarted you, love. So what if I let you do the dirty work for me? Thems the breaks. Now be a good girl and hand it over."

She glared at him knowing that he had the right of it, but not caring. "If you think you're getting this coin off me, you clearly don't know who you're messing with."

"But that's just it. Everyone knows who you are." His voice turned taunting, his leer making her skin crawl. "You're the High Lord's whore."

She flinched. Given Erebos's plans for her, the words cut deeper than usual. She'd been called worse, but the truth of how others saw her, how little they valued her, it stung.

Bannock wasn't the smartest man, but he was a predator through and through. She knew he caught her involuntary reaction, that it was like blood in the water to him. He crowded her, forcing her back into one of the alleys as he pressed his advantage and gripped her chin with his hand.

"You tired of spreading your legs for that prissy fuck, sweetheart? You wanna give me a ride instead?" His voice took on a musing and conversational cast, though nothing could disguise the threat in his words. "You know, that sounds like a fair trade to me. You want to keep that token so badly? Give me a taste. You make it good for me, you take my dick like the good little slut we all know you are, I might just allow you to finish this race. So what about it, Shadow? You ready to let a real man fuck that pretty little cunt?"

CHAPTER 15

RONAN

*H*e lost her the second she slipped past the city gates. Even with her head start, she was barely two minutes ahead of him. It may as well be two hundred. He'd been able to easily track her progress as she darted off to the east, but knowing her route was useless to him now that she was concealed within Glimmermere's walls.

Her in-depth knowledge of the city meant it had just become a whole new game. Finding her again before she reached the finish line would be next to impossible. If he'd been the one with the hometown advantage, it would have been no contest, but as was becoming increasingly clear, he was a long way from home.

As he approached the eastern gates Shadow had disappeared through, there was a notable lack of people. He supposed most folks were crowding around the palace so they'd be the first to know which competitors would be moving on. Still, it was unnerving to find the bustling marketplace all but deserted. It was as if the whole city had shut down for the day. He might have been worried something had happened if not for the fact that he could hear the distant roar of the crowd rumbling like incoming thunder, the steady buzz growing with every step.

He was almost there.

The knowledge provided a fresh wave of energy, which he greatly appreciated as he rounded the final bend in the road and zoomed through the gate. The guards posted there did little more than scowl at him, but Ronan barely had eyes for them as he searched for a glimpse of Shadow.

As suspected, she was long gone, but he did spot a familiar face.

Camille, the courtesan he'd met on his first day in town, gave a jerk of her head, beckoning him over as she darted between two stalls into what looked like some kind of alley. He had no idea whether the townsfolk were allowed to assist the contestants in any way, but given the effort she'd taken to remain discreet, he could only assume it was frowned upon.

Though who could really say? The High Lord and his cock— Ronan snickered at his preferred nickname for Dmitri—seemed to encourage underhanded methods. The irreverent part of him couldn't help but wonder how many people secretly referred to the flock as the Circle of Dicks. With its three members all sharing names beginning with the letter D, surely he couldn't be the only one? Then again, given his loathing for Kieran—or whatever the fuck he was calling himself now—perhaps that was simply his way of expressing his innate distrust for anyone who'd willingly bind themselves to that fraud of a monarch.

Ducking into the alley, he spotted Camille near the other end. Catching his gaze, she pointed a finger to the sky. "If it's the High Lord's Shadow you're after, look up."

Ronan narrowed his eyes, wondering how she'd guessed who he was searching for.

She chuckled, a soft, husky sound that spoke to an inherent sensuality. She was likely one of the few sex peddlers who truly enjoyed her line of work. Either that or she'd been doing it for so long she didn't know how to turn it off anymore. Given the laughter crinkling her eyes and the perpetual smile curling her lips, he was sticking with his initial assessment.

"Wondering how I divined your secret?" she asked with a knowing smirk.

Figuring it couldn't hurt to give into his curiosity since his token was still safely concealed, Ronan nodded.

"You know how everyone turns to watch the bride as she makes her way to the groom at a wedding?"

Ronan had absolutely no idea where she was going with the analogy, but he nodded anyway.

"Well, the smartest of us know that's the perfect time to steal a glance at the groom. So while everyone was busy gawking at the High Lord and Shadow as they made their grand entrance the other night, I was looking at *you*. I saw how you couldn't take your eyes off her. As soon as she appeared, it was as if no one else existed." Camille let out a wistful sigh. "What I wouldn't give to have a man look at me that way."

Her words made him feel oddly exposed, especially since it was the second time in as many days someone had commented on the way he looked at Shadow. He needed to do a better job hiding his reaction to her. If Erebos caught on—assuming he hadn't already—things would get that much more difficult. Ronan wiped a hand along the back of his neck, trying to laugh it off. "I'm sure plenty of men have looked at you like that."

"No," she softly disagreed. "Not the way you did. Not for keeps. Trust me, I wouldn't be in this line of work if there had been."

"Why look at me in the first place? You and I had barely spoken a word to each other. You had no reason to seek me out."

"You turned me down," she said simply. "That never happens, so I was intrigued." She lifted one shoulder in a slight shrug. "Then I saw the way you looked at her, and well . . . I had my answer."

"But why help me?"

"Because a man so clearly in love deserves to live long enough to act on it. I can't give you forever, but I can try to help you have tonight." She turned playful once more, winking at him. "Let me know if you need any tips on how to make the best of it, handsome."

Instinct told Ronan there was more to it than that, but now was not the time to press her further. Instead he placed a warm palm on her shoulder and feathered a kiss over her cheek. "Thank you, Camille. I owe you one."

She waved him away, appearing almost shy as she dipped her head and ran her fingertips along her cheek. "Just promise me you will tell her how you feel the next time you see her."

Reflecting on Shadow's lack of memory and nearly glacial reaction to him throughout the day, he didn't see that happening, but there was no point in mentioning it to Camille. Instead, he gave her a smile and turned toward a stack of crates. Using them as stairs, he sprinted up the teetering pile until he was balanced at the peak. From there, he jumped, grasping onto the edge of the nearest roof. His muscles burned from overexertion after the swim and climb, but he gritted through it and pulled himself up.

He knew the exhaustion he'd feel later was worth it as soon as he spotted Shadow's hair billowing out behind her like a flag as she darted across the rooftops.

Gotcha.

There were perhaps a dozen buildings between them, with only a couple more ahead of her in the row before she'd need to drop back down to the streets.

Calling on his gift of Air, he all but flew, closing the gap between them as he sprinted and leapt across the rooftops behind her. He only faltered once, landing not on a flat surface as he expected, but a pile of discarded supplies. Thankfully he recovered in time to see Shadow reach the end of the row. She glanced down, her gaze sweeping along the street before she jumped. She hadn't looked back once, so she had no idea he was hot on her trail once more.

Grinning, Ronan didn't let up his pace. If he was lucky, he'd catch up to her before she reached the palace. He couldn't wait to see the look on her face when he pulled up beside her and she realized she hadn't ditched him after all.

Reaching the end of the row, he copied her move, checking to make sure it was safe to drop down before jumping over the edge. Though the street directly beneath him was mostly clear, he hesitated. Shadow was nowhere to be found.

He glanced up and down the cobbled path. The palace was situated on a slight hill to his right. As he'd suspected, that crowd he'd been missing filled the streets, nearly blocking the route he'd need to take. Or they would have been if not for the sectioned-off trail down the middle. With his unobstructed view, he should be able to spot Shadow making her way to the finish. Even without it, her hair would stand out like a damn beacon. She wasn't there.

But why would she backtrack with the end in sight?

What game are you playing now, killer?

Dropping down, he caught a distinctly male voice just up ahead. He couldn't quite make out the words over the not-so-distant shouts of the crowd, but instinct had him walking in that direction anyway. Ronan knew better than to question it, especially once he caught the telltale clank of a buckle being unfastened.

He had no logical reason to assume the worst, but anxiety danced in his veins like a storm drifting in from the horizon. He was coiled, tense, a man on the verge of unleashing something catastrophic.

Finally he was close enough to make out the man's words.

"So what about it, Shadow? You ready to let a real man fuck that pretty little cunt?"

"B-Ban-nock, I-I—"

The stuttered response had Ronan seeing red. He was no longer a storm on the brink, but a raging inferno. Fury rippled through him, his Fire responding to the instinctive need to destroy. Usually his control over his gifts was absolute, but her soft sob and unmistakable fear shredded it entirely. He couldn't recall a time in his life he'd ever felt his anger quite this potent and all-consuming.

There was no time to do more than react as he moved into the darkened alley. Spotting the figures, he grasped the larger of the two by the neck and yanked him back. There was a second of recognition as his mind registered Bannock's stunned expression. Without hesitation, he cocked his arm back, slamming it into the other man's cheek. He would have shattered bone even without the aid of his Earth-enhanced strength, but raging out of control as it was, his gift turned the already punishing blow into something life-threatening. It was like smashing a piece of fruit with a boulder. The fucker didn't stand a chance. As soon as Ronan's fist connected, Bannock went limp, tumbling to the ground and straight into a pile of rubbish where he belonged.

Not caring whether the bastard was still breathing, Ronan spun around and grabbed Shadow by the shoulders. Panic continued to claw at his throat, choking him and turning his words into little more than a strangled rasp. "Are you all right?"

"Perfectly. I had everything under control," she snapped, scowling up at him. The familiar yet unexpected display of temper took his addled brain a second to translate.

"Under control," he repeated, the words feeling foreign in his mouth.

"Yes."

"But you were scared."

She snorted, gesturing angrily toward Bannock's unconscious form. "Does it look like I needed your help?"

Ronan shifted his attention to where she indicated, though there was a definite delay between the things she was saying and his ability to process them. He was still recovering from the surge of his power combined with some seriously turbulent emotions. It took a couple of blinks before he could make out the stain spreading across the other man's stomach.

Blood.

That's when Ronan noticed the blade in her hand.

"You cut him."

"I was trying to, but you knocked him out of reach before I could do more than scratch the skin." Her annoyance was unmistakable. "It's barely a flesh wound."

Here he was thinking he'd just stopped the unspeakable from happening, and she was pissed he'd stolen her kill.

It felt as though he'd turned the corner and found himself standing on the ceiling rather than the ground. Nothing was making a damned bit of sense.

"But I . . . I heard you."

She scoffed. "I was baiting him, you idiot. You heard the same thing I wanted him to hear, a weak terrified female playing the timid little mouse. Do you think so little of me that you actually believed I was scared of a man just because he uttered some crude words and is bigger than I am?" She laughed, but there was no humor in it. "As if that was the first time I've ever had to deal with an unwanted advance. I've dealt with countless men just like him since I was barely more than a girl. I'll let you in on a little secret. He wasn't even the worst. So please do not insult me with your alpha male, white knight bullshit." She gave another little disbelieving snort. "Do you really not know what I'm capable of? You know what? It doesn't matter. All you need to know, Butcher, is that I'm not some damsel in need of rescue. I fight my own battles. I slay my own dragons. I do not. Need. You."

Ronan stared down at her, his heart only just returning to something resembling normal. He didn't know what to make of her speech. Of course he fell for her act because the sound of her distress was so unexpected it sent him flying into action.

But she'd jumped to all the wrong conclusions. It wasn't some outdated misogynistic belief that had him jumping in to save her. He knew better than anyone she wasn't fragile or helpless. It was part of what drew him to her. When he looked at her, he saw an equal in every possible sense of the word.

He reacted the way he did *because* of who she was.

Anything to put that note of fear in her voice had to be a true threat. She may go by a different name now, but she was still the Night Stalker's queen. A warrior in her own right. An assassin whose reputation was unmatched in not one but two fucking realms. So if she was truly in fear for her life, how could he not swoop in and try to help her if it was in his ability to do so?

He let out a harsh exhale, relief leaving him shaky and out of sorts. Unable to find the words he needed to make her understand, Ronan shook his head.

"Yeah, that's what I thought," she muttered, the sound of her disappointment unmistakable. "Now if you'll excuse me, I have a race to win."

"Wait, that's it?"

She was already pushing past him. "What do you mean 'that's it'? It's the whole reason we're here. You had to know they'd make a target of me same as you. Just like you *should* have known anyone stupid enough to come after me wasn't walking away unscathed. That's not who I am. And I won't apologize for it."

"I'm not asking you to."

"Then stop looking at me like that."

"Like what?"

She pursed her lips, studying him for a second before some of the fight seemed to leave her. "I don't know who you think I am, Ronan," she said, her voice a tinge softer but no less cutting. "But it's not me. I won't pretend to be someone I'm not. Not for you, not for anybody. So whatever you think you're doing here, you need to let it go. Because if you keep coming for me, I promise your fate will end up the same as his." She glanced down at Bannock's unmoving form with a pointed stare.

Realizing there was nothing he could say, no way for him to make her believe him when he said he knew exactly who she was, he decided he needed to show her instead. It was the only way to prove not only that he respected her, but that he never doubted her or her ability.

Which was why he started running the second her eyes dipped away from him.

"Hey! You sneaky . . ."

Her words were swallowed by the wind as he called on his gift of Air once more. This time around, he had no intention of keeping pace with her. She was fast; he'd give her that. But he was faster.

He'd been checking his speed all day to keep her in sight. Despite whatever she may think, he'd known all along she'd be a target. It was the whole reason he'd stayed close. He wanted to keep an eye on her. Because while she was in this competition to win, he was in it only for her. If or when they made it to the end and had to face off against each other, they'd cross that bridge when they got there. Until then, he had every intention of keeping her alive and unharmed.

Hopefully somewhere in the middle of all that, he would make her remember him.

But right now? In this moment? He had a point to prove.

Ronan jumped forward on a magic-induced burst of speed, unapologetically using his gift. He shot down the road, barely registering the roar of the crowd. They could have been booing him for all he cared. It made no difference. He knew Shadow was close behind, but he didn't risk a glance back to see just how close. All that mattered now was winning.

She could accuse him of underestimating her all she wanted. The truth was, she underestimated *him*. Shadow had no idea how far he'd gone to get here. How much further he'd go before he gave up.

He'd nearly welcomed death when he thought he'd lost her. Now that she was within reach, that he knew she was alive, not even death would stop him. One way or another, he was getting his woman back. Even if he had to make her fall for him all over again.

The vine-covered arch that led to the palace's courtyard loomed closer, the faces in the crowd continuing to blur as he pulled his token free and shot through the opening and straight up the steps to where the High Lord and Dmitri stood waiting. There were perhaps a handful of other people with them, but not a single one of them was a competitor.

Dmitri held out a hand, so Ronan slapped his token into it with a smug grin. Then he glanced around, his lungs burning, his smile stretching. He hadn't just beat Shadow. He'd beaten everyone.

As she sprinted up the stairs not even a minute later, a look of absolute disbelief crossed her face as she realized the same.

It was on the tip of his tongue to goad her. After the tongue lashing she'd delivered, it was the least she deserved, but the words died on his tongue as he caught the High Lord's disappointed stare.

Shadow's shoulders stiffened as he took her chin in his hand and lowered his lips to her ear. To everyone else it must appear like a tender gesture. Ronan saw it for the act of dominance it was.

The bastard's growled words only proved it. "I expected better from you."

"You and me both." Shadow's voice was just as quiet but strained.

Erebos's hold on her chin tightened, and it took everything in Ronan not to gut him then and there.

"Do you think this is some kind of game?"

Shadow tipped her head back to meet his gaze. "Isn't it?"

Anger flashed in the High Lord's eyes. "You've made a mockery of us both. Go straight to your room. I'll deal with you later."

Without so much as a glance back in Ronan's direction, Shadow did as she was told.

If there was ever any doubt he had her under some kind of spell, that was the proof. Shadow didn't meekly obey anyone. She gave as good as she got. She fought tooth and nail. But for Erebos, she caved, trudging off to her room with all the enthusiasm of a naughty child bracing for punishment.

Ronan bit back a snarl, the High Lord's eyes meeting his as he turned away from Shadow's retreating back.

When I find out what you've done to her, you sadistic sonofabitch, I will repay your kindness tenfold. You'd better pray that when that day comes, the Mother takes mercy on your soul, because I sure as hell won't.

Erebos stiffened as if sensing the unspoken promise, and then his lips curled up in a sinister one of his own. As their eyes locked and held, Ronan would have sworn he heard the High Lord's voice echo in his mind.

"The only god I serve is Death."

CHAPTER 16

EREBOS

The sun had long set, but the trial remained unfinished. He'd retired to his private suite of rooms once it became obvious it could take all night. Since then, Dovina and Dominic had taken turns providing him with updates, and he was due for another any minute.

A muscle ticked in his jaw as he waited. He was not an impatient man by nature; he could appreciate better than most the effectiveness of biding one's time. But ever since learning of the presence of one of the Chosen in his realm, he was almost constantly on edge. Especially after that insignificant little *flea* dared threaten him so openly.

What's worse, where one went, more usually followed. Especially if they were associated with Luna's Vessel.

Just as he was about to do something truly pathetic to pass the time, like pace, the door slid open.

"Finally," he growled.

"Apologies, my lord," Dominic said, bowing slightly.

"Has there been a development?"

"Yes."

"Well?"

"Of the fifty-eight who started this morning, twenty have crossed the finish line, and sixteen have been killed."

That left twenty-two roaming around, only two of which could move on to the next trial.

Unaware of his mental arithmetic, Dominic continued with his update, "As of ten minutes ago, all tokens have been found. It's now a matter of strategy and daring."

"Any guesses who the last two will be?"

Dominic's expression remained neutral, giving nothing of his actual thoughts away. "All of our top picks have already finished. I suspect whoever is the most cunning will win out over the foolhardy or brave."

Meaning the general didn't care who else moved on since his favorites were already through. Fair enough. When he didn't offer anything further but continued to stare at him, Erebos raised a brow.

"Was there anything else?"

"Yes, my lord."

Dominic hesitated slightly, only further piquing Erebos's interest. He wasn't going to like whatever his general was about to say.

"I'm waiting."

"You should know that Bannock was involved in an altercation with Shadow."

The brawler had been among the last batch to cross the finish line. According to Dovina's report, he'd looked as though he'd had a rough go of it based on the bloody cloth wrapped around his torso and the broken bones in his face. But she hadn't said anything about Shadow, which was unlike his Raven. That could only mean Bannock hadn't been able to talk until the healer fixed whatever happened to his face.

"What kind of altercation?"

"He cornered her, touched her, threatened—"

Erebos was already moving. He didn't need to hear anything else.

Knowing Shadow had been threatened was enough. Her use to him had an expiration date, but no one else knew it. As far as they were concerned, she belonged to him. That meant she was off limits.

Period.

Anyone stupid enough to come after what was his courted death.

He prowled through the palace, his fury manifesting as darkness. Little black wisps swirled and coalesced all around him, cloaking him and dimming the well-lit corridors. It was the closest he'd been to his true form since taking over this body.

After years of playing a part, it was easy to forget he was the deity responsible for bringing mortality to this plane. The one who could latch onto a mortals' minds and twist the strands of their consciousness or shred it entirely. No one was more powerful than him, except, perhaps, his wife.

But Luna wasn't here.

For too long, he'd hidden his power, afraid of drawing her attention before he was ready. No more. With one of her Chosen near, it was only a matter of time before they crossed paths again. So while he may not be at his full potential in this body, he wouldn't be handicapped by his mortal trappings.

Death was his lifeblood. His language. His art.

No matter his form, he was a master. And while that meant he *could* make it quick and painless, today there would be no mercy. Not for the man who dared to come between him and his one true goal. So Bannock's death might be quick, but it would be far from painless.

With every step closer to his target, he reclaimed his power, calling it to him until it lapped along his skin like a lover's sweet caress. By the time he rounded the corner and could make out the sound of the brawler and his comrades speaking, the High Lord was nowhere to be found.

For the first time in a long time, he was the Lord of Death.

And he was here to take what was owed.

He slowed his steps until they weren't even a whisper on the floor. Not because he was hiding, but because there was always value in collecting information.

"I can't believe you faced off with the High Lord's whore and lived. You must be the only man in Empyria who can make such a claim."

Bannock grunted his agreement. "I don't think her heart was in it, to be honest."

"You saying she wanted to take you for a ride, Banny?"

"What pretty bird doesn't?"

Male chuckles rolled through the room before a new voice spoke up.

"You have to admit, though. It's kind of hot."

"Getting stabbed by a cold bitch?" Bannock asked.

"No. The thought of fucking the High Lord's prized piece of pussy. I mean, she has to be sweet if he keeps her so tightly leashed."

"I wouldn't mind putting a leash on her," the first man drawled.

"I wouldn't mind if she put a leash on me," the second shot back.

"What do you say, Banny, you want to finish what you started? We could take turns. You could go first."

"Fucking right, I'd go first. It's the least I deserve after the bitch left me her calling card."

"She stabbed you, so now you get to stab her?" This was the second voice again.

"Only seems fair."

With every word, the men sealed their fates. There'd never been hope for dear old Banny, but the other two might have been spared had they not opened their fucking mouths.

Now it was too late.

As a general rule, Erebos considered himself unbiased. He had no reason to be. Death always won in the end. But in the rare instances someone was stupid enough to garner his undivided attention, he gave it to them. And then he made sure they lived only long enough to regret it. As this mewling triad was about to learn.

The idiots were still laughing when Erebos swept into the room, the darkness peeling away from him like a cloud of smoke. Before the men even realized he was there, the smoke shot out, condensing into a pair of phantom hands as it grasped Bannock's two sidekicks by their throats and strangled the life right out of them.

Bannock wasn't as fortunate, though under other circumstances some might consider him lucky since he was one of the rare few who could claim to have gazed upon the true face of a god.

The brawler managed to get to his feet, his entire body shaking as he held out his arms. "P-puh-please H-High Lord. I-it was ju-just talk."

Erebos regarded him the way a giant might regard an ant. That is to say, not at all.

Bannock was still offering his stuttered apology when Erebos took him by the neck and lifted him straight into the air. It should have been an impossible move given the difference in their builds. But not for him. Not with death singing in his veins.

"You made a huge mistake."

Bannock tried to nod, his eyes bulging, his face turning a mottled red.

"You will not live to repeat it."

With that, Erebos tightened his grip until he crushed the other man's windpipe, though he didn't stop there. He continued squeezing until he grasped the top of the man's spine in his bare hand. Then he jerked his arm back and severed the spine in two.

He was already walking out of the room before the bastard's head hit the floor.

CHAPTER 17

RONAN

"Are you sure about that shirt?"

Ronan glanced down at the white tunic he'd tucked into his brown leathers. "What's wrong with my shirt?"

Bast scrunched his nose. "There's blood on it."

"So?"

"What do you mean 'so'?" he asked, looking horrified. "You've just received a royal summons."

"To go to a tavern."

"Perhaps you do not understand what the word royal means. Allow me to explain . . ."

Ronan had to swallow a laugh. If Sebastian ever learned he was not only intimately connected to royalty but he'd also issued his fair share of royal summons, the poor bastard would shit his pants.

"Dmitri knows what to expect. He's the one overseeing these stupid trials. If a little blood offends him, then he's in the wrong line of work."

"Still, it would not hurt for you to try."

"Sebastian, I'm not changing my clothes."

Bast lifted his hands in surrender, but his sigh was filled with exasperation. "You should work harder to endear yourself to the High

Lord's inner circle. You've successfully completed three trials as of today and are no closer..."

Ronan tuned the other man out, his temper sparking at the words. Not because Bast was wrong, but because he was fucking right.

It had been five days since this damned contest started. Five days, three trials, and two wastes of fucking time. He was no closer to helping Shadow regain her memories today than he'd been on day one. She'd avoided him at every turn since leaving him on the palace steps.

He'd hoped to find a way to force the issue, but the last two tests hadn't lent themselves to any sort of extended conversation. Shadow arrived at each one just as it began and took off as soon as she'd completed her task. Outside of contest-sanctioned events, she remained behind the palace walls, as unreachable to him as she'd been when they resided in different realms.

Unlike the first trial, which had been a bit of a free for all, the last two had been structured, meaning not only were the competitors mostly separated, they were supervised. Ronan had little doubt he was the reason for that. After his display at the party and then again with his upset of a win, he knew the High Lord wanted to keep a closer eye on him. The additional scrutiny also explained Shadow's icy behavior. Not that it required one. She'd made her feelings clear as crystal with the tongue lashing she'd given him. And then he'd taken it a step further and humiliated her by winning in her place.

Ronan let out a frustrated sigh. No, he couldn't blame her cold shoulder on the High Lord. He'd earned his spot on her shit list all by himself.

As for the trials themselves, the second had been intellectual in nature. The contestants were each placed in a sectioned-off area so they could not see or talk to one another and asked to solve a series of puzzles.

The brain teasers were easy. He coasted through them without issue. To be honest, after the drama surrounding the race, he'd been pretty underwhelmed by the whole thing. The most memorable part had actually been Bannock's absence. Rumor had it the brute managed to find a token and cross the finish line, but when he hadn't shown up to participate in the next trial, Ronan couldn't help but wonder what had really happened after he left that alley.

It was also why he questioned the fate of those who failed the second trial. Only the first twenty to finish moved on. The rest weren't seen again, nor were those who lost the race. Ronan had no idea if they'd been forced to leave town or if something more *permanent* had been arranged.

As for today's trial, it marked the halfway point, and the gloves were definitely off. The remaining twenty competitors had been paired up and made to take part in a head-to-head battle with the weapon of their choice. There were two ways to end the match. Submission or death. Given his competitors and the man they were fighting to serve, Ronan had little doubt mercy had been in short supply. He certainly hadn't shown any to the unfortunate soul he'd faced off against. Unless one counted a flaming axe through the throat mercy.

No, he didn't question the fate of today's losers. He was much more interested in learning about the winners. Since the fights happened behind closed doors, with only Erebos and his flock as witnesses, there was no way for him to know who else had won or lost. He could only assume Shadow and the handful of others he'd singled out continued to perform well.

"Are you even listening to me?"

"No."

Bast threw up his hands. "Why do I even bother with you?"

"I've been asking myself the same question about you since we met."

"Lies. You love me."

Ronan raised a brow. "You think so, do you?"

"Everyone loves me. I am undeniably loveable."

"What you are is a pain in my arse."

Bast waved a hand. "It's the same thing."

Ronan didn't bother with a response, choosing instead to move toward the door of their room. He knew he didn't have to share the cramped quarters with Bast anymore, thanks to the stipend he earned as a participant, but he preferred having a place to return that wasn't associated with Erebos or the other contestants. He didn't trust anyone with ties to the contest.

He didn't much trust the manwhore he roomed with either, but Bast was far closer to earning it than anyone else in Glimmermere. He'd at least proven himself loyal thus far.

"You coming?"

"That depends . . . You sticking with the bloody shirt?"

"It's a few spots, Bast. No one is going to notice."

"*I* noticed."

"Of course you did."

"What do you mean 'of course'?"

Grabbing his cloak off the hook by the door, he tossed it over his shoulders and shot Sebastian a cheeky grin. "You're clearly obsessed with me."

Bast's jaw dropped. "*Pardonne moi?*"

Ronan laughed, beyond pleased he'd finally managed to catch the other man off guard. "Come on, Sebastian. I'm buying."

"Next time, lead with that."

IT WAS full dark by the time they reached the Scarlet Siren, the upscale tavern located clear on the other end of town from their boarding house. He and Sebastian exchanged knowing looks as a carriage rolled by, the matching pair of thoroughbreds as much a testament to the wealth of the people inside as the wheeled vehicle itself.

"I told you to change your shirt," he hissed.

"I stand by my decision. If the Siren's patrons are too prissy to handle a few drops of blood, they can go elsewhere."

"You're going to stand out like a pig with tits."

"Excuse me?"

Bast let out a long-suffering sigh. "As someone who doesn't belong."

"But nursing sows *do* have tits."

"Must you logic everything to death? It is an expression, Ronan."

"If you're going to insult me, at least do it well."

Ronan was sure he was doing just that when Sebastian started grumbling in his native tongue. Unfortunately for him, the lyrical words lacked the unflattering edge of a proper putdown.

"A fancy bar is still a bar, Bast. I'm sure I'll blend in just fine."

"It's your funeral."

Rolling his eyes, Ronan pushed open the door and stepped inside. "Speaking of blending in," he murmured, taking in the gleaming floors and chandeliers, "could you please at least try not to fuck the first person who breathes in your direction?"

"I mean, I could, but where's the fun in that?"

"Bast . . ."

"I know, I know. Behave." He gave a little huff. "You seem to forget that I've been in town longer than you, Ronan, and haven't ended up on the wrong side of a cell yet."

"Not for lack of trying," Ronan muttered under his breath as a blissfully unaware Sebastian continued speaking.

"I'm perfectly capable of conducting myself in an appropriate manner. I was raised in court, after all."

"Appropriate is not a word I would choose to describe you or your behavior."

"Fair." Bast grinned, taking the words as an unintended compliment. "Come to think of it, neither would I."

They moved deeper inside, Ronan taking in every detail of his surroundings. Everything spoke to wealth and excess. The gleaming floors, their honey-colored planks unmarred by so much as a dirty bootprint, the red, paper-lined walls with their subtle damask pattern, the lack of a tavern's usual aroma. Instead of stale beer and vomit, there was a spicy tinge in the air, as if the owner of the establishment had found a way to pump cologne through the space without it becoming overpowering.

The place was also three times the size of the hole in the wall where he'd met Bast, meaning it was impossible to see everyone in attendance with only a single sweep of his eyes around the room. But he did spot a few familiar faces, which supplied him with answers to his earlier question about who else had won their matches.

Dichen's veiled figure was seated at a table he would have selected for himself. She sat with her back to a corner, her dark eyes focused on the door. No one would be able to sneak up on her there, and she had an unobstructed view of the room at large. The woman kept to herself, so he hadn't seen her in action yet, but he had little doubt she was as skilled as everyone claimed. He almost looked forward to testing his blade against her own. Almost, because it would be a pity to kill one with such talent.

He also spotted the muscled blonde beauty, Marin, who was chatting animatedly with one of the bartenders. He couldn't make out their words from where he was standing, but it was clearly a topic she was passionate about. She held a knife in one hand and a fork in the other, looking a bit like a conductor as she waved them around to emphasize her point. More than once, the bartender's eyes nervously darted down as if to ensure she wasn't about to use her silverware as weapons.

They'd nearly completed their circuit around the room when Bast stopped dead, his eyes flaring wide and a flush stealing up his neck. Ronan followed his gaze, his own lips twitching when he found the object of Bast's fascination.

"If I'd known all it would take to shut you up was to get you in the same room as him, I would have made a point to seek him out," Ronan drawled with a smirk.

"I will have you know that by all accounts, Loren is a lovely man and a very skilled warrior."

Ronan cocked a brow. "So am I, but you aren't rendered suddenly mute by my mere presence."

"Perhaps you're not nearly as impressive as you believe yourself to be."

"Doubtful. My ego is well-deserved, thank you very much."

Sebastian glared at him. "Oh, piss off."

"If you insist."

His friend's eyes widened with panic. "Ronan, stop. Where are you going? No. Wait," he pleaded, trying and failing to pull Ronan back as he made his way over to the table where Loren was holding court with his adoring fans. "Ronan!"

He ignored the whispered shout, giving Bast no option but to follow him or go off on his own. Which, come to think of it, was a dangerous gamble, but he couldn't resist the chance to find out what happened when Bast was forced to interact with the city's favorite hero.

Ronan couldn't pretend to know Loren well. Outside of a handful of grunted pleasantries, they hadn't interacted at all. Which seemed to be the status quo among the contestants. What was the point of getting to know someone you might have to kill in a few days' time?

Despite that, Loren's smile seemed genuine when he noticed Ronan's approach. "Excuse me, friends," he said, breaking off in the middle of whatever story he'd been telling. "It would appear the stars are watching over me. I'm finally going to get my chance to learn about the mysterious fire mage." He clapped one of the men on the shoulder and walked the rest of the way to Ronan. "So, Butcher, was it? Are you here to ferret out my secrets?"

"That depends. Are there any you're willing to part with?"

The other man grinned, revealing an unnaturally white set of teeth. "None. You?"

"I'm fresh out of secrets."

"Now that I find hard to believe. You're one walking mystery, aren't you?"

"I've always considered myself an open book."

"Yes, you would. Wouldn't you?" Loren laughed, his amber eyes twinkling with amusement. "We have no secrets from our own selves, so I suppose your opinion of yourself is as valid as mine."

"And what's yours?"

"Undecided. After that little display in the hall, I'm willing to bet your fire is the least of what you've got up your sleeve."

The man was far more perceptive than he had any right to be. Ronan made a mental note to tread carefully. He may play the role of amiable city son, but he was every bit as ruthless as the others. The nice ones almost always were. For what better way to lure in an unsuspecting victim than with honey?

Loren's eyes shifted to a starstruck Bast who hovered nearby, nervously clutching his velvet cap in his hands. He'd nearly shredded its feather beyond repair, completely oblivious to the fact he was anxiously plucking at the plume while staring up at Loren with absolute adoration.

"Who's your friend?" Loren asked, his lips hitching up.

"Oh, allow me to introduce you to—"

Before Ronan had a chance to finish his introduction, Bast cleared his throat and swept into his most elegant bow. "Sebastian Jean-Rene Villehardouin of Colvers, at your service. But please, call me Bast."

"Nice to meet you, Bast."

His friend nearly vibrated with pleasure at the sound of his name on his idol's lips. His praise was effusive as he began prattling on like he'd never been intimidated at all. "It is a pleasure to make your acquaintance. I've been following your accomplishments with great interest."

"Is that so? I do love meeting a fan," Loren said, leaning forward and giving Bast his full attention. "What's your favorite?"

"Oh, the time you slayed the sea monster. Without question."

"Which time?" Loren asked with a flirtatious quirk of his brow. "There's been several."

Ronan half-expected Bast to clam up given how he'd acted earlier, but he shouldn't have been surprised the opposite was true. Flirting was practically the man's first language. He was more comfortable than ever when he held Loren's gaze and murmured, "You do know your way around a *tentacle*, don't you?"

"I consider myself an expert."

Realizing he'd just become an unwanted third wheel, Ronan stepped away without another word, leaving the men to their mutual worship of Loren and his many exploits.

Ronan couldn't help but chuckle as he made his way toward the bar. Leave it to Bast to abandon him at the first sign of a willing bed partner. Not that he was surprised. The man had a fucking gift for turning any conversation into a seduction. More power to him. Maybe he'd learn something about Loren over the course of the evening that Ronan could use to his advantage later on. If so, Sebastian might just turn out to be his secret weapon.

He was so preoccupied with his thoughts that he didn't see the robed figure until he walked into him. It was a reminder that he needed to stay focused. This was not the time or place to be getting sloppy.

"Apologies," Ronan said, taking a couple steps back.

"It was my fault," the man replied smoothly, his eyes an unnerving shade of deep red. "I don't believe we've been formally introduced. I'm Cedric Aldair."

"The blood mage," Ronan said, wondering if the man had purposely run into him in order to gain an introduction. It was a move he'd used himself many times before, especially when wanting to gather access to a mark. The reminder had him instantly on guard.

"I see my reputation precedes me."

"That is usually the case for men with gifts like ours."

"Mages are rare in this part of the continent. You're only the third I've come across, and I don't believe I've ever encountered any with command over the elements. Is fire your only one, or can you control the others as well?"

Ronan gave him a tight-lipped smile which Cedric returned, though it was noticeably cooler.

"I don't mean to pry. I'm simply curious. I'll give you a little demonstration if you return the favor."

Learning how Cedric worked his gift would be valuable intel, but Ronan didn't trust the man as far as Bast could throw him.

"Maybe some other time," he said, with a slight incline of his head. "My friend is waiting for me."

Then he stepped around the blood mage and headed to the other side of the room, intending to snag a table near Dichen while they waited for Dmitri to show up and finally tell them why he'd summoned them. Ronan was betting they were going to learn what was required for the next trial but lost his train of thought when his eyes landed on Shadow. She was hunched over her table, expression pensive, drink untouched. She wore her pale hair pulled up into a messy bun, several long strands falling out and making her appear far more innocent than an assassin queen had any right to.

Realizing this might be his only chance to speak to her, he booked it in her direction, but before he made it halfway, fingers lightly grazed his arm. It was too intentional a caress to be ignored, so he checked his steps and glanced down, whatever he was about to say dying on his lips as his eyes found Camille's.

She looked pointedly at the empty table next to him. Not mistaking the demand—for it was certainly not a request—Ronan took a seat.

"What are you doing here?" he asked as she set a stein filled with amber liquid in front of him. "You moonlighting as a server now?"

"I'm whatever I need to be," she said, giving him a look that spoke volumes.

Not only did it say he should know better than to ask stupid questions, it confirmed a suspicion he'd had ever since she'd mentioned attending the High Lord's party. As far as he knew, only the competitors and Glimmermere's social elite had been in attendance. There was no reason Camille should have been invited, unless she had ties to the High Lord.

"You're one of Dovina's little birds," he said, his voice dropping low to ensure it didn't travel beyond the two of them.

Her gaze swept down, and he took her silence for the admission it was, though her ties to Dovina and the High Lord puzzled him. Not because she worked for them, but because it made her willingness to help him—and put herself at risk in the process—even more shocking. He was the last person she should be looking out for, and yet . . . here she was again.

"I have a message for you."

"For me?"

She nodded, pretending to clean his table, which was already spotless. "I'm here to remind you that there are eyes and ears everywhere."

She flicked her gaze to the left. Ronan subtly did the same, his eyes landing on Calix, the poisoner. "You cannot trust anyone."

"Not even you?"

Her lips twitched. "Today you can. But watch what you say, and who you say it to, lest that information be shared. That's your message."

"You haven't exactly told me anything I didn't already know, Camille."

"Perhaps not, but maybe there's another question you should be contemplating."

His body tensed, instinct warning him that the real clue she was giving him was not in the message itself.

"There are many who are not as impressed with you as I am."

He dipped his chin in a nod, having known that to be true the second he signed up for the competition.

She tipped her head as discreetly as possible to the table Shadow was seated at. "I do not suggest going over there tonight. Everyone knows the best-laid traps have the sweetest lures."

"Thank you for the advice, Camille."

"You're not going to take it, are you?"

Ronan smiled, trying to take the sting out of his admission. "No."

He truly did appreciate her sticking her neck out for him, but the truth was, his course had been set the second his eyes landed on her. This was the first opportunity he'd had in days to speak with her. He had to take it. He was running out of time.

"But my stubbornness doesn't make you any less of an angel."

"Stars save me from the egos of men," she muttered, clearly exasperated as she abandoned all pretense of cleaning his table. Straightening, she offered a cryptic, "The celestials are always watching over us."

"What the fuck is a celestial?"

But she was already gone, vanished into the crowd so thoroughly he wasn't even sure she was still in the tavern at all.

He made to stand, his eyes landing on the stein of ale she'd brought him. Recalling Calix's presence, he debated the safety of drinking it.

The glass hadn't been out of his sight since Camille set it down, and after the lengths she went through to protect him, he didn't think she'd bring him something tainted. Still, this should probably be the only drink he accepted for the night.

Even mostly certain it was safe, he gave the cool liquid a cursory sniff. Smelled like ale.

He took a tentative sip. Tasted like ale.

When he didn't immediately start choking or fall over in painful spasms, he downed half of it in one go, telling himself it would be rude to waste it. And if he did die of some slow-acting concoction, well, he had only himself to blame.

Recalling Camille's parting words, he wondered if by celestials, she meant gods. He knew better than most that the Mother absolutely watched over her Chosen. Effie's timely arrival at Nightshade's was proof enough of that.

Perhaps it was naïve, but he couldn't help but believe that his goddess wouldn't have ensured he made it this far only to let him be felled by something as insignificant as a pint. Not when she so clearly had a purpose in store for him. A purpose involving the beauty seated a mere three tables away from him.

He found it interesting that no one else approached her, especially since none of the guards who'd been all but breathing down her neck since the first trial were anywhere to be found.

Shadow was well and truly alone.

Even without Camille's warning, he would have recognized the bait for what it was. But then, he'd never been one to run away from anything with his tail tucked between his legs, least of all a challenge. And he'd definitely never cared about playing by someone else's rules. If Erebos was trying to scare him off or send a message, he was failing spectacularly.

And he would continue to do so because Ronan would not be stopped. He wasn't going anywhere until he had Reyna back where she belonged.

With him.

In his arms.

In his bed.

Whether she knew it or not, this woman was his future.

Comforted by his little pep talk, Ronan stood and purposefully strode over to her. Shadow stiffened without turning around, sensing his presence. He was inordinately pleased to learn she was still so attuned to him. That she knew he was near without looking.

"Have you come to gloat?" she asked, sounding resigned.

"No, I've come to tell you a story."

That got her attention.

She slowly lifted her head, tilting her chin to the side so she could look up at him over her shoulder. "A story? What kind of story?"

He claimed the empty seat across from her with an unapologetic smirk. "I figured it's past time I tell you how we met."

CHAPTER 18

SHADOW

*R*onan's sunshine and ember scent washed over her. It was so uniquely *him* she knew he was near without having to check. In fact, the second he'd entered the tavern, she'd known exactly where he was, as if her body now existed in orbit to his. She wondered if it was the same for him.

Despite her harsh words in the alley, the man intrigued her. For the first time she could recall, she felt truly *seen* by someone else. Not just seen—valued. And not as a shiny toy to be paraded around or as a monster used to frighten others into submission. Valued for the simple fact she existed at all.

It was a novel experience. One she hadn't quite wrapped her head around. One that left her filled with questions whose answers she could never pursue.

It's why she pushed him away—or rather ran away—after blowing up at him in the alley. At the time, she'd meant each and every word. But left with nothing but time on her hands after Erebos sent her away, she weighed the man's actions against her accusations, and . . . they didn't add up.

He'd been a steady presence at her side through the entire race. He'd never interfered *until* he thought she was in danger. The relief and resulting shock on his face couldn't be faked. Ronan truly believed she'd needed help. And instead of laying into her when she accused him of being a misogynistic prick, he'd gone on to show her how wrong she was.

If anyone was the judgmental ass, it was her. She'd thought she'd had him pegged. That he was just another overbearing, alpha male asshole who was all talk without the necessary skill to back it up. And he proved her wrong.

Not just wrong, completely fucking wrong.

Ronan didn't just back it up; he'd downplayed his talent. He was far more skilled than he'd ever even alluded to. But the part that really rankled? She'd bought it. She never once considered him a true threat when the fact was, *he* was better than *her*.

He'd beat her.

No one beat her.

Shadow hadn't gotten her ass kicked in a skill test like that in years. There was a reason she was the best. She worked ten times harder than anyone else to ensure it. Proved it so often that she would never have to prove herself again.

Until now.

It was an exhilarating proposition, especially considering it very well meant the two of them would be facing off against each other in the end. Though the thought of besting him didn't sit as easily as it once did. Killing was easy. She'd done it for as long as she could remember. But nothing about ending Ronan's life would be easy.

The simple truth was, he didn't deserve to die.

She considered herself quite the expert at reading people, and intuition told her Ronan was a good man. A little rough around the edges, perhaps, but who in her world wasn't? It wasn't enough to garner a death sentence. Or to even be on the receiving end of her undiluted temper.

Shadow owed him an apology, or at the very least an explanation, but he'd get neither. Because no matter how drawn to him she was, nothing had changed. They were enemies, fighting against each other for the same prize, and only one of them could win. All she could offer him was a fair fight and try to protect him from Erebos.

His shadow moved across her tabletop, and she tensed, knowing this conversation was unavoidable and dreading it anyway. But he couldn't keep sniffing around her. He was going to get himself killed —and not by her. She'd at least guarantee him a quick and painless death. The same could not be said for the others, least of all Erebos.

The Butcher had piqued the High Lord's interest. That was rarely a good thing. One of two outcomes came to pass when he discovered a rare and unusual creature. He tamed it, or he killed it, and Ronan didn't strike her as the kind of man who could be tamed.

Why did the thought send a bolt of lust shooting through her?

Annoyed by her uncontrollable reaction to him, she didn't bother with a greeting. "Have you come to gloat?"

She felt like a coward sitting there, unable to even look at him. She knew he'd already guessed that she'd been avoiding him, but not for the reasons he might suspect. He probably thought she was off nursing her injured pride. The reality was so much more complicated than hurt feelings.

When his answer came, she wasn't prepared for it. Not the way his warm voice caressed her ears or for the words themselves.

"No, I've come to tell you a story."

She straightened in her chair, the wood creaking softly as she pushed back so she could look over at him. "A story? What kind of story?"

For all that Ronan seemed to be a straight shooter, she knew next to nothing about him. And if she was being honest with herself, she both loved and hated how much space he took up in her mind as she tried to fill in the blanks. There was no way she was going to pass up an opportunity to finally get some answers if he was willingly handing out information.

He claimed the empty seat at her table and sat down without invitation, splaying his legs wide and resting one arm on the back of it. "I figured it's past time I tell you how we met."

And here he goes again. The man was either delusional or truly in need of a healer. He refused to let go of his belief that they knew each other.

Suddenly exhausted, Shadow let out a heavy sigh. "What's to tell? I was there, right?"

"You were, though you went by a different name at the time."

She rolled her eyes, adopting an unaffected air, though there was no denying she was curious. Perhaps she was about to learn just who this mysterious Reyna was. Jealousy speared her at the reminder of the other woman, and a wave of frustration built on its heels as she berated herself for the unwanted emotion.

What does it matter, Shadow? He can never be yours.

An even softer voice in the back of her mind chased the reminder. *But you wish he could.*

Ice filled her veins as that little revelation crashed into her. She had no business *wanting* anyone. Least of all him. No, *especially* him.

As if he'd picked up on the direction of her thoughts, Ronan smiled, his eyes flashing with mischief as he rested both forearms on the table so he could lean in and invade her space. His sudden proximity set off a little flutter in the center of her rib cage, telling her she was fooling herself. It was too late; she was already a long way from *wanting*.

Stars, she was in trouble.

Why? *Why* was this happening?

She'd never responded like this to any man. Why now? Why *him*?

Shadow mentally threw her hands in the air and let out a scream of frustration. She didn't even know him, for darkness's sake.

He stretched out a finger, running it along the back of her hand. "Don't you want to hear my story?"

The small caress had her jerking in her seat like she'd been hit with a cattle prod. She caught the quiet rumbles of laughter rolling through him as he noted her reaction.

Ass.

"You mean your made-up story about our nonexistent past? Sounds riveting."

"Oh, but it is."

"You're wasting my time."

"You're stuck here until Dmitri shows, so you might as well pass the time with me."

"I don't require a clown to entertain me. I'm not a child."

"No, you certainly aren't."

Shadow had to fight the urge to squirm as his appreciative gaze raked down her body. "And I quite enjoy the time I spend alone."

"Mmm," he hummed, his eyes darkening as they lifted back to hers, his smile turning wicked. "So do I. But *alone time* doesn't hold a candle to the fun that can be had with a friend, does it?"

She stopped breathing, her mind emptying of everything except the way he was currently staring at her like she was a bunny and he was a wolf ready to pounce. She blinked, clearing her throat before she could ask, "Why'd you say it like that?"

"Like what?" He'd adopted his most innocent tone, but she knew he was intentionally baiting her.

"All"—she waved a hand at him—"you know."

"I'm afraid I don't. Please, enlighten me, kitten."

She barely had a chance to register the endearment before she blurted, "Smolder and sex."

His eyes widened, and he snickered. "Smolder and sex?"

She gave him a jerky nod.

He loosely clasped his hands together and regarded her with a slight shake of his head. "Now that's interesting."

"What is?"

"That while I was simply suggesting a friendly chat while we wait for our host, your mind automatically turned to sex."

"I ... but you ... I did *not*."

"You did, kitten."

She scowled, hating the way his sinful smirk had birds taking flight in her belly. "Don't call me that."

"Killer, then. Does that suit you better?"

"It's at least accurate and less offensive."

"Kitten is offensive?"

"I don't particularly enjoy being compared to a weak and pathetic creature."

"Oh, kitten. There's nothing weak or pathetic about you."

"Exactly."

Those fucking lips of his twitched again, and she had to fight hard not to lean forward and nip the bottom one with her teeth. Shadow drew in a shaky breath, feeling a bit like she'd been hypnotized. Surely these urges weren't coming from her? Someone needed to sew that perfect mouth shut. Its seductive curl and the innuendo-filled words that came out of it were a menace to society.

"What was that?" she asked, realizing she'd missed whatever he'd been saying.

"I said you seem to be forgetting how fierce kittens can be. How even the smallest among them can shred a man to ribbons, leaving him bleeding and absolutely shocked by the fact . . ."

That did sound like something she would do.

". . . and even bleeding out, the little one will still have the man at her mercy the next time she comes around wanting to play."

"There you go making it sexual again."

"Are you sure that's not your doing, *kitten?*"

She gritted her teeth. "I am not your kitten. For one thing, I don't have claws." She lifted her hands, giving him a tight smile as she showed off her neatly trimmed nails.

"Don't you? Those blades of yours have certainly shredded a man or two."

She sighed but ceded the point. "All right, but I certainly don't walk around meowing in an obnoxious demand for attention."

"No, you're too stealthy for that. Stalking your prey in silence until it's time to pounce."

"You've given this comparison of yours a lot of thought."

"What can I say? Kitten suits you."

She watched his lips curl around the words, goosebumps erupting down her arms as his tongue swept across his bottom lip.

He leaned forward until their faces were less than an inch apart. "Shadow?"

"Hmm?"

"You might not meow, but I bet I could make you purr."

She gaped at him, her mouth falling open as she was rendered completely speechless.

His gaze dipped from her eyes down to her lips. "Would you like that, kitten? For me to reach under this table and pet you until you were little more than putty in my hand?"

"You . . ." That was the best she could manage, because fuck it all, she did. She wanted *exactly* that. "I think we've gotten off topic."

He sat back in his chair, blue eyes searing her with their heat as he folded his hands over his flat stomach.

She mourned the loss of him, even as she welcomed the breathing room. The man was damned potent. A few innocuous words in that sexy growl of his, and she was reduced to absolute rubbish. What would it be like if she let him make good on his offer?

No, Shadow. Absolutely not. You will get him killed.

She didn't give herself the opportunity to consider why she was more concerned with his death than her own.

His lips twisted with knowing amusement, but rather than continuing with his teasing, he surprised her by saying, "Our tale begins in the Forest of Whispers."

So he hadn't been using the tale as an excuse to talk to her. He really did want her to hear it. That alone was enough to renew her interest in the story, though she couldn't resist a little dig first. "Oooh, the Forest of Whispers, how fitting. A pretend setting for the made-up story of our past."

"Be quiet now, killer, or I won't tell you how the queen of the Forsaken nearly gelded me."

Now *that* had her lips snapping shut.

"Glad to see I finally have your attention."

There was no 'finally' about it. The man had held her attention hostage from the second he set foot in her city. Not that she'd ever dare admit it.

"An impostor declared war against the rightful queen of the Chosen—"

167

"The Chosen?"

"That was short-lived."

She shrugged in apology. "Just trying to get the facts."

"The Chosen are those blessed with the gift of magic." He wriggled his fingers, little flames dancing above each of them before vanishing.

"Your people. You're one of the Chosen."

He nodded.

Her brows furrowed. If there were more like him, why had she never heard of them before? *Because this story isn't real, Shadow. It's just make-believe.* Mollified, she gave in to the willing suspension of her disbelief.

"The Kiri, Helena, was in desperate need of allies, which was why after centuries of exile, she sought out those previously declared her enemies."

"The Forsaken?" she guessed, since he'd mentioned the forest lady being another queen.

"Exactly, but when she and her Circle arrived—"

"Circle?"

"You're not very familiar with how storytelling works, are you?"

"You're the one leaving out pertinent details."

He chuckled. "Fair enough. The Circle is a group of five elite warrior mages sworn into service of the Kiri." He stared expectantly at her as if waiting for her to ask another question, though instead of relief when she didn't, he let out a little sigh. "Anyway, when they arrived at the edge of the forest, the Night Stalkers were not very happy to see them."

"I thought you said they were called the Forsaken."

"They are both. The Night Stalkers are just one clan that makes up the Forsaken."

Shadow nodded. "Okay, I'm following. Go on."

"You don't make anything easy, do you?"

"Only death."

"I walked right into that."

She smirked.

"As I was saying, once the Circle entered the Night Stalker's territory, they were surrounded without even realizing it. They didn't know they were in any danger until the famed assassins dropped from the treetops they call home, appearing for all the world to step out of the very darkness itself. And then the air rippled and parted like a curtain to reveal their dark-haired queen, her face and arms decorated with swirls of black paint."

Shadow was enchanted, completely swept up in Ronan's story. She knew for a fact it wasn't one she'd heard before, but there was a quality to it that had her feeling like she had, maybe a long time ago as a child. The images his words invoked weren't quite déjà vu. They were distant and hazy . . . not memory exactly, but more like a remembered affection.

"What happened next?" she asked, leaning forward and resting her cheek against her fist.

Ronan matched her position, dropping his voice as he continued with his retelling. "Helena made her plea. She held nothing back, openly admitting that her people were in danger. That she needed help to face off against an enemy of unparalleled strength. The Night Stalkers listened, some more mistrustful than others. But their queen saw an opportunity of her own, for only a few days prior, one of their villages had been attacked. The land was restless and corrupted, the spirits of their clansmen trapped and unable to find peace. And so a bargain was struck. In exchange for help cleansing the land and releasing the souls of the dead, the Forsaken agreed to help the Chosen defeat the impostor queen."

"Get to the part where this queen held a knife to you."

"Patience is a virtue, you know."

"We're running out of time, Dmitri could get here any second, and I want to know how the story ends."

His answering smile was smug. "Very well. Fast forward a few months. I saved her life, she saved mine, we butted heads at nearly every corner, and somewhere along the way, the assassin queen fell helplessly in love with me. The end."

Shadow scoffed. "Now I know you're full of shit. No assassin worth her blades would fall for your nonsense. I certainly wouldn't."

"I did say we butted heads. The woman held me at knifepoint more times than I can count."

"That sounds more like it." Shadow laughed, feeling a kinship with this queen. "How'd you talk her out of killing you?"

"I am *very* persuasive."

The way he said it had heat curling low in her belly. "Oh please, more like she didn't want to deal with the political fallout your death would cause."

"That's entirely plausible. But I like to believe her feelings for me wouldn't have allowed her to go through with it in the end."

"Because you're deluded. I still can't believe such a woman was won over by your subpar attempts at seduction."

Ronan quirked a brow. "Subpar? Oh kitten . . ." He inched closer. "You haven't begun to be introduced to my attempts at seduction."

Shadow opened and closed her mouth. *Fuck.* "Nor do I care to."

"Liar."

"More like I am embarrassed on your behalf."

"Or you're secretly terrified I'll find out you're not as immune to me as you'd like to believe."

Shadow let out a little sniff but didn't correct him.

"I can prove it to you if you wish."

"That won't be necessary."

"Scared of being proven wrong?"

"Hardly."

"Let's make a wager then, shall we? If you win, I promise not to bother you anymore. And if I win . . ."

She eyed him warily, though that had more to do with the sudden ache in her chest at the thought of Ronan making good on his promise. "That's a tempting offer, but the answer is still no."

"Aw, come on, kitten. Play with me." He reached out, trailing a finger along her lips, holding her gaze, all manner of carnal promises burning in their depths.

It was on the tip of her tongue to give in. To say yes. To beg.

But before she could be that stupid, the velvet curtain separating the main room from the back was pushed to the side, revealing Dmitri.

Just like that, reality came crashing back down, shattering the moment between them. They were seated mere inches from each other, but suddenly everything stood between them. The contest. Erebos. Her future . . . his.

It was too much.

Shadow shot backward, quickly standing and stepping away from Ronan, desperate to put some space between them.

"Killer, wait—"

She shook her head, holding out her hand to keep him at bay. "Story time is over, Ronan."

CHAPTER 19

SHADOW

She could feel Ronan's eyes on her as the contestants moved into the small side room, willing her to join him.

Not going to happen, Butcher.

She moved instead to the opposite side of the room, trying to put as many people between them as possible. With only ten contestants remaining in the competition, there weren't enough bodies to properly shield him from her view. She tried to focus instead on studying the room. While she'd never been back here before, she knew it was used for private parties or the like. It was perhaps only a quarter of the size of the main bar area and had been cleared of all furniture save a couple of chairs, which had already been claimed.

Loren was man-sprawled across one of them, his lips lifted in a soft smile as he played with a sorry-looking teal feather. Dichen was in another, the black veil concealing everything but her eyes, which were intently peering about the room. The third and final chair had been claimed by a rather waifish man who didn't seem to belong at all. *Calix.* Her memory provided. *The poisoner.*

She scanned the other faces in the room, unsurprised to see who remained, though she scowled as soon as her eyes landed on Ronan, who was still staring at her.

Stop looking at me, you buffoon. It was like the man wanted people to wonder what was going on between them. Was he really that stupid? Or did he simply not realize how dangerous his obsession with her was?

You're just as obsessed as he is, Shadow. He wasn't sitting at the table alone. You were right there, all but going into heat because of a few sexy whispers.

Gritting her teeth, she subtly shifted her body until he was completely blocked from view.

"Looks as though we are all here," Dmitri said, stepping up onto a small stool so he could be seen by everyone. "Congratulations on your success thus far. The High Lord is very impressed by what he has seen. As am I.

"Your next trial will take place at the palace tomorrow evening beginning at sundown. Each of you has been given a unique mission that must be completed before sunrise. Anyone who does not successfully complete their task will not move on to the final round. I have cards for each of you detailing the specifics of your assignment. Please do not open them until you are alone."

"Did you really call us here to pass out a few letters?" Aldair asked, derision heavy in his tone.

Dmitri raised his brow. "As I said, the letters contain the specific details. These details are to be kept *private*. If, at any time, you share the task that has been set out for you, you will be disqualified. This is an individual challenge, meaning if anyone other than you completes the task, you will be disqualified."

Shadow frowned at Dmitri's phrasing. It almost sounded like he was hinting at a means of sabotage.

"If you do not show up tomorrow in the appropriate attire, you will be disqualified."

"Excuse me, but what do you consider 'appropriate attire'?" Marin asked.

Dmitri released a sigh, looking for all the world like he wished he could be anywhere else. "The details are in your letter. Part of your assignment is procuring the required items. If you fail to do so—"

"We will be disqualified," Aldair interrupted. "Yes, we get it. Now, are you actually going to tell us anything useful, or can we get on with our evening? I had this lovely filly in my sights, and I would rather enjoy getting back to her."

A few chuckles rang out at his words. Ever since Bannock's departure from the contest, Cedric had taken his place as the resident heckler. Shadow caught Dichen's gaze, and the other woman rolled her eyes as if to say, *'Can you believe this asshole?'*

Her lips twitched as she nodded her agreement.

Unaware of the silent conversation taking place around him, Cedric continued, "Besides, since I could very well die tomorrow, I much rather spend my night buried between a pair of willing thighs. Go out with a bang, if you know what I mean."

He held up his hand for a high five that no one returned, though Loren did smile in agreement.

Dmitri ignored him and reiterated the pertinent terms of tomorrow's trial. "Dress as is outlined in your letter, be at the palace by sundown, complete your task without anyone becoming the wiser before the sun rises, and you will move on to the final round. Any questions? No? Perfect. Come collect your letters."

Shadow's frown deepened. This trial was sounding stranger by the second. Less like a physical test and more like one of the assignments Erebos sent her on. That made sense since he was ultimately searching for her replacement. Following that train of thought, she started to piece together a vague idea of what they might be doing.

If she hadn't already known Erebos was throwing a masquerade tomorrow night, she'd wonder what in the darkness he was up to giving them specific outfits to wear. But if this *was* like one of her missions, they would need to blend in and not draw any attention to themselves.

At a masquerade that meant masks and costumes, which would also serve a second, less obvious purpose. Whatever creature or color they'd been assigned would allow the High Lord and his flock to easily pick them out without their identities being discovered by the other attendees. It would be one of the only ways to keep an eye on them while they completed whatever task they'd been assigned.

She wondered if they'd be expected to kill someone or steal something. Neither was an issue, but if she was expected to take someone out, it did help to know when planning her outfit. Some weapons were easier to conceal than others.

Plucking up the midnight-colored envelope bearing her name, Shadow turned and made her way to the exit. As she tucked the envelope inside her shirt, a sudden thought struck her, filling her veins with ice.

What if Dmitri was lying when he said each task was unique? It would be just like Erebos to make them all believe they had a chance to move on, only to give two contestants the same set of instructions, meaning half would automatically be cut once their partner completed the task.

Sneaky. Underhanded. It had the High Lord's name written all over it.

And given what had been going on between them, Shadow had little doubt who she'd have to face off against.

As if he could hear the thought, Ronan's eyes found hers. *Wait for me*, they seemed to demand.

It was tempting, especially with the way her body was still buzzing from earlier. She wanted him to make good on every one of his promises, but allowing this *thing* between them to go any further would be the height of foolishness.

If there was any chance she might be competing directly against him tomorrow, she couldn't allow her infatuation with him to sway her. Not when her freedom was on the line.

But there was another reason the thought of beating him before the last round was so appealing. If she could take him out now, she had to try. Because the final battle would surely result in his death. If there was a way to avoid that outcome, if there was a way for both of them to live, she had to go for it.

And the only way she could do that was to stay as far away as possible. Somehow, she needed to rediscover the icy indifference which had once come so easily. And if she couldn't find it, at least a little distance would help her fight through this sexual haze his mere presence trapped her in.

So even though her body protested every step, Shadow walked away. Away from temptation. Away from the promise in those ice-blue eyes.

Away from *him*.

And she hated every fucking second of it.

CHAPTER 20

RONAN

*A*s soon as he'd confirmed Calix had taken his leave, Ronan grabbed a seat at the bar and ordered the bartender to open a fresh bottle of the house liquor—no glass required.

He was in the mood to get pissed, so he didn't bother with the fancy stuff. He wanted alcohol. A lot of it. So long as it wasn't poisoned and got him pickled enough he could finally stop picturing the look of unmitigated *need* on Shadow's face when he'd asked if he could pet her, he didn't care what the fuck it tasted like. Which was good because it was little better than mint-flavored piss. And was that . . . glitter floating around in it? What the fuck was wrong with these people?

"Are you sulking, Ronan?" Sebastian asked with a laugh as he claimed the stool beside him.

"I don't sulk."

"*Non?* What do you call this, then?"

"I'm drinking."

"I can smell that. But I'm pretty sure this pouty lower lip of yours" —he reached out and flicked Ronan's lip—"is what we refer to as sulking."

Ronan grunted.

"Okay, fine. We will call it something more manly. Brooding, perhaps?"

Ronan took another pull of the foul liquid, knowing he was already well on his way to being absolutely tossed. The stuff was potent; he'd give it that. It was about all it had going for it.

"So why are we *brooding*, Ronan?"

It was on the tip of his tongue to tell Bast to fuck off, but instead he found himself admitting, "I almost had her."

"Had her? We're talking about the lovely Shadow, I presume."

He didn't bother confirming. There was only one woman he was interested in. "I just know if I can kiss her, she'll remember."

Bast clutched his heart. *"Que c'est romantique!"*

"What are you muttering about now?"

"True love's kiss. How romantic!"

He rolled his eyes at the over-the-top dramatics, though he found it endlessly amusing that Bast was a closeted hopeless romantic. One would never suspect with how he was determined to plough his way across the continent.

As far as true love's kiss was concerned, Ronan hadn't thought of it in quite those terms. Given the way Shadow responded to him, it was obvious to him that her body remembered him, even if her mind didn't. One was the key to the other. It's why he was certain that if he could kiss her, everything was bound to come pouring back.

"Maybe you did it wrong."

Ronan's back stiffened, his lip curling up in a sneer. "Impossible." That wasn't ego talking; there was simply no mistaking the look in her eyes when he'd offered to make her purr.

"Show me."

"What?"

"Show what you did. Maybe you said something to turn her off. Try it out on me, and I'll tell you."

A disbelieving laugh escaped as he grabbed the bottle and drank deep. "I'm not going to seduce you, Bast. No matter how much you beg. What happened to Loren? He seemed willing enough."

Bast ignored his attempt to change the subject. In a surprising display of strength, he took hold of Ronan's stool and turned it until they were face-to-face. "This is important. Let me help you win your lady love. You won't find a better judge than me."

"Bast, you're the least discerning person I know. You'd tumble in the sheets with anyone. How are you any sort of judge?"

"Fine," he huffed. "We'll get you a woman." Catching the eye of a pretty blonde with ample curves and a wild cascade of curls, he shouted, "A second of your time, *ma petite?*"

Blushing, she pointed to herself. "Me?"

Bast nodded encouragingly. "But of course."

Ronan shook his head and took another drink. Either he was drunk, or this was actually starting to taste good.

Ducking her head, the woman quickly crossed over, nervously tucking her hair behind her ear. "What can I do for you, gentlemen?"

Bast was all charm as he murmured, "We need to settle a bet. Would you mind helping us?"

She shifted her guileless blue eyes between them. "What kind of bet?"

"Well, my friend here thinks he's an expert at seduction. I, however, know that the title rightfully belongs to me. We're hoping you'd put the matter to bed"—he winked, making her blush even harder—"and tell us which one of us has the right of it."

"You want to s-seduce me?"

The note of hopefulness in her tone had Ronan clenching his teeth. What the hell was Sebastian doing? He hadn't agreed to any of this.

"If you wouldn't mind."

"Not at all!" The blonde practically jumped into Sebastian's lap.

He didn't bother hiding his smirk. "All right, Ronan. You're up first. Pretend she's your Shadow and give her your best chat-up line."

"Bast . . . I'm not doing this."

"Then you'll never win her back, and all of this will have been for naught. Is she not worth a little piece of your pride, Butcher?"

Of course she is.

"I just don't want to humiliate you."

"Oh . . . you won't. Now, fire away."

Ronan drained the last of his bottle, grimacing as he set it back down. Clearing his throat, he stood, a little surprised to find his legs weren't as steady as they should be. More worrisome was the fact that there were currently two blonde girls swimming on Bast's lap.

"Which one am I talking to?" he asked.

"Oh, this is going to be amazing," Bast murmured, giving the girl a kiss on the cheek. "Stand up for us, *mon ange*. Right here in the middle."

She giggled and obeyed. Bast gripped her hips and twisted so each man had access to one of her ears.

"There you go, Ronan. And to show that this is truly for your benefit, I'll give you some free advice. Whatever you say, whisper it. Everything sounds better in a whisper." He was grinning down at the blonde, who was enthusiastically nodding her agreement.

"Whispers. Definitely. Brings to mind the bedroom," she said breathlessly.

Bast ran his finger down the length of her nose. "Exactly."

Feeling like an absolute arse, Ronan searched his mind for some-thing—anything—he could say. Vaguely recalling Kragen successfully using something similar, he dropped his voice and gave it a go. "Have you been covered in bees recently?"

"N-no?"

"Hmm . . . you look sweeter than honey."

She giggled. And not an 'I want you to lift my skirt and have your way with me' giggle, a 'Mother's tits, this man is absurd' giggle.

Fuck, he needed another bottle.

"Well, it's no wonder why you struck out, Ronan. You're absolute shit. Have you ever even been with a woman? You need to do it like this." Bast tipped the girl's chin up until he was peering down at her, his expression filled with smoldering intensity as he whispered, "Do you believe in love at first sight, or do you need me to walk by you again?"

A breath stuttered out of her. "I-I believe."

He grinned and straightened, practically giving Ronan whiplash with how easily he switched out of his role as seducer and back to his usual cheeky countenance. "Try again, Ronan."

Ronan grappled for another line. This was far from his usual MO, but now it was a matter of pride. Anything Bast could do, he could do a thousand times better. Resting an elbow on the bar, he leaned down, his voice a seductive purr, "Do you have a mirror in your pocket? Because I can easily see myself in your skirt."

"Ugh, it's like you're not even trying," Bast scolded. Taking the girl's hand, he ran it down his torso. "Go ahead, *mon ange,* feel my shirt. Can you feel it?" She gave him a jerky nod, her teeth biting into her lower lip. He pulled her lip free as he whispered, "It's made of boyfriend material."

The blonde swooned. "Are you sure? Feels like husband material to me."

"Let's not get ahead of ourselves." He tapped her playfully on the nose when she fisted her hand in the velvet and tried to pull him down for a kiss. "Not yet, *ma petite.* Bet first, then kisses."

She pouted and looked to Ronan.

Oh, fuck it all.

Pretending it was Reyna's green gaze peering up at him, he gave it another go. "Your eyes are bluer than the Empyrean Ocean, and I don't mind being lost at sea."

This time there were no giggles, just a soft, "Oh."

Running a thumb along her cheekbone, Bast lowered his head and whispered, "*Je rêve de tremper ma baguette dans ta soupe.*"

The blonde licked her lip. "Stars . . ."

"Oh, come on, you're cheating. Everything sounds better when—"

"When I say it," Bast interrupted with a laugh.

"When it's foreign."

"What does it mean?" the blonde asked.

Bast wrinkled his nose. "It loses its magic when translated, but roughly I said, 'I dream of soaking my baguette in your soup.'"

She giggled. "You're right. It sounded much sexier the first way, but I suppose it still has a certain kind of charm."

Ronan inwardly groaned. How in the Mother's name could she find *that* sexy?

Clearly enjoying this little game far more than he was, the girl looked over at him with a wide smile. "Your turn."

Channeling his inner Bast, Ronan lowered his voice once more. "Do you remember me? Oh, that's right, I've only met you in my dreams."

She pressed a hand to her chest and swayed toward him.

Not to be outdone, Bast breathed, "I was wondering if you had an extra heart . . . because mine was just stolen."

"Mine too," she fervently agreed, looking up at him like he hung the moon. This poor, sweet girl. She had no idea what she was getting herself into.

Too into this game of theirs to feel foolish, Ronan tipped her face back to his. "If I had to rate you from one to ten, I'd give you a nine, because I'm the one you're missing."

"Okay," she agreed.

"Oooh, he's getting better, isn't he, *mon ange?*" Sebastian asked with a grin. The blonde gave an eager nod as he tucked some more hair behind her ear. "All right, since he's gotten the hang of it, I'll give you one last one, and then you pick your winner. Okay?"

She nodded.

Ever the consummate actor, Bast blinked a few times, pulling away from her and then leaning in close. "There must be something wrong with my eyes."

"Oh, no! What's wrong?" she cooed, leaning into him.

"I can't take them off you," Bast finished with a wink.

Ronan barely suppressed a groan. He wasn't sure it was possible, but Sebastian sounded stupider with every line.

Running his knuckles down her cheek, Bast softly informed her, "So which one of us impressed you most?"

"W-why choose when you're both right here and so clearly up to the task?"

Bast gave her a wicked grin. "You promised, *mon ange.* Don't get greedy."

"Um . . . well . . ." Her gaze darted between both of them, finally landing on Bast. "I choose you."

Sebastian's eyes went wide, and he let out a little laugh. "I won even after throwing the last line. Ah well, better luck next time, Ronan." He clapped him on the shoulder. "At least now you've seen a professional at work. Hopefully you can put your new skills to use, and next time it will be you who gets the girl. But as they say, to the victor go the spoils, *non?*" He curled his arm around the blonde's waist. "So what do you say, *mon ange?* Are you ready for me to spoil you?"

She nodded eagerly. "Oh yes. Quite ready."

Ronan watched them walk away with a glower, his words definitely slurring as he called after them, "You only won because my heart wasn't in it!"

When he returned his attention to the bar, he found a fresh bottle of the shimmering liquor waiting for him. He looked up with a frown, not recalling asking for another. The bartender stood at the other end of the bar drying off a glass but met his searching gaze with an amused grin and a shrug. As if to say, 'It looked like you needed it, mate.'

Ronan barely suppressed a groan as he realized there had been a witness to his shame.

This night just keeps getting better. The only silver lining was that none of his friends—or Shadow—had been here to see him. Von would never let him live it down. Helena or Effie either, for that matter. They'd probably take turns smacking him upside the head for uttering such nonsense in the first place. Thank the Mother for small favors.

Grasping the bottle by the neck, he drank long and deep, trying hard to shove Sebastian's mocking words from his mind.

'Maybe you said something to turn her off.'

'It's no wonder why you struck out . . . You're absolute shit.'

Ronan pinched the bridge of his nose. Fuck. What if the smug bastard was right?

Was he *that* out of practice? Did he imagine Shadow's reaction earlier?

No.

There was no mistaking the desire burning in her eyes. He just needed to come up with a better plan. Something that would guarantee their next encounter ended with his lips on hers.

Having enough remaining sense to realize he was in no state to come up with said plan in his current condition, Ronan let out a heavy sigh. *Tomorrow, then. At the trial, perhaps.*

Realizing he hadn't so much as unsealed the envelope he'd been given earlier, Ronan pulled it out and tapped it on the counter a few times, wondering about its contents. He wasn't near drunk enough to open it here and risk getting disqualified. Probably best to head home. Sleep off the humiliation of the night and get his head on straight for tomorrow. Yes, that's what he should do.

Tucking the missive away, his eyes fell back on the bartender's consolation prize.

Well . . . maybe he'd have just one more for the road.

CHAPTER 21

RONAN

"*G*et your fat ass up!"

Sebastian's annoyed shout was punctuated with the slam of a pillow atop Ronan's face. He sat up, sputtering and spitting little bits of downy fluff out of his mouth.

"What the fuck, Bast? I was sleeping," he growled, peeling a bleary eye open to glare at the current bane of his existence.

"Yes. I can see that." Bast stood in the doorway, arms crossed and mouth twisted in a scowl.

"What crawled up your arse and died?" Ronan asked, sitting up and rubbing at his eyes. His head hadn't pounded like this since . . . hell, he couldn't remember the last time he'd been this hungover.

"Do you seriously not remember our conversation"—Bast stormed across the room and flung open the windows, nearly blinding Ronan with the flood of sunlight—"almost three hours ago?"

Pressing the heels of his palms to his eyes, he groaned. "No?"

"No? No! Ronan, you have a trial in four hours. You've been in bed squealing like a hog fifteen minutes into his orgasm since I came back. Why aren't you up yet?"

"What is it with you and the swine analogies?"

"Ronan!"

"What?" he snapped, his temper slipping free. He couldn't recall a fucking thing after Bast left him at the Siren the night before, but his head felt as if an entire war band had taken up residence inside it.

Spying the black rectangle beside the bed, Sebastian stomped across the room and threw it at him. "You haven't even read your instructions yet!"

"Oops," he offered with a slight shrug because really, what else was there to say?

"Oops? Ronan," he cried, throwing his hands up in exasperation, "it's like you aren't taking this seriously at all. The fact that I, of all people, am acting more responsibly than you should be indication enough how very wrong things are here. Do you have any idea how appalling that is?"

Well, when he put it that way . . . But it seemed Sebastian was just getting started.

"You know how I abhor responsibility. *I* am the drunken but loveable rogue. *You* are the respectable one. Do not force me to trade places with you." Bast stomped his foot indignantly. "I did not sign up for this."

"You're the one who couldn't pay his debts."

"I am your *guide,* not your . . . your . . . manservant. It's bad enough you sent me on an errand you don't even recall."

"Peace, Sebastian. You've made your point. Quite shrilly, I might add."

"Have I? Because you. Are. Still. In. Bed!"

He tried to toss another pillow, but Ronan caught it mid-air and bared his teeth in a snarl. "Watch it, Bast."

Sensing he was pushing it, Bast adopted a different tack. "Have you given up, then? Is that it?"

"No. Of course not."

"Are you sure? Because this"—he gestured at Ronan's disheveled state—"does not look like a man intent on winning back the love of his life he spent the last five years searching for."

"So I got a little drunk—"

"A little? You smell worse than an entire fucking distillery. If I were to light a torch, the room would go up in flames. It's a good thing you didn't accidentally fart fire in your sleep and set yourself ablaze."

Ronan had to press his lips together to keep from laughing. It wasn't funny, not really. The man made a series of excellent points. He just had a truly colorful way of going about it.

"It was a rough night," he finally mumbled, having no other explanation for his behavior.

"It would serve you right if you failed tonight."

He didn't think he could withstand any more of Bast's tough love. "I'm opening my letter, all right? Will you shut up now?"

Sebastian pursed his lips. "That depends. Can I read it?"

"That depends," Ronan mocked, "can you keep your fucking mouth shut? You're not secretly working for the High Lord, are you?"

Something flickered in Bast's eyes. There and then gone. "I'm allergic to responsibility, remember? Besides, I'm too good looking to work for anybody but myself."

Ronan started to roll his eyes, but it made his stomach swoop, so he blinked and winced instead. "Come here then, but if you breathe a word of this to anyone, I will hunt you down and make your insides your outsides. Understand?"

Bast shuddered. "I liked you better when you were unconscious."

Breaking the wax seal with its tiny constellation of stars, Ronan pulled out a thick piece of parchment, his eyebrows climbing higher with each word he read.

You are cordially invited to attend the Lunaris Festival. The party will begin at sundown with a night-long masquerade celebrating the heavens themselves. As we pay our respect to the chaos from which we were created, let us look to the sky and revel in the glory of the stars.

In honor of the celestials who gave us life, please dress to impress as one of your most beloved creatures of the night.

BENEATH THE FORMAL invitation was another message, this one bearing the instructions Dmitri referred to the night before.

BUTCHER ~

THE MASQUERADE IS A FORMAL BALL. DRESS ACCORDINGLY USING YOUR CREATURE'S INSPIRATION TO SELECT YOUR MASK. YOU MAY NOT REMOVE YOUR MASK AT ANY TIME, NOR REVEAL YOUR IDENTITY TO ANY OF THE GUESTS IN ATTENDANCE. THE TERMS OF YOUR TRIAL ARE BELOW. HEED THEM WELL, AND MAY THE STARS BE IN YOUR FAVOR.

YOUR CREATURE: THE BAT

YOUR TASK IS TWOFOLD.

1: ACQUIRE THE LADY DOVINA'S BROOCH (THE ONE ON HER PERSON, NOT ONE FROM HER COLLECTION)

2: PREVENT CALIX FROM COMPLETING HIS TASK

BOTH THESE ITEMS MUST BE SUCCESSFULLY COMPLETED BEFORE SUNRISE TO MOVE ON. IF YOU GET CAUGHT, YOU WILL BE DISQUALIFIED. TELL NO ONE OF YOUR ASSIGNMENT. PROOF OF COMPLETION MUST BE PROVIDED TO THE MASTER OF CEREMONIES.

RONAN DROPPED the paper into his lap. "Well, what do you make of it?"

Bast slapped a hand on his shoulder. "It was nice knowing you, Ronan."

"You doubt me?"

"Did we not just read the same missive? You have to steal from the

Raven herself without getting caught." He barked out a harsh laugh. "You'd have better luck copping a feel of the High Lord's flaccid dick."

"I guess it's time to use those skills of seduction you taught me last night."

Sebastian looked horrified. "You're going to get yourself killed. Or worse. Are you forgetting she's part of the flock? She's going to know who you are and what your task is. Stars, anyone who catches sight of your hair will know you the second you set foot in the palace, masked or no. This is an impossible task, Ronan. They set you up to fail."

Ronan clenched his jaw, already perfectly aware of the fact. Someone had it out for him. Someone who was feeling a little territorial over their precious Shadow.

Too bad for them because so was he—and she belonged to him first.

"Bast, any idea where I can get a mask?"

Sebastian raised a brow. "You can't seriously intend to go through with this."

Ronan held his stare without saying a word.

Releasing a heavy sigh, Bast glanced out the window. "There are a few modistes who might have something on hand or the skill to fashion one. But you're a large man, Ronan. I doubt there's enough time for them to make you a full set of formal attire."

Thankful for his foresight, Ronan glanced at the bag he'd brought with him, recalling the formalwear safely tucked inside. "Leave that to me."

SHADOW

SHE FASTENED the clasp of her earring and then took a step back to look at herself in the mirror and let out a soft gasp. Not even she was immune to the picture she painted.

Her card had simply instructed her that she was to portray the lady moon. So her color palette for the evening was a combination of silver and white. Not that she had much say in the matter. Erebos had left the outfit he expected her to wear on her bed. Much as he did for any court-related gathering.

Her dress and mask were a matching set. The strapless bodice was made of overlapping gossamer fabric only layered until it was thick enough not to be transparent. The skirt was composed of dozens of strips of the same silver fabric along with gray and white tulle. The glimpse of silver through the white reminded her of the way moonlight spilled through the clouds. The sheer fabrics hinted at the shape of her legs when not providing little peeks of bare skin with every step she took.

As if that wasn't enough of a statement, Dovina had sent her personal maid to help Shadow with her hair and makeup. Shadow quite liked how the moonlight-colored strands were twisted up into an intricate mass of curls and braids. And as if anything else were required, diamonds decorated her ears and neck, and a shimmering powder had been applied to any exposed skin, meaning she sparkled with every shift of her body.

"You are breathtaking," Erebos said with reverence, stealing into her room without invitation. As he so often did.

She waited for him to reach her, knowing he would want to see how they looked standing beside one another.

He'd also dressed with care, though he was all in black. He'd even gone so far as to dye his hair for the evening, and the contrast was . . . stunning. Erebos was an incredibly handsome man, but there was something about seeing him wear the colors of darkness that seemed *right*. Even his eyes seemed darker. More a deep forest green than their usual jade.

"Moonbeam," he whispered, resting his hands on her shoulders as he stared at her reflection in the mirror. "You are exquisite."

She offered him a smile, appreciating the compliment though her heart yearned to hear it from someone else.

"I brought you something."

"I think you've already done enough," she said, not sure what else she could possibly need. Her gem-encrusted half-mask covered all but her lips.

"This is the pièce de résistance. Trust me."

"Always."

He walked to her closet and pulled out a large black box. He must have stashed it there earlier when dropping off her other garments. Setting the box on her vanity, he set the top aside and retrieved a glittering crown.

"My lord, it's too much," she breathed as he walked toward her holding the array of stars.

"Nonsense."

He placed it on her head, the cluster of metal and gems surprisingly light.

"Look," he ordered softly. "Not even Luna herself would shine brighter than you tonight, Shadow mine."

"Luna?"

"The Lady of Light." His lips gave a wry twist. "The moon goddess herself."

Shadow turned back to the mirror, her breath catching at the sight. Erebos was right. The crown was the perfect final touch. It just brought everything else together, lending her ensemble an elegance and regal quality it had been lacking.

"Thank you, my lord."

He pressed a kiss to her shoulder. "The Lord of Night could hardly walk into a ball without his Lady to guide him, could he?"

Any delight Shadow had taken in her appearance dimmed at Erebos's not-so-subtle reminder of his intentions. She had been caught off guard by her task for the evening, but not because it had been difficult. Quite the opposite. It felt as though he'd gone easy on her. All she had to do was acquire one of Dominic's rings. Child's play. The man would simply give it to her if she asked sweetly. No questions asked. Hardly a test of her skills. She wouldn't need an hour, let alone the entire night.

"I'm surprised you didn't give me an impossible task so I would be forced to leave the competition," she found herself saying.

The skin around his eyes tightened, and he ran his hands down her arms until he grasped her elbows none too gently. "I will not see you end in disgrace. You wanted to make a point. You wanted to prove you are the best. Fine. Prove your point. But know that even after the contest ends, the only title you will hold is that of my Lady. Just because you win, Shadow darling, doesn't mean you get to keep the prize. But surely you knew that?"

Her heart dropped, and it took every considerable effort to hold on to her impassive expression as she held his glittering stare in the mirror.

"You belong to me, and I will never let you go."

There was a sinister quality to the words, a possessiveness that filled her with ice.

"I would expect nothing less, my lord."

"Good girl." He gave her a satisfied smile and held out his elbow, waiting for her to curl her arm through his. "Now, we've kept our guests waiting long enough. Let's go."

CHAPTER 22

SHADOW

As she'd suspected, her task was complete in a matter of minutes. She hadn't even said a word. Shadow simply held out her palm and gave Dominic an expectant lift of her brow. He handed his signet ring over with a slight quirk of his lips. It was too big for her to slide on one of her own fingers, so she'd tucked the trinket into the bodice of her dress and walked away as if the exchange never happened.

With her assignment out of the way, she was left with plenty of time to, well, not blend in exactly. There was no *blending* in this outfit, but she was still able to observe. Which suited her just fine. She was more than a little curious what the others were up to because as certain as she was that she'd been given a ridiculously easy mission on purpose, she knew the opposite would be true for them.

Unlike her, *they* were actually being tested. She resented the special treatment, especially after the High Lord publicly promised he wouldn't. Still, the knowledge didn't confirm her other suspicion: whether she and Ronan had been given the same task. What was laughable for her would be a true feat for him. All she had to do was turn in the ring, and she'd have her answer. If she was right, it would be over. Ronan would be spared.

So why wasn't she seeking out Dmitri right now? Why was she moving through the room like a ghost, trying to remain undetected while she sought out the one man she should avoid at all costs?

Because you are a fool, Shadow. No better than a silly girl with her first crush.

She didn't bother to deny it. She'd never been one for lying. Not even to herself. And the simple truth was, his words from last night had been replaying through her mind on a constant loop. She could recall, with perfect clarity, the velvety rasp of his voice when he called her kitten. The way his ice-blue eyes had darkened with desire. How he'd sat close enough that she drew in the very air he'd exhaled—as if in doing so she could draw the man himself inside her. As if *he* was the nourishment her body required.

So even though every instinct warned her against it, Shadow moved through the ballroom, ignoring the lavish decorations and beautiful strains of music as she scanned the crowd for a certain chiseled face.

The masks did little to hide the identities of most of the guests— not that they were actively trying to conceal the truth. For them, the masks were a suggestion, unlike the contestants. Either way, Shadow knew she'd have no trouble finding Ronan in the crowd. The man lured her like a siren. Ending up at his side was inevitable.

Even if it was the height of lunacy.

It wasn't long before she spotted a few of the other contestants. Loren was the first to catch her eye, his wide grin all too recognizable even with most of his face concealed behind his wolf mask. The next was Dichen, who'd been assigned a cat. Shadow had never seen the woman unveiled, but there was no mistaking the absolute grace of her movements. She flowed between dancing bodies like water, her slight form slipping in and out of view as she maneuvered through the crowd. And the owl could only be Cedric, the blood mage. His burgundy eyes were a dead giveaway.

But no Ronan.

With a little growl of frustration, she narrowed her eyes and started her search again. They landed on Dovina almost instantly, the dark feathers and pointed beak of her raven mask not exactly subtle. She was talking to someone, her lips curving into a frown at whatever they were relaying.

A slight movement to Dovina's left pulled Shadow's focus. Out of habit, her eyes darted over to the cause of the disturbance, then up to inspect the stranger's face. As soon as she started to look away in disappointment, her eyes snapped back up.

Ronan.

"What in the darkness are you wearing?" she whispered.

It wasn't the clothes she referred to—he was impeccably dressed. His shirt was form-fitting black silk, its buttons a series of twinkling onyx gems running down the length of his torso. She wasn't sure there was a man alive who could make silk appear so utterly masculine. It was the same for his pants, the dark fabric hugging his muscled thighs and disappearing into a set of knee-high boots in a way that made her mouth water. No, she wasn't referring to his sinfully sexy—albeit unexpected—outfit.

It was the skull cap with its long, pointed ears and the scrunched and flattened nose that had her fighting a laugh.

No wonder she hadn't spotted him straight away. He'd hidden his flame-colored hair beneath the leather of his . . . helmet? She wasn't sure what word to assign to the mask that not only concealed the better part of his face but also wrapped around the rest of his head.

If she hadn't been studying him at that precise moment, she would have missed the gentle flick of his fingers and the way his jaw tensed with concentration.

"What are you—"

She didn't need to finish the question—not that he was near enough to answer it anyway. As she watched, a small bauble floated over to him and straight into his waiting palm, causing his lips to curl up in satisfaction.

There was no explanation for what she'd just seen, except that fire must not be the only element Ronan had access to. That . . . and her assumption they'd been given the same task was wrong. For whatever trinket he'd just stolen was surely part of tonight's trial.

Before she could wrap her head around these new discoveries, Ronan pocketed the item and spun around, heading for a set of double doors that would lead him to a walkway filled with darkened alcoves.

The perfect place for couples to slip away if they were feeling particularly amorous.

"Now what are you up to?" she whispered, her curiosity well and truly piqued.

Sparing only a quick glance in either direction to ensure no one was paying attention to her, Shadow followed.

RONAN

HE WASN'T sure what was more embarrassing, this fucking mask or losing a flirting match to Bast. The answer came to him immediately.

The latter. *Definitely* the latter.

That said, the mask was undeniably heinous. When Sebastian first handed it to him, Ronan took one look at it and laughed. "Ha ha, very funny. Where's my real mask?"

"That *is* your real mask."

Even now, hours later, he still wasn't convinced it wasn't a prank. Not that there was anything he could do about it. It was wear the damn mask or lose on a technicality. And he was not losing anything else this week, thank you very much.

With the first half of his task completed, it was time to seal the deal. Calix had wandered off this way nearly twenty minutes ago and had yet to return to the ballroom. Now was the perfect opportunity for Ronan to sabotage the man's task without the watchful eyes of the other guests tracking his every move.

The light was dim enough in the corridor he felt fairly confident that he could move about undetected. Keeping his ears trained for any slight sound, he prowled down the walkway, eyes scanning the dark recesses lining either side for any hint of a person. It wasn't until the hall started to turn to the right that he realized it was U shaped and likely came back around to connect to the ballroom on the other end.

He let out a little growl, frustrated it wouldn't be easy to sneak up on the poisoner after all. Resigned to returning to the main room and sniffing out his target another way, he continued walking, his footsteps faltering when he spotted the steel-gray tip of a woman's shoe.

He crept closer, a tingle of warning whispering down his spine. It was too early in the evening for people to start passing out from overindulgence, and he was too intimately familiar with death to mistake the stillness for anything else. What he couldn't yet discern was whether the one responsible was still nearby.

Instead of calling out and alerting anyone to his presence, he continued with his stealthy prowl, crouching down when he was next to the woman so he could inspect her more thoroughly. Her body had been dumped in one of the little alcoves, her back propped up against the wall, her head lulling obscenely to the side.

Out of habit, he pressed his fingers to her wrist to check for a pulse. He'd just reached out to tilt her face toward him, so he could see if there were any clues as to what killed her, when a soft voice reached his ears.

"She was poisoned."

Ronan tensed, a defensive protest springing from his lips unbidden. "I didn't do it."

Shadow quirked a brow, her mask dangling from her fingers. "I didn't say you did, Butcher. Poison's not your style."

He thought she kept talking, but his heart had somehow lodged itself in the vicinity of his throat, and he was having a hell of a time pulling air into his lungs.

She was absolutely radiant, an angel crafted from starlight. If he was a man prone to verse, he might say he was in the presence of the divine—or as close as his sorry arse would ever get.

Shadow's lips twitched up. "See something you like?"

That's when he remembered he was still wearing the fucking mask. He quickly ripped it off his head and tucked it into the back of his waistband, simultaneously trying to smooth down his hair with his other hand. The quiet shake of her shoulders told him it was too late on both counts. Though it was hard to care when the subtle movements made her skin glimmer like it had been dipped in stardust.

His mind emptied completely, and he had to blink a few times as he stared at her. Even then, the best he could manage was a reverent, "Kitten . . ."

Ignoring him, she stepped forward and knelt down beside him. He had to swallow back a moan as the entire expanse of her toned leg was exposed by the slits in her skirt. Unaware of what she was doing to him—or perhaps she simply didn't care—she pointed toward the body, speaking softly, "See the darkening of the veins by her eyes and along her neck? Poor Marin. It wasn't a kind way to go."

It took considerable effort for Ronan to take his gaze off Shadow and follow the direction she'd indicated. He didn't know what it said about him that he'd been so entranced by her, he'd fucking forgotten what he'd been in the middle of.

Who did that?

A man who'd grown impervious to death, that's who.

Or one who was starved for any sign of affection from a woman who didn't even remember him.

He wasn't sure which was worse.

Refocusing on Marin's body, Ronan studied the discoloration Shadow mentioned, his eyes roaming over the dead woman's pale skin. There was a hint of red marring the wrist curled in her lap that gave him pause.

"I don't think it was poison."

"Why not? This is clearly Calix's handiwork."

"No," Ronan said slowly. "I think this might have been the blood mage, disguising things to look like she'd been poisoned."

Shadow's brows pinched together. "Aldair? Really? But why?"

"We were all given secret assignments tonight. As far as I know, none of our instructions were accompanied by a reason."

"So you think Cedric was told to take out Marin?"

"It's certainly possible. My task involved another contestant."

He could feel her eyes on him. "Who?"

"You know I can't tell you."

They both stood. Shadow bit her lip, her eyes taking on a faraway cast as she tried to make sense of their discovery. "Okay . . . but Calix could have poisoned her hours ago and just came to check on her progress."

"He could have, but I doubt it." Ronan pointed out the patch of dried blood inside Marin's wrist. "If that had been the result of the poison, it would have come from her mouth or nose, or even her eyes. Not her wrist. The blood was intentionally spilled. There's only one person we know who requires blood to cast spells. Besides, Calix has only been out of my sight for twenty, maybe thirty minutes. She's been dead at least an hour, perhaps two."

"How could you possibly know that?"

"Her temperature."

"Hmm," she hummed, appraising him.

"What?"

"Brains and brawn. I'm impressed." She studied him, and he recognized the determined gleam in her eyes. She was puzzling things out in her mind. "Calix is the one you were coming after. That's the real reason you don't suspect him."

"Let's just say I have a good idea what he's up to, and it does not involve Marin."

"I see. And how did you come about this information?"

"Does it matter?"

"Consider it professional curiosity."

Ronan weighed his words carefully, settling on a neutral, "Dovina isn't the only one who knows how to come by sensitive information."

Thanks to Bast—who'd spent a rigorous afternoon with the cleaning girl responsible for Calix's lodgings—he'd found out the details of the man's task before setting foot in the palace. The poisoner needed to find Dmitri's flask and leave it in the High Lord's private suite. Ronan's plan had been to relieve Calix of the item before he could plant it without the man ever being the wiser. Now it seemed

Ronan would have to recover it from Erebos's room and deliver the flask along with the brooch to Dmitri. Not impossible, but significantly more complicated.

Unless Shadow could sneak him up there.

He had a feeling she just might if he played his cards right.

She continued to study him but thankfully didn't press him further for information they both knew he couldn't give her. "I see," she said simply, walking away.

"Are you just going to leave her here?" Ronan asked, tipping his head toward Marin's body.

"She's not our problem."

"Fair enough."

Ronan was sure there were plenty of people who would be appalled by her cavalier dismissal, but he wasn't one of them. He'd been touched by death too many times to be precious about it. Unless the corpse belonged to one of the handful of people he cared about, it didn't much affect him. Shadow, given her profession, must feel the same way. To them, the discovery of the body was just another day at work. It just came with the territory. Truth be told, he was grateful they didn't have to dispose of it. Now they were free to enjoy the rest of the evening's festivities.

Just as soon as he completed the second part of his task, that was.

As if she could sense the direction of his thoughts, Shadow smirked and toyed with the ribbons of her mask. "I saw you, you know. For as fancy as your magic is, Butcher, it's not very subtle."

Ronan chuckled. "I could have done more to hide what I was up to, but I was in a hurry."

"You're lucky I was the one who caught you. According to the rules . . ."

Warmth bloomed beneath his ribs as she teased him. He was equal parts pleased and embarrassed to learn she'd been keeping such a close eye on him. Pleased because despite all her protests and the walls she tried to erect between them, she couldn't stay away. Embarrassed because he should have sensed the tail straight away. He couldn't afford to be so careless.

Hope ignited within him, burning through his veins and filling him with renewed purpose. Bast was wrong. He hadn't turned her off and ruined his chances; he'd *scared* her off. Shadow was afraid of what she felt around him, but not so afraid that it outweighed her curiosity.

She wanted him.

The relief Ronan felt at those words, at the proof of them as she continued to steal quick glances up at him and offer small, flirty smiles.

It was working.

If he just kept chiseling away, eventually he would break through the last of her defenses. It wouldn't be long now. He could feel the truth of it in his bones.

He *would* win.

And she . . . she would be his.

They finished walking the length of the arch and were about halfway through the final straightway when the music floated to them on the breeze. Realizing that this might be his only opportunity to press his advantage and make use of the fact they were currently alone together, Ronan reached out a hand and stopped her movement.

"Dance with me."

She let out a little laugh. "Funny."

"I'm serious."

Her brow furrowed. "What, here? Do you even know how to dance?"

"Of course I know how to dance. Anyone can sway to a beat."

Some of the laughter faded from her eyes as she realized he was serious. "I'd pay to see that, but you know we can't, Ronan."

"Why not?"

"Oh, I don't know, one of a hundred reasons. Because we're in the middle of the hallway? Because anyone could come along and see us? Because you and I *cannot* be seen together."

He closed the distance between them, catching a whiff of the intoxicating scent he'd come to associate with her—night-blooming jasmine and a hint of cedar—as he pressed a hand to her lower back and drew her body so close it all but touched his.

"So what?"

"So what?" she parroted.

He took a few steps sideways, towing her with him as he moved them into the darkness of one of the alcoves. "Better?"

"Ronan . . ." But he could tell her heart wasn't in the protest. Already her mask had fallen to the floor so she could rest her palms on his shoulders. She wasn't attempting to push him away; she was clinging to him.

There was just enough light in the private nook for him to make out her features. She was staring up at him, her expression a mix of wistfulness and confusion. He knew she didn't understand this pull between them. She'd been fighting it, but her resistance was crumbling.

This was it.

This was the moment he'd been waiting for. His chance to break Reyna's memories free of the prison Erebos trapped them within.

Heart thundering in his ribs, Ronan cupped her face in both his hands. Dipping his head down until his forehead rested against hers, he swept his thumbs over her cheeks and whispered, "Do you have any idea how long I've searched for you? What losing you did to me? I barely survived it the first time, kitten. I know I won't make it through a second."

Her lips parted, but he pressed his finger against them, halting her words.

"If this is the last time I get to hold you, if this is my last chance to know what it feels like to be whole, I don't care how many reasons there are why we shouldn't. I refuse to spend another second pretending my heart isn't yours."

With those words hanging between them, Ronan's lips crashed down on hers.

CHAPTER 23

SHADOW

The second his lips met hers, the chaos of her mind fell silent. Instead of a litany of all the reasons she should get as far away from here as possible, there was only him and the warmth of his hands cupping her cheeks . . . the press of his thigh between the vee of her legs . . . the velvety scrape of his stubble against her skin . . . the taste of him on her tongue . . . the soft growl of need rumbling through his chest and into hers.

"Mine," he breathed against her lips before claiming her mouth once more.

Yes.

She might have spoken the word aloud; she wasn't exactly sure. She wasn't sure of anything, really, except how perfectly they fit together. It was like he was the key and she the lock. He was the only one in existence with the power to crack open the shriveled black muscle she called a heart. The only one who could teach it how to love.

It should have scared her. If she'd been thinking clearly—or at all— it would have.

But there was no thinking.

Only him.

Only Ronan.

She was lost to the sensation of him. Helpless to do anything but follow wherever he led while her heart beat erratically in her chest, like a tiny bird learning to take flight. She'd been kissed before. But not like this. Nothing compared to the soul-awakening experience that was Ronan. It was so much more than two mouths fumbling against each other in the dark.

It was a confession.

A promise.

A claiming.

He pulled away, and it took a few seconds before Shadow could recognize the uneven pants surrounding them as her breaths. Still holding her face, he tipped her chin up, peering down at her with a reverence usually reserved for holy men praying to their gods.

"Reyna . . ."

A dozen tiny things happened at once. The icy burn of anger replaced the warm pulse of desire in her veins. The winged creature soaring in her chest fell from the sky—dead once more. Her hand dropped from his shoulder to the dagger sheathed at her thigh, seam-lessly releasing the weapon and digging the tip of the blade into his stomach.

Her face felt frozen, but Ronan's was a concert of conflicting emotion.

Relief. Hope. Disappointment. Despair. Confusion.

And then, finally . . . acceptance.

"You still don't remember me, do you?" he asked, his desire-deep-ened voice tinged with regret.

"I don't know how many times I have to tell you. My name. Is *not*. Reyna!" She spat the words, furious that he would kiss her like that . . . make her feel those things . . . while thinking about, and dreaming about, and *loving*, someone else. The truth of it eviscerated her more brutally than she had ever managed while wielding one of her beloved blades.

He didn't want *her*. He'd never wanted her.

She was a replacement. A stand-in for the woman he'd lost.

Shadow didn't know it was possible to hurt like this. To feel cracked open. Raw. Bleeding and broken. All while remaining perfectly untouched and whole.

She wanted to pummel him, to claw his face and shred him into a million pieces just as he'd done to her. Instead she sucked in a breath and did nothing, working hard to pick up and tuck away every last shattered piece of her pride. He didn't deserve her pain. He didn't deserve anything.

Completely unaware of the gathering storm within her, Ronan swept the pad of his thumb over her lip. "I'd hoped . . . but then I guess it doesn't matter." He started to lean down, his mouth feathering against her.

"No." She jerked in his arms, fighting against his hold like a feral cat. "No!"

"Yes," he growled, pushing her back against the wall and pinning her in place with his body. "*Yes*."

Shadow didn't even realize she'd cut him until the coppery tang of his blood hit the air. He didn't react to the wound with so much as a hiss of pain. He was wholly focused on taming her, and she wasn't nearly strong enough to resist.

But that didn't stop her from trying.

She twisted her face away, attempting to ignore the tickle of his lips over her skin as he breathed kisses along her jaw. Her voice shook, losing its edge as her chest rose and fell with desperate breaths. "You don't get to kiss me like that and pretend I'm someone else."

He gripped her chin and turned her head until she was holding his gaze once more. "There is no one else. Only you. Just you." He punctuated each declaration with a kiss. "Your name doesn't matter. Your memories . . . your past. None of it matters. They change nothing. Because you."

Kiss.

"Are."

Kiss.

"*Mine*."

The next time his lips met hers, she melted into him, her weapon falling forgotten to the floor. She hated how completely he'd taken control of her body. How it responded to him with no regard to her wishes. Mostly, she hated how much she *didn't* hate him. If anyone else ever dared manhandle her the way he was, she'd have them castrated and bleeding out at her feet. But with Ronan? She couldn't get enough.

Her hands tangled in his hair, fisting in the silky strands and gripping hard. He grunted into her mouth, his thigh settling more firmly between her legs. She rocked against him without conscious thought, and she moaned as the subtle friction sent tiny sparks shooting across her body.

"You keep making noises like that, you'll draw a crowd, kitten." As if that's exactly what he wanted her to do, he shifted his stance, grinding the steely band of muscle along her center and pulling another needy moan from her. "Or is that what you desire? Do you want everyone out there to know what I'm doing to you? How good I make you feel?"

Shadow bit down on her lip, trying to contain her whimpered pleas as he continued to rub against her, setting her blood on fire with her need for him.

"I think that's what *you* desire." It was harder to form the words than she'd expected, her breath hitching as he hit just the right spot once more.

He grinned against her neck. "So what if it is? So what if I want everyone to know that while you may walk at his side, it's *my* name you cry out?" He kept one hand anchored in her hair while the other roamed down her body. When his fingers did little more than graze the tops of her breasts, she couldn't contain her protest.

"Ronan," she panted.

"I know, kitten. I wish there was time for me to explore you properly. Next time, I promise. Tonight we'll have to make do with you coming on my fingers. I know you want me to peel you out of this dress so I can lavish each of your perfect breasts with the same attention I'm giving your lips. That you want me to bite and suck and lick my way down your body until I'm kneeling before you, worshiping your exquisite fucking cunt with my tongue. I want that too. I want to make you come so hard the only thing keeping you upright is my hands on your body."

His palm ran the length of her torso until it hit the exposed skin of her thigh. Shadow was so lost to sensation, she couldn't form a coherent sentence. "Please . . . I . . . darkness . . . Ronan . . ."

"Have I told you yet how gorgeous you look in this dress?" He slid his hand between her legs, his fingers replacing his thigh as he ran them along her slick center. "You'd look fucking edible in anything, but what I really love about this gown is that it's so . . . *convenient*," he breathed as those nimble digits pushed aside her undergarments and spread open her folds.

She gasped, her eyes rolling back.

"Look at me, kitten."

Shadow forced her eyes open, her pulse racing in her ears as she locked gazes with him. As soon as her eyes met his, he slid two thick fingers inside her.

"Fuuuck, you're already dripping for me."

"Oh, stars," she cried as he curled his fingers before dragging them back out, the invasion everything she craved but still not enough.

"I wish it was my cock you were gripping so sweetly, but my fingers will have to do for now."

"Ro-nan," she brokenly moaned as he thrust in and out of her.

He released her hair so he could press his hand over her mouth, muting the sound of her ragged moans. "Fuck, I have to taste you."

She moaned against his palm as he pulled out and then sucked his fingers clean.

"Fucking delicious," he growled in approval before lifting his hand and bringing his mouth to hers. "Taste yourself." He licked into her mouth, swallowing her cries as the thrust of his tongue against hers echoed the rhythm of his fingers between her legs. His breaths stuttered out of him as he dropped his forehead against hers. He wrapped his hand over her mouth once more, continuing to play with her as he confessed, "I wish we didn't have to be quiet. I want to hear you scream for me. I want you shouting my name while I fuck you so thoroughly your body never forgets the feel of me buried inside you."

"I want that too."

Muffled as she was by him, she didn't think he could hear her actual words. But he seemed to understand the sentiment, because he grinned.

"Will you scream for me, Shadow? If I was to remove my hand, would you shout out my name so loudly that even the heavens above know who owns this pussy?"

She nodded, tears pooling in her eyes from the intensity of the climax building inside her. Shadow couldn't remember the last time someone other than herself had gotten her off, let alone one who sent her hurtling toward the edge so quickly. But with every dirty word and sweep of his fingers, her orgasm loomed closer. A tidal wave about to break.

"Should I do it? Shall I release your mouth? I hear footsteps. People are walking by right now. They don't know what I'm doing to you here in the dark, but all it would take is for me to lift my hand and they would."

As if the words alone conjured them, Shadow could suddenly sense eyes on them, peering into their private alcove from the other side of the darkness. But instead of fear, the sensation only ramped up her pleasure.

Ronan's breathing grew labored, as if he was just as affected by what he was doing to her as she was, but somehow his voice never lost its sensual rasp. "They'd hear your cries and imagine a thousand scandalous scenarios that could cause a woman to lose herself to her pleasure so completely. And they'd know I was the one to give it to you. That I own you. Do you want that, kitten? Do you want to be owned by me?"

"Yes!" she screamed against his hand, her body shaking as her orgasm slammed into her. An hour ago, Shadow didn't want to be owned by anybody, but the mere suggestion of belonging to Ronan sent her toppling off the cliff.

"That's it. Give it to me."

He continued to fuck her with his fingers, sending her climax through wave after wave until she could barely stand. Then he held her quaking body tightly against his, lending her his strength while she fought for breath. Once her heart had returned to a somewhat normal rate, he tipped her chin up and feathered one last kiss over her lips.

"Your body always knew you were mine, kitten. Now you know it too."

≈

EREBOS

TENDRILS of black smoke peeled away from him like angry clouds as he watched his prized possession be mauled like a common back alley whore. His vision grayed at the edges as the darkness claimed him, his true visage trying to break free. It took all his substantial control to retain his grip on his current form, his hands shaking and his jaw ticking from the strain.

To transform now would leave him vessel-less, the dreamer's body reacting to the sudden outward expansion the same way a balloon too filled with air violently pops. And no one had time to deal with that.

Still, it would serve her right if he destroyed the object of her obsession right before her eyes. If he made her watch as he flayed the flesh from his bones and then tore him into a million tiny pieces before making her eat them. If she wanted him so badly, he'd let her have him. Or perhaps he'd go with something more classic and rip his head from his body and place it on a pike outside her door as a warning. Then again . . . mummification was always fun. She could keep him propped in the corner of her room as a reminder of what happened when she disobeyed her one true god.

With every malicious thought, more wisps broke free, filling the space with misty darkness. The mist took shape when she came with a muffled shout, the cloud fragments forming two skeletal hands.

No.

The hands curled into fists before dematerializing. He would not make it easy for them. Shadow would never learn if he didn't make this hurt her every bit as much as it would kill *him*. So instead he remained concealed in his cloak of shadows, teeth bared in a feral snarl as his nemesis carefully helped his toy place her mask back on.

"You look like a dream in silver, kitten. Too bad it doesn't hide blood anywhere near as well as black."

For a heartbeat, Erebos wondered if his control slipped and he'd accidentally lashed out. But then Shadow let out her own soft growl of frustration.

"Dammit, I can't go back out there like this."

"Perhaps I can escort you to your rooms so you may change."

Her voice turned mocking, but there was a flirtatious edge Erebos didn't recall her ever aiming his way. "Do you honestly believe I have a spare ball gown just hanging about my closet?"

Oh, the ways I am going to make you pay for this, Shadow mine. I thought you had learned your lesson. Apparently I will have to be more thorough this time.

"Perhaps not of this caliber, but certainly there's something you can use for the occasion."

"You just want to get me alone so you can have your way with me again."

"We're alone right now. If that was true, I wouldn't need to take you anywhere."

"I suppose that's true . . ." The rustle of fabric told him *exactly* what had interrupted her flow of words. As did the breathlessness of her reply when she spoke next. "Tell me the real reason you want to go upstairs, and I'll take you."

His Shadow may be a faithless whore, but she was clever. Even after succumbing to her lust, she still managed to sniff out the bastard's ulterior motive as easily as a bloodhound. There was a reason she was the queen. Or that she used to be, anyway.

"It's the only way to complete the second part of my task. But I won't lie, kitten. Getting you near a bed is reason enough."

She laughed, a low husky chuckle that had a man's blood rushing south. "Fine. Follow me, but if we get caught, don't act the hero. I can take care of myself."

You just keep piling on the sins, don't you, Moonbeam? Does your betrayal know no end? It's like you want me to punish you.

Erebos took a few steps back, even though there was no way the lovers would see him unless he wanted them to. The darkness could hide all manner of secrets, but never from him. He saw every detail, and his veins burned with jealous rage at the well-loved state of his toy. Her lips were swollen, skin flushed, hair mussed. She'd been a fucking goddess when he'd brought her down here tonight, but now she was ruined. Defiled by a common piece of filth.

And it wasn't the spray of blood splashed down the side of her skirt he was referring to. That macabre accent simply served to further accentuate how perfect she was. A warrior queen who only accepted payment in the form of blood.

No, he referred to the invisible stains left all over her skin by that cretin.

How dare the worm reach so far above his station? How dare a mere mortal play at being a god?

Erebos watched them move slowly away from him, their soft voices only stoking the flames of insanity he was lost in. As a plan took shape, his temper coalesced into dark satisfaction.

A low, sinister chuckle rolled out like thunder. "Oh yes . . . that will do nicely."

Not only would he get what he wanted, he'd take out one of Luna's precious children in the process, and his Shadow would finally learn a very valuable lesson.

She belonged to him.

And Death did not share.

CHAPTER 24

RONAN

"They really didn't tell you anything about what to expect today?"

Ronan shot an annoyed glare in Bast's direction. "The answer hasn't suddenly changed in the fifteen minutes since you last asked me."

"It just seems odd, doesn't it?"

"No odder than the first day."

Bast chewed on his lower lip. "Yes, I suppose you're right, but a notecard with a time and location feels a little anticlimactic for the grand finale. With it being the last trial, and with all those sponsors in attendance, you'd think the High Lord would want to ensure a good show. I mean, they paid a lot of money for the privilege of attending. The money he made off their bets alone . . ."

"Don't think I don't know about the bets *you've* been making."

"I bet against you. Get over it. I won and offered to share the winnings with you, didn't I?"

"How kind of you to offer me *my* money."

"Your money? You didn't win the bet."

"No, but you still owe me from the card game."

Bast let out a dismissive huff. "I've more than paid you back for that."

"You think so, do you?"

"Have I not been your loyal and faithful companion these last weeks? My friendship is priceless. Now, back to the trial . . . What are you going to do if it comes down to you and your lady love?"

"I don't know," Ronan answered honestly. He was no closer to figuring a way out now than he'd been the day he signed up. "I guess I'll improvise."

"Improvise? Improvise! Ronan. The arena probably has ten thousand people—"

"Ten thousand, Bast? Really. No wonder you're a shite gambler. You can't fucking count. There will be a couple thousand, tops. And that's assuming people traveled for the occasion."

"You know they did. You could see the tents and caravans from our window. They've been coming in droves to watch today's death match."

"We don't know it's going to be a death match."

That was true, if they were being technical about it. No one had actually spoken the words out loud, but it wasn't exactly a secret either. From day one, it had been hinted that the finalists would face off against each other in a battle to the death. And just because the other trials hadn't explicitly demanded murder, there was no doubt in Ronan's mind that the missing contestants hadn't got up and left town after losing their various tests. One of them? Sure. All of them? Not fucking likely. Just because no one had discovered a body yet— Marin's notwithstanding—didn't mean there wasn't a pile of them rotting somewhere.

Death had always been a foregone conclusion.

It was simply a matter of whose.

"Are you sure we're going the right way?" Ronan asked, glancing around the unfamiliar buildings. His involvement in the contest hadn't given him a lot of time for exploring, but he was fairly certain the arena they'd constructed to hold today's trial was in the opposite direction, just outside the western gates.

Bast reached in his pocket and pulled out the card someone had left under their door. His brows dipped as he scanned the address printed on the back. "It should be just ahead on the next block, but . . ."

Intuition was a harsh buzz in Ronan's veins. The street wasn't exactly deserted, but it was close. Though that wasn't unexpected with the city's population making its way to the arena. It certainly hadn't aroused suspicion . . . until now.

Still staring at the building with a frown, Sebastian asked, "Do you think they asked everyone to meet here? Or maybe they have you all spread out, and you'll have to race to the arena and fight it out there?"

There was no knowing what Erebos had up his sleeve, but Ronan had a feeling his being sent here wasn't quite so innocent. The rules were clear. Any contestant not present at the start of a trial was automatically disqualified. It wouldn't be difficult to send him a fake set of instructions to get him out of the way.

"It's a trap," he growled.

"Are you sure? Maybe someone is waiting for you inside."

"Oh, I'm counting on it."

"Wait, what? And you're still going in there?" Bast tried to grasp Ronan's arm but was no match for the pure fury propelling him forward.

"I'd hate to disappoint whoever worked so hard to get me alone."

"Ronan . . ." Bast muttered a series of fervent curse words before following after him.

"What are you doing?" Ronan snapped, barely sparing him a glance as he pulled the Butcher's famed sword, Souleater, from his bag.

"Getting myself killed, apparently."

"No. Stay outside. Better yet, get to the arena and see if there's any way to buy me some time."

Sebastian's gray eyes filled with an intensity Ronan hadn't seen from him before. Everything was a joke with him. Life was a game to be played and enjoyed, never taken seriously. Never real. But he was deadly serious now.

"Where you go, I go."

The declaration floored him. "Bast . . ."

Sighing heavily, Sebastian eyed the door to what seemed to be an abandoned apothecary and then pulled it wide open. "Come on then, Ronan. Death waits for no man." He darted inside, leaving Ronan with no option but to follow or let him walk into the ambush like a lamb arriving at slaughter.

SHADOW

"LOOKING FOR SOMEONE?"

Shadow stiffened, her entire body going on high alert as the High Lord's voice caressed her ears. How he made three little words sound so threatening was beyond her. It was a skill she would have worked hard to master under other circumstances.

Peeling her eyes away from the gate and the people still flooding in, she gave a slight shake of her head. "No one in particular."

"Liar," he breathed.

Her heart stuttered in her chest, but a lifetime of practice kept her expression wiped free of emotion. "I'm merely curious where the other contestants are. Or did only four of us complete the last trial?"

Her eyes drifted over Dichen and Cedric before coming to rest on Loren. His attentive stare surprised her. He wasn't even trying to disguise the fact he was eavesdropping on her conversation with the High Lord.

Recalling the man's soft smile and the way he'd played with that familiar teal feather the other night at the Siren, she couldn't help but wonder if she wasn't the only one on the lookout for Ronan. Or rather, the Butcher's handsome friend.

They should be here by now. Actually, Ronan should have been here nearly an hour ago to be debriefed by Dmitri with the rest of them.

She knew damn well he completed the last trial. They'd broken every rule to ensure it. Removing their masks. Revealing the details of their tasks. *Working* together . . . among other things. If Erebos found out . . . but of course he had. Erebos knew everything. He had eyes and ears everywhere.

She was such an idiot.

He'd been avoiding her since the ball. She should have known it wasn't a reprieve.

Fuck.

A bell chimed, signaling the approach of the hour. Only fifteen more minutes until the start of the final trial. If Ronan didn't show up soon, it was over. She should feel relief at the thought. At least he'd be spared the fate of the others. But it wasn't relief she felt. It was panic.

Still looking at Loren, she spotted one of Dovina's best girls weaving through the crowd and coming up to tap the crowd favorite on the shoulder. He leaned down with a frown, his expression turning thunderous as he listened to whatever she whispered in his ear.

But then Erebos chuckled, and the sound of dark satisfaction set her teeth on edge. It was the first time she could ever recall feeling openly hostile toward the man who'd been her hero since the day he saved her.

"What have you done?"

Erebos gave her a slow, cruel smile. "No less than he deserved."

Her heart sank, and she had to clamp down hard on the urge to pull her blade. Knowing there was nothing she could do, not at the moment, Shadow looked away and prayed that luck would continue to favor the stranger who'd wormed his way into her every waking thought. She didn't want to see Ronan harmed because of his involvement with her, or worse.

There was no future for them.

No way they could ever have more than a stolen moment in the dark.

But hidden deep in her heart—the part of her that had come alive for no one but him—there was a wish she could never voice. A single hope-filled, and equally hopeless, word.

Forever.

She wanted it—fiercely. An entire lifetime to spend with each other unraveling the mystery of these *feelings* he'd unleashed with one life-changing kiss. In so many ways, it felt like she'd woken from a dream. Like she'd been holding her breath under water and finally allowed herself to break through the surface and suck in the oxygen she so desperately needed.

Ronan made her feel alive in ways she hadn't even begun to wrap her head around. And she wanted to know *why*. What was this hold he had over her? How could he make her feel so much in so short a time? Was it only infatuation? Lust? Something more? And why was it a man she'd just met felt more familiar to her than one she'd known for years?

Why him?

Why now?

Why bring him barreling into her life only to rip him away days later?

It wasn't fair. None of this was fair. The one thing she craved was the one thing she could never have: Time.

Time to figure this all out.

Time to explore these new feelings.

Just more time . . . with him.

Throat tight with unfamiliar emotion, Shadow glanced back at the other contestants only to come up short.

Loren was gone.

RONAN

IT WAS WORSE than he thought. That fucker Erebos hadn't sent a lone assassin after them. He sent the whole damn fleet.

It was Nightshade all over again, but this time Ronan didn't just have to keep his own arse alive; he was responsible for Bast as well. Having never seen the man in a fight, he couldn't speak to his skill. But he didn't hold out much hope the boulevardier from Colvers was a master swordsman. If the man's reaction to a little blood spatter on a shirt was any indication, this was *not* going to end well.

Releasing a heavy breath, the Butcher pushed away everything that made him Ronan, welcoming instead the blessed numbness he'd need if he had any chance of seeing them both through unscathed—or as close to that state as he could get.

Drawing his weapon, the Butcher looked around at the dozen or so masked men surrounding them. "Well, what are you waiting for, an invitation?"

Bast surprised him by picking up a forgotten fire poker and giving it a few test swings. "Perhaps they're shy? Shall we show them how it's done?"

Sharing a look filled with unspoken messages, none of which there was any time to decipher, they nodded and dove into battle as if they'd done it a thousand times before. In Ronan's case, that was a fairly accurate assessment. But it was the ease with which Bast did the same that was so shocking.

With no time to focus on it, Ronan lost himself to the familiar dance of blade and blood. Step, swing, pivot, thrust. On and on it went, his Earth-infused shield protecting him from the worst of the blows. These men were good. But they lacked the proper motivation.

They were here because of an order.

Ronan was fighting to save lives. Not his, he was pretty indifferent to his own, but Sebastian's and then, hopefully, Shadow's.

Since their stolen moment, he'd stopped thinking of her as Reyna. The shattered look in her eyes when he'd whispered the name would haunt him for the rest of his days—or minutes, depending on how things went. Either way, he never wanted to be the cause of that kind of hurt again. He may never get Reyna back, and that was okay. His woman's soul was the same. That was all that mattered.

It was impossible to keep track of how many men were left. The swarm felt never-ending, but they were falling fast, so the fight couldn't have lasted very long. With victory in sight, Ronan faced off with one of the last men standing while Bast held his own with the other.

The man grinned, oddly cocky despite the fallen state of his comrades. "Erebos sends his regards." He gave Ronan a two-fingered salute and took a step back as if to leave.

"Not so fast." Ronan bared his teeth, the heat of his Fire pulsing through his veins. He'd already known that rat bastard had been behind this, but hearing the confirmation sent him boiling over. He roared, his Fire manifesting down the length of his blade as he swung, severing the man's head from his body.

He spun, ready to help Bast dispatch the last of the rubbish, when he was brought up short.

"Move, and I gut him like a fish."

Since his back had been to them, he had no clue how Bast had managed to get himself in a headlock, but his head was pulled back at an awkward angle, one of his arms stretched up behind him in the assassin's hold.

"Don't listen to him, Ronan."

"Shut up, Sebastian," he growled, his eyes never leaving the masked face of the assailant. He'd taught countless warriors how to assess an opponent. How to seek out any manner or weakness in a matter of seconds. How something as simple as the way a man breathed could tell you everything you needed to know about his intentions.

This one was playing a game. He had a blade pressed against the exposed skin of Bast's throat. He could have killed him several times over by now if that's what he planned. That's when Ronan realized this rendezvous had never been about killing him—that would have been a bonus.

This was about delay. Keeping him busy as long as possible, so he had no choice but to forfeit. And then, without the watchful eyes of the entire continent on him, Erebos could come after him and do whatever twisted things he had in mind.

Ronan was fucked if he didn't make it to the arena in the next few minutes. Frankly, it would take a miracle to get him there at all.

Dousing the flame of his blade, Ronan slowly set it down and lifted his hands in the air. "Let him go."

"No, I don't think I will." As if to prove the point, the man dug the blade into Sebastian's skin, carving a line straight down the side of his throat, not stopping until he reached his sternum.

Bast tried not to cry out. His fever-bright eyes held Ronan's stare as he fought against the pain. But he lost the battle, eventually screaming when the man dug the blade deeper.

Ronan vibrated with the need to act, but every idea he had to get rid of the assassin would end up with Sebastian getting hurt. He couldn't take the chance.

If you don't do anything, he'll die anyway. He deserves better than a meaningless death when all he wanted to do was stand at your side.

A subtle shift in the darkness along the wall caught his eye. Ronan tensed but didn't look away from the man grinning manically. The flash of blond shocked him. As did the face it belonged to.

Loren.

But was he friend . . . or foe?

It was hard to be sure. Everyone in this town had an agenda.

Catching his eye, Loren lifted a finger to his lips and took a tentative step forward. He would have sworn the man was silently telling him to keep the assassin occupied. Ronan prayed he wasn't reading the situation wrong. He'd never forgive himself if Bast paid the price for his hubris.

Well . . . he'd said it would take a miracle. Maybe the Mother wasn't done looking out for him yet.

"Tick tock, Butcher."

Pouring every ounce of derision in his voice, Ronan crossed his arms over his chest and tilted his head to the side. "I'm sorry. Were you waiting on me for something? I thought you told me not to move."

The assassin blinked, his dark eyes clouding with confusion. "I-I did."

"Was that a question? Are you asking me?"

"No."

"You know, for a man holding the knife, you sure don't seem to know what the hell you're doing. I don't think you're very good at this, mate."

It was obvious the assassin wasn't used to his victims talking back. Or not expressing any fear. Frustrated, likely seeking to reclaim the upper hand, he made a wild slash from Sebastian's shoulder to hip.

Fuck.

Bast swallowed back a scream, his entire body jerking in pain as blood poured down his shirt. The unexpected spasm caused the assassin to lose control of his weapon, and it slid deeper into Sebastian's belly.

Fuuuck.

Stomach wounds were dangerous. They were almost always fatal if the blade caught an organ. The man's inexperience was showing, but somehow his incompetence was every bit as deadly as actual skill.

Loren used the momentary chaos as his opportunity. He jumped forward, kicking the assassin in the side of his leg and sending him toppling over, away from Bast. The dagger, still lodged in his stomach, didn't fall.

But Bast did.

Without the other man supporting him, he dropped to his knees with a ragged groan. Not wasting a second, Ronan set the would-be killer ablaze and rushed to his friend's side. Loren was already there.

"Go," he said tersely, none of the champion's usual swagger or charm on display. "You can still make it if you run."

"What about you?"

"I said fucking go!"

Ronan looked to Bast, pale and covered in blood. "Sebastian—"

"It's okay, Ronan. This is the way it's supposed to be. Go get your girl."

"But—"

"GO!" they shouted in unison, though Bast's shout was a weak imitation of Loren's resonant boom.

"If anything happens to him . . ."

"Other than being nearly disemboweled? I think we've probably dealt with the worst, but I'll take care of him and get him to a healer. You have my word. Go. Finish this, Butcher."

Holding Loren's gaze for one drawn-out moment, he gave a curt nod. He stayed only long enough to pick up his weapon, a flicker of relief and gratitude filling him at the sound of Sebastian's voice. Any manner of things could have gone differently, even a second's hesitation and he may have never heard it again. Somewhere in the last couple of weeks, while he hadn't been paying attention, the mouthy little fuck had wormed his way into being one of the few people Ronan actually gave a shit about.

Thank you.

Someone was watching out for them, which meant there was still a chance. This wasn't over. He started walking toward the exit, unable to help but hear the men's hushed conversation.

"You saved me. How . . . heroic of you."

"Well, I *am* a hero. It's what we do."

"This is hardly your usual job. I doubt it will even make the headlines."

"I don't care."

"You really are a hero." Ronan was nearly at the door but glanced back in time to see Bast cup Loren's cheek. "*My* hero."

Loren's laugh was low but pained as he dropped his forehead to Bast's. "When I'd heard what happened . . ."

"How did you hear?"

"Camille found me. She saw you go inside, guessed the rest."

"So you came to my rescue? Why?"

"I guess one night wasn't enough."

The Bast he knew would have laughed, tossed back something flirty like 'that's what they all say' but *this* Sebastian, the one Ronan was starting to suspect might be the man beneath the façade, fisted his hand in Loren's hair and yanked his face down with a growled, "Good."

Knowing he was needed elsewhere and assured that his friend was in good hands, Ronan threw open the door and ran like his life depended on it.

Because it did.

CHAPTER 25

SHADOW

Shadow couldn't make herself look away from the gates. Nervous energy unlike anything she'd ever known had her heart pulsing in an uneven tempo, the first beat a slow lurch and its echo occurring at triple speed. That couldn't be a good sign, but she didn't know how to access her usual unaffected mien. She was too busy simultaneously willing the bell to toll and praying Ronan appeared.

"Don't fret, Shadow mine. This isn't the last you'll see of your play-thing. I have quite the reunion in store for you."

Her poor abused heart tumbled straight to her feet, and her gaze followed. Defeat was a cold, bitter taste on her tongue.

This is what you get for daring to stray. You knew better. The High Lord's will is law. You live to serve. Your wishes mean nothing.

As her mental tirade continued, the crowd gave a surprised shout and took up a slow chant.

"Bu-tcher."

"Bu-tcher."

"Bu-tcher."

Shadow's head snapped up in time to see Ronan jogging up to her, a smile tugging up the corner of his mouth.

"Sorry I'm late."

The bell rang out, and Shadow gave the tower a pointed look. "I'd say you were just in time."

"Oh, goodie. You made it," Erebos said from his place beside her, his voice dripping with disdain. "We were *so* worried about you."

"I'm sure you were." Ronan ran a hand down his black shirt, his palm stained crimson when he pulled it away. "As was the welcoming party you left for me."

Apparently these two weren't even going to pretend they didn't despise each other anymore. Good to know that the game—if not over exactly—had taken a definite turn. It would also seem there'd already been a number of casualties. Why did that make her bones buzz in warning?

Ronan moved in until he was right next to her, sandwiching her between him and Erebos. He pitched his voice low as Dmitri took center stage, ready to address the crowd and kick off the main event. "Did you miss me, kitten?"

Is it considered missing you when I've thought of little else than the velvety growl of your voice when you call me 'kitten' or the way just the whisper of your lips on my skin makes me forget how to breathe? What about when I've spent the last hour terrified I'd never see your face again when I haven't been afraid of anything since I was a child? What have you done to me? What have you awakened, and how do I put it back to sleep?

Unable to say any of that, she kept her voice even and her tone dry. "No more than I would a rash."

He chuckled. "What did I miss?"

"You mean you haven't guessed?" she asked, keeping her eyes trained on Dmitri and her voice low.

"I'm assuming there's going to be some kind of fight."

"A battle royale," she confirmed. "We are all facing off against each other. The last one standing wins."

"Good thing I'm already warmed up."

She risked a glance up at him. His expression was unreadable, but a muscle ticked in his jaw. Sensing her gaze on him, his eyes shifted to hers. They didn't exchange a word, but an unspoken agreement passed between them. They wouldn't turn on each other unless—until —they had to.

The backs of his knuckles grazed hers. She wasn't sure what the small touch implied. Was he apologizing for what was about to happen? Reassuring her? Something else entirely? Stars, she was exhausted from trying to decipher this new language he'd introduced her to. Things were so much simpler before he came into her life.

Simpler, but also without color or nuance.

She honestly couldn't say which she preferred.

Frowning, Shadow turned her focus to Dichen, her mind still a riot of unanswered questions. *Will I ever be able to go back to how things used to be after today? Do I want to?*

Shadow knew 'after today' was code for 'if he dies' or 'if I kill him.'

Remember what you're fighting for. Remember why you are doing this. After today, you will be free.

Somehow the encouragement didn't help put things in perspective the way it usually did. Nor were the words particularly comforting. After the High Lord's insistence that not even winning would spare her from the future he'd set for them . . . she wasn't sure what exactly she was fighting for anymore.

If it was up to him, freedom would never be hers. Which meant everything she'd done in the name of winning would be for nothing. Each choice . . . each death . . . utterly meaningless.

A quiet but insistent voice slithered through the back of her mind, its words so unexpected—so treasonous—she could hardly believe them to be hers. *Why continue to obey the rules of a man you no longer respect?*

Despite the mid-afternoon sun, a chill ran through her body, causing her to break out in goosebumps.

Where had *that* come from?

She didn't always agree with Erebos, but she still respected him . . . didn't she?

Worried the High Lord would somehow be able to sense the trai-

229

torous direction of her thoughts, she shut them down, turning all of her attention to her first opponent. With Loren disqualified, only Dichen and Cedric were left. Since Shadow had no magic to counter the blood mage's, Dichen was the clear choice.

This should be interesting.

They were well matched, but both of them were used to carrying out their assignments under the cover of darkness. It was going to be a change fighting out in the open, with nowhere to hide and nothing to grant either of them the element of surprise.

"Contestants, you've fought brilliantly thus far. Each trial was created with the intention of testing not only your limitations but your suitability to take on the role of the High Lord's Champion. You have risen to each and every challenge. Your adaptability, strategic thinking, strength, stamina, and perseverance are the very highest of calibers. Today we test your heart. And so I ask you this, who wants it most?"

A few weeks ago, Shadow would have known the answer to Dmitri's question without hesitation. It was her. Today, the words lacked the conviction that would prove them to be true. Thankfully, no answer was required.

At least not from her.

The crowd roared in response to the Master of Ceremony's speech, everyone screaming out the name of their favorite. She took what comfort she could from the fact that there were others out there that still believed her to be the most deserving.

"Contestants, please take your place in the center of the ring. No matter which of you leaves victorious, you've all earned your place amongst the stars."

As one, the final four descended the stage and moved to the dusty arena that would soon be baptized by their blood. There wasn't much in terms of decoration, though none was truly needed. The contestants were the entertainment. Their slaughter of one another a sort of living—or perhaps in this case killing—theater. Not much was required for that, save their weapons of choice.

A wide selection waited for them on the wood-paneled walls that encircled them. Dichen wasted no time, grabbing several shurikens and other blades intended for throwing. Shadow already had all her favorite daggers concealed on her body, but she made a show of inspecting the offerings if for no other reason than to study what the others were doing. Ronan, not surprisingly, chose the broadsword strapped to his back, though he also picked up a double-headed axe and slung it through his belt. Aldair made the most shocking selection —choosing a triple-headed flail with nasty-looking spikes. She could only guess what use a blood mage would have for such a specialized weapon, but she was certain she was about to find out.

There was a stretch of anticipation-filled silence as the contestants moved into the center. Once they were all in a loose semicircle, Erebos made a show of slowly settling into his throne. His eyes were pinned on her.

This is what you wanted, he seemed to say. *Enjoy it while it lasts.*

She lifted her chin. *Oh, I will.*

Erebos dipped his head in a slow nod, giving Dmitri the signal he'd been waiting for. "Let the battle begin!" the High Lord's Peacock shouted, throwing his hands into the air.

The crowd went wild, but Shadow barely heard them. Her entire focus was on the woman sprinting straight toward the paneled wall. She saw a blur of red in her periphery as Ronan lunged for Cedric.

Teach them all why you call yourself the Butcher.

Why she was sending any sort of affirmation his way wasn't quite clear in her mind. It hadn't been a conscious choice exactly. More a reflex. As nonsensical as it was, she couldn't help but wish him well. If this was the end, she wanted to be the one to face him. She would give him a death to be proud of. An end befitting a warrior of his station.

Nearing the point where she either needed to stop or run face-first into the wall, Dichen leapt straight up, landing as nimbly as a cat on the thin ledge looping along the top. The people closest to her gasped in shock as she straightened and kept running, selecting one of her silver stars and letting it fly.

So that's your plan.

It was a smart move for an assassin prone to sneak attacks.

Without height or darkness to aid her, range would be her greatest advantage. As would her speed.

Shadow grinned, already anticipating the match. It would be a true test of her skill. A win to be proud of.

She dodged the assassin's blade, taking off in a sprint of her own, knowing a moving target was far more difficult to hit. Dichen took aim and let two more of her stars fly. One nicked Shadow's bicep, and the other landed somewhere behind her.

The veiled woman wasn't the only one with impressive aim. Freeing one of her blades, Shadow anticipated where it needed to be and set it free. It caught Dichen in the thigh, causing her to stumble, but not lose her footing, as she continued sprinting along the top of the ledge that separated the crowd from the center of the arena.

Dichen threw three blades in quick succession. Shadow dodged the first and then caught the others. Dichen's eyes widened in surprise when Shadow immediately flung them back.

Running out of ledge, Dichen braced herself for a jump that would take her over the sixteen-foot walkway that separated the two halves of the arena to where the ledge picked back up on the other side.

Seeing her opportunity, Shadow pulled two more daggers from their hiding place along her rib cage. Waiting for Dichen to go airborne, she took aim and fired.

There was a collective intake of breath as the crowd waited to see what would happen. Then a startled cry as the hilt of the first blade smashed into Dichen's temple. The second slicing through the arm she instinctively lifted to protect her face. The shift in her body's momentum sent Dichen crashing to the ground instead of sailing through the air.

Four more blades followed, faster than anyone could track, landing with absolute precision as they sank through the fabric of her veil and clothing, pinning her to the dirt.

It wouldn't hold her for long, but it didn't need to. Shadow just needed the woman to stay in one place long enough that she could end it. Dichen struggled in earnest, working to pull herself free. She'd only managed to release two of the daggers before Shadow was upon her.

Holding one of Shadow's knives in her hand, Dichen lashed out, but Shadow was faster. She caught the woman's wrist and halted the movement, using the weight of her body to keep Dichen pinned to the ground.

Both women were breathing hard, trickles of blood running the length of Dichen's youthful face and Shadow's arm.

"Any last words?" Shadow asked, not as a taunt, but as one master of the craft honoring another.

Dichen's pulse fluttered in her throat, but her dark eyes were calm. "There is glory in death for those of us who serve Him. At long last, I return home."

"May the stars welcome you."

"Not the stars. Tul Mort Jateh."

Shadow's breath hitched, and she shuddered as invisible fingers reached out and trailed the length of her spine. Fear, potent and all-consuming, held her in its grasp. It was pure instinct that made her react.

Still holding Dichen's wrist hostage, Shadow shoved it down, stabbing the assassin through the throat with the same weapon she had intended to use to slit Shadow's. For some unknown reason, a smile lifted Dichen's lips even as blood bubbled up between them. Then with a sigh that sounded like pure contentment, her eyes fluttered closed, and she fell still.

Shadow's heart raced and her limbs trembled. Swallowing, she pushed herself off the other woman and scrambled away. There was no basis for the intensity of her reaction. But there was no ignoring it either.

What the hell had Dichen said?

And why did the unknown words fill her with such terror?

CHAPTER 26

RONAN

*P*rimed from his earlier fight, it didn't take more than stepping onto the killing field to set the hunger for violence surging back to life. One would assume his inner monster would be sated, but the Butcher had been born in darkness and forged with blood. His craving knew no end.

Having never gone up against a blood mage, Ronan had no frame of reference to pull from, but he wasn't worried. Much about battle was universal. No matter what Cedric threw his way, he'd be ready.

At least, that's what he thought before Dmitri's shout rang out and the mage raised his weapon and turned it on himself.

Ronan was already moving, his sword aloft and aimed to strike, but his steps faltered as the metal heads of the flail arced up over Cedric's head and down toward his back. The crowd's shocked cries gave voice to Ronan's own surprise as the mage staggered forward, drops of crimson raining down onto the dirt below.

What in the Mother's name . . .

And then the unexpected act of self-harm made a twisted sort of sense, for what was the source of a blood mage's power?

Blood.

A lot of it.

The more of the empowering liquid he had at his disposal, the stronger the magic he could wield. The flail provided him with the means of drawing a significant amount of it in a short time, granting him access to a whole library of spells he would not otherwise be able to perform.

Understanding this in theory was a world away from experiencing it firsthand. Ronan was no stranger to formidable magics; he served the most powerful woman in his home realm and was capable of awe-inspiring acts on his own. But even still, he was utterly defenseless against the full brunt of the man's gift.

Between one faltering step and the next, everything Ronan knew to be real came under attack. Reality was suddenly no longer a known entity, but an ever-shifting landscape at the mercy of the man currently trying his best to kill him.

It wasn't as drastic as night replacing day or the arena transforming into an ancient forest. He could still feel the warm kiss of the sun on his face and smell the metallic tang of Aldair's freshly spilled blood. But now, instead of one mage, Ronan was surrounded by twenty nearly identical replicas. With every step he took in any direction, the circle spun, making it impossible to know which was the *true* Cedric.

Ronan came to a standstill with a low growl, eyeing the ring of impostors for any clue he could use to his advantage. The mages acted independently of one another. Some grinned at him; others adjusted their grips on a wide variety of weapons. There was even one beckoning him forward while the man beside him scratched his arse.

One broke free of the group, then a second and a third. Ronan knew trying to fight the decoys would be an effort in madness. Not only were they not real, but all he would succeed in doing was tiring himself out and making himself an easier target for the mage.

What he needed was a way to identify the real Cedric. Something he could do to test all of them at once. Ronan grinned as the answer came to him.

He needed to fight fire with Fire.

He was only going to be able to pull off a stunt like this once, so he had to make it count. Ronan dropped deep into the heart of his power, drawing as much of the Mother's gift into him as he could without risking a loss of control—or worse, a depletion of his reservoir. His well ran deep, but it wasn't bottomless. A full drain would render him unconscious, likely for days. He wasn't Helena, with the ability to draw on the magic within others to replenish himself. He needed to ration his gift carefully, especially in a situation where weakness equated death.

That said, he also knew when a gamble wasn't only advantageous but necessary.

This was such a time.

He continued to pull the Fire into him until it felt like he could see the neon glow of the flames flickering beneath his skin. When he was near vibrating from the effort of trying to keep hold of all that unchanneled power, he released it in a powerful arc, throwing his arm out like he was flinging a boomerang, and then he kept spinning, the molten flame pouring out from the palm of his hand in one continuous stream until he completed his circle.

The magical flames did nothing to the fake mages, though their agonized cries sounded authentic enough. Ronan ignored them all, along with the bloodthirsty screams of the crowd. They were here for a show, and he was certainly giving them one.

He raked his gaze around the circle of potential enemies, landing on the man frantically batting at his arms and legs with a ravaged shriek. The smell of char and burning flesh hit his nose, and Ronan knew he'd located his intended target.

He didn't hesitate. Fire still laced his veins, and he threw it outward, turning Cedric into a pillar of living flame. The magic-powered fire burned so hot, so fast that the mage was consumed in seconds. Knowing Shadow was still out there, along with thousands of innocent people, Ronan drew on what was left of his magic, this time focusing on the Air branch. He grabbed hold of all the oxygen, starving the flames so they couldn't spread. With the fire extinguished and the mage's illusions gone, all that remained in the wake of the firestorm was a Cedric-shaped statue made entirely of ash.

Needing to do something with the air he stole, Ronan channeled it through his body, letting it pour out of his mouth in one powerful stream aimed straight at Cedric's remains. He didn't let up until the mage was nothing more than a flurry of ashes drifting away on the breeze.

Rid now of the borrowed air and his opponent, not to mention nearly all his magic, Ronan took a few shuddering breaths and turned to face the stage housing Erebos's throne.

What he expected to find was the High Lord's furious gaze trained on him. What he found instead was Shadow, every inch of her exposed skin freckled with blood.

Pride at her win was quickly replaced by grim acceptance.

The reckoning was finally at hand. And this time, there was no escaping the truth.

One of them had to die.

CHAPTER 27

SHADOW

Fate wasn't something she'd ever put much stock in, but if it was real, if there was some goddess watching over them all, spinning her threads and plotting their destinies, she was a cruel, sadistic bitch with one hell of a mean streak.

Shadow had only just caught the tail end of Ronan's battle with Cedric—if you could even call it that. From what she'd seen, it had been more of a one-sided slaughter. One second the mage was there; the next, he vanished. Reduced to nothing but soot and dust as he rejoined the heavens above.

Even she could admit the display was intimidating.

And yet, there was no way out of what had already been set in motion. Fated or not, she made the decisions that landed her here. Now she had to see them through. No matter how much she wanted to run in the opposite direction.

Ronan held her gaze, sweat dampening his dirt-streaked brow. He held nothing back as his eyes locked with hers. Not the slight tremor in his hands, the harsh rise and fall of his chest, or the cascade of emotions rolling through him. He let her see every one, telegraphing them in his icy-blue irises: panic, regret, anticipation, lust—for violence or her or both—and hope. It was the last that kept her rooted to the ground.

"What are you waiting for? Kill 'im," a woman in the crowd shrieked. Several other voices took up the call and shouted variations of the same.

"Well, kitten. Looks like we've reached the end of the road."

"It was always leading us here."

"True. There's a beauty in inevitability. A freedom that comes when you give in to fate."

Shadow quirked a brow, surprised to hear him pull the word almost directly from her thoughts, even if his opinion was the complete opposite of hers.

Ronan took a step forward, and her breath hitched, her entire body coming alive in response to his proximity. If she dared look down, she was willing to bet the little hairs on her arms would be on end, all straining to reach the man who'd drawn her to him with his magnetic presence since that very first day.

"Promise me something?"

Mouth suddenly dry, Shadow licked her lips and jerked her head in a nod.

"Don't go easy on me."

"I wasn't planning on it."

"Good. I'm rather looking forward to seeing what you've got," he said with a bemused grin as he adjusted his grip on the pommel of his sword.

"You may not feel that way when you're bleeding out at my feet," she warned him, reaching for two fresh daggers as they began to circle one another.

"I've always wanted to draw my last breath beneath a beautiful woman."

"Then today must be your lucky day."

His chuckle washed over her the way a spring breeze rustles through blades of grass. Still holding her gaze, he smirked. "To be fair, in my fantasy, we were engaged in a very different kind of swordplay."

Her heart kicked up at the admission. "Well, then. I guess you'll die as you lived—in disappointment."

DRAWING ON HER CONSIDERABLE SPEED, Shadow darted forward, moving in close and landing two quick slices along his arms before dancing away behind him.

Ronan laughed as the crowd roared in approval. Up close and personal was an assassin's bread and butter. It's where their skills truly shined. A sword might be fancy, but it wasn't much use when it couldn't strike its target. A dagger, on the other hand, could cause considerable damage in any number of ways.

Realizing her intention, Ronan tossed his sword on the ground and ducked low, grabbing a fistful of dirt and tossing it in her face. She anticipated the move and twisted away, but he must have used more of that damned magic of his, because the dirt chased her, flying up into her eyes anyway.

"Cheater."

"Am I? Or am I just clever?" He used her momentary blindness to disarm her and steal both her blades.

Shadow reached behind her and pulled two new ones free from the sheathes hidden beneath her shirt. "You're going to have to do a fair bit more than that if you want to beat me."

"Oh, I intend to," he growled before tipping forward and tackling her.

Agility was no match for sheer bulk. She toppled ass over tea kettle, the breath knocked out of her as she landed flat on her back. If not for the years of muscle memory instinctively guiding her, she would have quickly found herself trapped beneath him. Instead, she rolled to the side and kicked out, knocking Ronan onto his side, and scrambled to restrain him. Expecting the move, he wrapped her in a bear hug and flipped her over his head until they were both lying in the dirt, trying to catch their breath.

It went on like that for several rounds. Each time one of them seemed to gain the advantage, the other easily countered it. It was a

241

constant back and forth with no real leader. They weren't just evenly matched; they were perfect foils. Their methods both complementary and made to neutralize each other.

Ronan's style was composed of straight aggression, his attacks brutal and heavily reliant on his strength. Hers, in contrast, were stealthy displays of speed and dirty street tricks. It wasn't long before they were both dripping sweat and blood, bruises already blooming on her cheek where his skull cracked against the bone. She was pretty sure it was an unintentional hit because his eyes immediately flickered with apology. She used the slight lowering of his guard to slam the heel of her hand into his nose and then solar plexus. Ronan dropped with a pained grunt.

Shadow was back on top of him in a second, freeing a blade tucked into a hidden sheath at her thigh and bringing it up to his throat. Instead of slitting it and ending both his life and the trial, she hesitated.

Ronan knew it too, because he taunted her. "I can't help but feel like you're toying with me, kitten. Is your heart even in this?"

She wiped a forearm over her brow, baring her teeth in something far too unkind to be a smile. "Is yours? You've stopped even pretending to go on the offensive."

"Maybe I'm just waiting for you to tire."

"Maybe. Or . . . you're letting me win."

Ronan did something with his hips that sent her tumbling over. "Is that what you think? Are you sure it's not the other way around? You're Empyria's greatest assassin. How is it you can't manage to take out a lone man?"

Shadow bared her teeth, adjusting her grip on her weapon and reaching around to cut Ronan behind the knee. "What makes you think I don't have you exactly where I want you?"

Pain flared to life behind his eyes, and she shoved him off, retaking her position on top. Chest heaving, sweat dripping in her eyes, Shadow once again placed her dagger at his throat.

This time there were no teasing words. No cocky smiles. Ronan stared up at her, his eyes raking over her face as if he was attempting to memorize it.

She spoke without conscious thought, the words pouring from her before she even realized it. "I never wanted this."

"I know."

"It's the only way."

"I know."

Sudden frustration replaced the heavy weight of guilt pressing into her chest and making it impossible to breathe. "Dammit, stop lying there giving me permission to end you."

"What would you have me do, Shadow? Kill you instead?" He shifted just enough she could feel the tip of the dagger he'd stolen pressed against her rib cage.

"Yes," she hissed. Not because she wanted to die, but because it might alleviate some of this fucking guilt.

His expression was surprisingly tender for a man about to have his throat rent open. "I could no more harm a hair on your head than I could a child. I've always known this was going to end one way if we reached this point. But my goal was never to win."

"It wasn't?"

"I've only ever had one mission, to reunite with the woman who pieced my broken heart back together. You were the one who taught it to speak your name. It beats for you." He dropped the dagger and reached up to cup her cheek. "Mission accomplished."

"Ronan." Her voice broke around his name.

"Do with me what you will, kitten. My heart, my life, they're yours. They've always been yours, because without you to share them with, they mean nothing at all."

"I—"

"Finish him!"

Erebos had remained mostly silent until now, a seething sentinel bearing witness to their ruin, but it would seem the clock had just run out on his patience.

"Do it." Ronan's gentle order hit harder than the crack of the High

Lord's command. "It's okay, I promise. If this is all we get, it's enough. Loving you is more than enough."

A tear broke free and splashed down her cheek at his tender reassurance.

"Don't cry, kitten." He curled his hand around her wrist, reinforcing her grip on the dagger at his throat. His lips twitched up in a sorry attempt at a smile. "This is what I wanted, remember? To draw my last breath underneath a beautiful woman. All you're doing is fulfilling a dying man's wish."

"I'm sorry," she whispered, her eyes falling closed as she sucked in a ragged breath and blindly slashed out.

The crowd that had been a near-constant roar in the background fell as silent as the man beneath her, their shock rendering them speechless.

It was over.

Now she had to find a way to live with what she'd done.

CHAPTER 28

EREBOS

He could no more ignore Luna's pull now than he could in the days he and his goddess had meant more to one another than a means to an end. Since visiting her in the garden upon his release from the tomb she'd trapped him in, his conniving wife had made a point to stay far away. Her presence now, when she could have come to him any number of times in the last five years, could not be a coincidence.

With Shadow fully engaged in battle against the veiled Night Stalker, Dichen, he allowed himself to slip away, leaving his vessel and projecting his consciousness to the celestial plane.

"You rang?" he droned, even as his body reacted to the sight of his nubile bride. He was no more immune to her now than he'd ever been. She'd been crafted for him from the very stars themselves. Her glittering perfection was a stunning contrast to his rippling darkness.

She stiffened at the sound of his voice, her head tilting slowly as she turned to look at him, sweeping those iridescent colored eyes over his body, her regal countenance giving nothing away.

"I wasn't sure you'd come."

"Don't I always come when you call?"

She bit her pouty lower lip, and he had to battle the instinctive need to pull it free and replace her teeth with his own. He loved to hurt her, his shining star. There was nothing he enjoyed more than her tears, except perhaps her sweet moans. Luna came to life under his touch. She quite literally glowed during her climax—it was the main reason one of her better-known monikers was the Lady of Light.

"I stopped counting on you long ago," she said eventually.

Anger at her betrayal roared to the surface, as it always did when she dared accuse him of being the villain. She was the one who locked him up. He was the forsaken one, not her. *Him.*

"Still singing that old worn-out tune, sweetheart? How disappointing."

She crossed her arms, the moving plumping up her already perfect breasts. Darkness, he ached for the feel of them. How many centuries had it been since he'd claimed her body? Oh, there had been others, but she was *his.* No one could tame the wild chaos of his immortal soul the way she did.

And that was the heart of the matter, wasn't it? For all that, she was his. He was *hers.*

And she didn't want him.

Oh, it rankled. He'd never forgive her for throwing him away. As if he were nothing.

As if *they* were nothing.

Everything he did now was to prove to her just what a mistake she'd made. For the light could only shine in the darkness. Meaning Luna was *nothing* without him. A queen without a queendom. A mother without her children. A goddess of sweet fuck all.

Yes, he was bitter. No, he didn't care.

Guilt was a mortal entanglement. He had no use for it.

Anger, on the other hand? Along with its good friends jealousy, rage, and lust . . . well, those suited him just fine.

"What are you doing here, Luna? Have you finally come to beg?"

"Beg? Oh, you'd love that, wouldn't you?"

"You on your knees before me, yes, I'd quite enjoy that. Almost as much as you would, I'm sure."

Luna shivered, her nipples pebbling beneath her gossamer gown. He didn't bother hiding his smile. For all her feigning, his dear wife wasn't any less affected by him than he was by her.

"To answer your question, no, I'm not here to beg. I wanted to see the look on your face when you realized you were going to lose."

"Lose? What are you talking about? It's already over."

"Is it? You're that confident your little Shadow is still fully under your control?" There was no mistaking the bitterness as she spat out the name.

"Ah, Luna, are you jealous?"

"Of a mortal?" she scoffed. "Not remotely. Though, I find it incredibly twisted that you'd dare dress your plaything up as me and call her by my name. That's depraved, even for you."

"Oh, you have been keeping a close eye on things, haven't you?"

Her smile was sharp enough to cut. "I always watch over my children."

"So you did send the boy. I'd assumed, but he's hardly a worthy tribute, and he's certainly no match for mine."

"I wouldn't be so sure," Luna said, her smile turning smug.

"Is that so? And what, pray tell, makes you so confident?"

"Isn't it obvious? You will fail now for the same reason you always fail."

"Oh?" The lone word was little more than a bitten-off growl. "Please do enlighten me."

"Gladly." She took a few steps closer, lifting a hand to poke him in the chest. "You are doomed to fail because the one thing you've never seemed to understand, darling husband, is a woman's heart."

RONAN AND REYNA'S adventure is just getting started. Pre-order your copy of Queen of Whispers & Mist, book 2 in the Forsaken series, to find out what happen when the Lord of Death tries to come between these fated mates.

ACKNOWLEDGMENTS

To my readers who love my characters as much as I do, thank you for giving me a reason to write this story.

To my friends who are my cheerleaders chapter by chapter (and some days page by page), without you ladies rooting me on I don't know if this book ever would have made it on time. Kim, thank you for the brainstorming sessions and letting me ramble on about my love for Bast. Sarah & Ruhla, thank you for being my alpha readers your reassurance in those early stages is priceless.

To my narrators who's talent inspires me to write wild scenes like oh say a #whisperoff and who I trust enough with my characters to only write things like 'have fun' in the character description. I love you guys. You don't know how much it means to hear you bring my words to life. Your voices are magic and they make everything sound infinitely better.

To my husband and our fur babies, thank you for the unconditional love, and for making sure I'm looked after on the days I'd otherwise forget to eat or sleep.

And finally, to William Goldman who's masterpiece *The Princess Bride* has inspired me in more ways than I could ever list.

THE CHOSEN UNIVERSE

PRISONER OF STEEL & SHADOW

QUEEN OF WHISPERS & MIST

COURT OF DEATH & DREAMS

ALSO BY MEG ANNE

**BROTHERHOOD OF THE GUARDIANS /
THE NOVASGARDIAN VIKINGS**

UNDERCOVER MAGIC

(NORD & LINA)

A SEXY & SUSPENSEFUL FATED MATES PNR

HINT OF DANGER

FACE OF DANGER

WORLD OF DANGER

PROMISE OF DANGER

CALL OF DANGER

BOUND BY DANGER (QUINN & FINLEY)

THE MATE GAMES: WAR

A SPICY PARANORMAL WHY CHOOSE ROMANCE

CO-WRITTEN WITH K. LORAINE

OBSESSION

REJECTION

POSSESSION

TEMPTATION

THE MATE GAMES: PESTILENCE

A SPICY PARANORMAL WHY CHOOSE ROMANCE

CO-WRITTEN WITH K. LORAINE

PROMISED TO THE NIGHT (PREQUEL NOVELLA)

DEAL WITH THE DEMON

CLAIMED BY THE SHIFTERS

CAPTIVE OF THE NIGHT

LOST TO THE MOON

GYPSY'S CURSE: THE COMPLETE TRILOGY

A PSYCHIC/DETECTIVE STAR-CROSSED LOVERS UF ROMANCE

VISIONS OF DEATH

VISIONS OF VENGEANCE

VISIONS OF TRIUMPH

THE GYPSY'S CURSE: THE COMPLETE COLLECTION

ABOUT MEG ANNE

USA Today and international bestselling paranormal and fantasy romance author Meg Anne has always had stories running on a loop in her head. They started off as daydreams about how the evil queen (aka Mom) had her slaving away doing chores, and more recently shifted into creating backgrounds about the people stuck beside her during rush hour. The stories have always been there; they were just waiting for her to tell them.

Like any true SoCal native, Meg enjoys staying inside curled up with a good book and her cat, Henry . . . or maybe that's just her. You can convince Meg to buy just about anything if it's covered in glitter or rhinestones, or make her laugh by sharing your favorite bad joke. She also accepts bribes in the form of baked goods and Mexican food.

Meg is best known for her leading men #MenbyMeg, her inevitable cliffhangers, and making her readers laugh out loud, all of which started with the bestselling Chosen series.

Printed in Great Britain
by Amazon

13244770R00155